ATLAS SULKS

W.W. MUNK

Published by
ScreenPlay Novel. com

ISBN: 0989719103

ISBN-13: 9780989719100

Library of Congress Control Number: 2013912950
ScreenPlay Novel com
South Burlington, VT

Cover design by Marcia Blanco

This work is dedicated to R. K. Dandy.

I admit it my friend; you were right all along.

BSY, B.

It is said satire can tell the Truth by making Fiction seem like Fact.

It is also said satire will make some people laugh and others not.
Still, it's better to laugh.

Anon

Chapter I
Thesis

"What is he doing?"

Dabny's eyes followed the words. Yes, the spelling was correct and each word was in proper sequence. But those inky black characters couldn't really mean what they did.

"Are you sure he wrote it this way?"

"He told me to keep it a secret," answered Leona Parks. The executive assistant nervously looked at the office door to confirm she'd closed it all the way. "I knew you'd want to see it."

She was right. Those inky black characters warned of trouble ahead. Now, having read all of them Dabny wanted to rush across the hall to the CEO's office. But her father had left early today. She'd have to wait to confront him and waiting wasn't her way to conduct business. Taking immediate action, she believed is better than waiting for a later opportunity; sometimes those opportunities never present themselves. Or when they do, they sadly go unanswered.

"I want you to hold onto this," she said, handing the paper back. "Don't tell him you showed it to me. And don't send it out."

As Leona quietly left the room, Dabny Talbett, President of the Atlas Radio Company, fumed over the offending memorandum.

August 10, 2012

To: The members of the Board of Directors.

If ARC is to remain the leading broadcaster in Talk Radio, our only option is to forgo our campaign to privatize the radio airwaves. Though it is a good and noble effort, and necessary to free our company from government intrusion into our business practices, the costs of continuing this initiative are presently more than our bottom line can bear. We have exceeded the allocated budget and our costs continue to mount. The possibility now exists we may not be able to continue to employ the talk show Hosts who bring listeners to our nine hundred and seventy three stations. If that happens, we will lose our advertisers and their advertising revenues. As CEO of Atlas, I cannot allow that to happen. Since we, the stewards of Atlas are responsible for the making of profit and the payment of dividends to the shareholders, we must act in the most responsible manner. Therefore, I will instruct our lobbying firm to cease its activities regarding the privatization campaign. Perhaps in the future Atlas will again fight for ownership of the airwaves and when we win, we'll take control of our destiny.

Signed, Jamesford Talbett, CEO

Aggravated yet in control of herself as always, Dabny walked to her floor to ceiling windows, seventy five stories above the scurrying specks below. Deep in thought, she contemplated her boundless world, a spectacular landscape of glimmering high rise towers. Inside, smart men and women were crunching numbers and working deals and creating wealth. Those smart deal makers make money, a lot of it and they deserve every dollar. Their efforts contribute mightily to the profitable functioning of the capitalistic process. Sure, that process creates pain for the uneducated and unskilled. But the winners realize the rightful gain from the output of their brains and talents. That's the way Nature works, she reflected. It's the way the System should work, as well.

Then, while gazing at the monuments to unchained free enterprise she began to devise her plan. It had to be foolproof. It had to be doable and of course, it had to work the first time. She wouldn't get a second chance. But then second chances are for second rate losers. She believed a person with intelligence and drive is entitled to succeed. She only needs to be free from the government's constraints. That's all. People like her, guided by the principle of enlightened self-interest, can and will prevail. A Talbett never asked for a handout or a government subsidy or any demeaning corporate welfare. Success comes to those who work for it and aren't bothered by the envy of the also rans.

Convinced she needed to act right now, she nodded in agreement with herself. She walked back to her desk and pressed the intercom button.

"Leona, I'll be leaving to take care of a business matter. I won't return today."

She opened the desk's top drawer and brought out a fine calfskin address book. Turning to the 'R' section, she found the desired name and instantly memorized the number. After that, she opened the next drawer and took out a file folder. Then she picked up her purse and left the office.

Chapter II
A Link is Forged

Blessed with more than her share of beauty and brains, Dabny took on the business world undaunted by the regulatory forces opposing her. Those forces were outdated and defective. She was laser focused and driven to achieve extraordinary objectives. Every day her emerald eyes watched for traps set by her devious competitors and beneath her raven hair her brain was constantly alert, refining and refining again her artful plans and strategies. She anticipated every obstacle that lurked in her path and she possessed every talent she needed to acquire anything she wanted.

"Not every girl is an only child," she'd like to say to her sisters in Alpha Alpha Alpha, "and not every girl is born to parents like mine, so I made the most of the genes I inherited."

So far, in her thirty-four years Dabny made the most of every gene in her genetically endowed life. In her childhood private schools and during her Ivy League days she worked hard and earned high praise from her instructors. She led the debating team to an undefeated record and she excelled at swimming and lacrosse. Every term she made the dean's list and during her senior year she was elected president of her sorority's chapter. And, at the height of 5'4" she captained the women's volleyball team, again to an undefeated record.

"I never want to know," she'd often declare, "what it's like to be a loser."

On this afternoon, still churning over her father's wretched memo she drove her sleek Mercedes to the near West Side. The route took her out of the city's most sought after real estate: top priced commercial properties where all those soaring office buildings merged into an upscale shopping district: boutique after chic boutique with windows displaying the latest offerings in roped 24 Karat necklaces and diamond studded tennis bracelets as well as the hottest fashions in women's wear. When she had the time, she'd descend on that trendiest of neighborhoods and, in a flurry of exalted excess she'd purchase a season's worth of the latest styles and perfectly matched accessories. Today however, she had other plans.

While she motored along elegant Park Crest Boulevard, she switched on the radio which was preset to W4, a station owned by the Atlas Radio Company. "It's all a big lie," sulked the talker named Rapid Roy Limerick. "It's more of the same outrageous lies from the lying, leftist Liberals. They want you to believe everyone in this country, just because they happen to live here has the so-called right to vote early…and without a picture ID! They think everyone has the right to own a house and to go to a public school and have the government pay for their health care. Believe me, I looked in the Constitution and I sure didn't see anything about any of that. I mean it! Who says some dirtbag skid row bum or a wetback illegal immigrant has the right to waltz into a hard working doctor's office and demand treatment for their West Nile Virus? And they expect you and me to pay for it! Those lies from the lying leftists are not what good Americans think. Liberals hate our country and they'll say anything to get what they want. People, we have to demand action from our leaders! Call your congressman today and demand that he votes against the public health care bill."

Hearing that, Dabny laughed out loud, not because what he said was funny but because Rapid Roy Limerick couldn't be ignored. He was the biggest talker on Atlas. In fact, he was Talk Radio's biggest talker. Rapid Roy, along with Ted Brundy and other Atlas Hosts were the reason the Talbett family was the most powerful in the radio business. And after Dabny accomplished her plan, Atlas would become an invincible empire. She envisioned a time when the entire broadcast industry was borne on the immense shoulders of Atlas, which would never know exhaustion or complacency, or meekly submit to pinhead bureaucrats. Right now however, she needed to reach her current destination, Café De' Le Aura. Arriving there, she entrusted her Mercedes to the red jacketed valet and entered the swank bistro.

"Ah Miss Talbett," exclaimed the startled maître de, "if only I knew you were coming!"

"If you don't have my table, Emile," she politely replied, "I'll take the one in the corner."

The maître de bowed and said, "your private table is always available for you."

Once seated at her favorite spot, she settled herself. At this time of day, the bistro wasn't half full with the regular clientele of corporate lawyers and their partners, and high level business executives and their pretty female associates, conversing quietly in private booths. She liked this place. During the day the sound system played the tranquil compositions of Debussy and Satie while a soft mist of sunlight floated languidly in the air, creating a shimmery ambiance which pleased and relaxed her. Yes, her life was good, so much better than most of humanity's and she was thankful for it. She'd drawn a lucky card; her days were rich with possibilities, brimming with the finest prerogatives.

Those prerogatives came from hard work. The long hours in the office, the numbing spreadsheets and interminable meetings and the irksome memos made this little bit of luxury possible. Here and now were the right place and time, the precious few years when the world's potential is available to a person with her abundant abilities. Life had given her all the breaks and one day she'd return the favor. Perhaps she'd build a museum. It would be a fabulous monument that exhibited hard work's rightly deserved rewards: the finest examples of Art Deco and modern sculpture, architectural designs in the post-modernist style and futuristic drawings of tomorrow's shining cities. These gifts she'd give willingly, the only way a gift can be given. No one should ever give anything if it's merely from ingrained habit or social coercion or for the sake of time worn tradition. To follow tradition, she'd say, is to let the past do your thinking. And thinking makes us who we are, and who wants to live in the time worn past? One day, she'd create a scholarship fund for promising students who'd freed themselves from rusted out traditions. They'd be the very brightest young people with the potential to create great wealth. That's the kind of endowment munificent achievers make to their alma mater. But right now she'd do what she had to while Opportunity presented itself. With that thought in mind, she called the number she'd memorized.

After the second ring, a young woman answered, saying, "HR Consulting."

"This is Dabny Talbett. I want to speak with Mister Roache."

She had to hold for fifteen seconds, longer than she liked to wait. But she knew the man was constantly busy, and constantly in demand. Hondo Roache used his intelligence, as well as his congressional connections to create a company that was unequaled in the industry. His clients were some of the country's largest corporations and he'd select his new clients from a waiting list of the country's other largest corporations. Today, when he came on the line his mellifluous voice sounded happily surprised and very curious.

"This is unexpected, Miss Talbett."

"I'm at Le Aura," she said to him. "I want you to come here."

He didn't respond right away. Then he said, "is this something I should prepare for?"

"I need you as you are."

"Twenty minutes," he said and hung up.

Satisfied with the call, she ordered a glass of Château Cheval Blanc. It was her favorite wine, smooth and subtly tart with a clean and brisk aftertaste. She allowed herself to savor a first swallow, only one because she had to concentrate on the document in her hand. She began to read. The top of the first white page was titled The Freedom to Own and Operate: The Exercise of Inalienable Commercial Rights through Smart Congressional Lobbying, by Hondo Roache, CEO. Her thoughts took on sharper focus as her eyes followed the words.

Legislators are like compliant, yet sometimes sly and duplicitous canines that, in order to gainfully serve their function in the world need a wise and authoritative master. Once they are properly trained, such canines (read: legislator) will slavishly obey their master's orders. They will even charge into mortal combat if they are so directed. It is important to note that every legislator will invariably seek the path that leads to the greatest reward for himself and his prospects for re-election. I know this to be true because I was such a legislator. I cast my votes so as to benefit my contributors and my political party (Republican, of course) as well as my own best interests.

"Is that homework or are you reading for pleasure?"

Peering down at Dabny was a man in his sixties, immaculately attired in a charcoal gray, pinstriped suit set off with a red and gold tie in a perfect Windsor knot. With a full head of silver hair, a face chiseled by experience into a sharp edged sculpture and gleaming blue eyes that sparkled with a wealth of wisdom he personified an icon come to life.

"Jason!" Dabny exclaimed. "I thought you were in London."

"Jumped the pond last night," he said. "Still feeling a bit jet laggy."

She rose to embrace him then motioned to a chair at her table. "You look your usual hearty self," she said with an idolizing smile. "You know of course, I wholly embrace your ingenious principles."

"And you, dear Dabny," he replied, "are one of my favorite acolytes."

She uttered a delighted chuckle and leaned closer to him. "Now then," she said lowering her voice, "the last time we spoke you mentioned an exclusive club of sorts. It all seemed terribly hush-hush."

"Not a club," Jason Gild said. "It's something quite different, but really I can't talk about it at this moment."

"I hate it," she sulked, "when you keep secrets from me."

In reply, Gild's lips curled upward, slyly provocative. "I will only tell you this," he whispered. "A magnificent new way of doing business is in the offing." He held up his hand to fend off her pouty glare. "You'll understand," he said, "when the appropriate time comes. I promise it will be worth the wait."

"I hate to wait," she said, "for anything."

He responded with an understanding nod, like an indulgent uncle and then he changed the subject. "How's Jamesford? I hear there's a lull in your efforts with congress."

"My father is ready to throw in the towel," she replied, "and it breaks my heart. We're so close to getting a majority. The Republicans are happy to give us ownership of the radio bandwidth, but two Democrats won't budge. If you ask me that whole party is nothing but a vulgar mob of socialists."

"Government shouldn't control us," Gild avowed. "We need to cut it down to size, so it will fit inside a shoe box. Then at the stroke of midnight, when the moon is on the wane we'll bury that box in the backyard so deep it can never claw its way out."

It was the kind of comment he would make in his frequent interviews in the Wall Street Journal. That and other financial media sought his quotes on how laissez faire capitalism is, in fact, the motor that should drive every decision that affects the nation's existence. Gild would assert in his famously inscrutable manner that government, wielding its obsolete laws only inhibits the country's growth. By its very nature, government hogties the real producers of wealth, the men and women who dare to achieve great things.

"They like to say the People own the airwaves," he said to Dabny. "But the crazy truth is the bureaucracy does. It's the Law of the Land, whether we approve or not. "

"Government shouldn't own my wavelength," she said. "I need it to maximize earnings for Atlas, and the shareholders of course. But to do that, I have to utilize every second of airtime.

I'm wasting it on those insipid Public Service Announcements, and I don't want to worry about the bureaucrats yanking our license. "

"It's been many years since a corporate owned station lost its license," Gild said. "Isn't the renewal process merely procedural?"

"It has been in the past," she answered. "But in the last year we've seen more of those damn nuisance challenges from grubby left wing activists. They never get far with the Communications Council," she went on, "but we have to go through the motions. Our biggest station is in renewal right now, and there's the usual issue with Crystal ComCo."

Jason Gild knew about the other big player in the Talk Radio format. In the last few years CryCom, as the company was commonly called, hired several top Hosts away from Atlas and took twelve percent of its market share. That big of a loss and the threat of losing still more couldn't be sustained, even by a company the size of Atlas. Today, Dabny and Jamesford Talbett were battling on two fronts: one with their guileful business adversary, the other with a handful of mulish civil servants in Washington.

"We'll win both wars," she said, "when we take ownership of the spectrum. Then I'll use every dial position to monetize the bandwidth's untapped potential."

Her words evoked a shiny gleam in Gild's gleaming eyes. He bent nearer the young woman. "To win that war," he said, "you'll have to fight very hard and dirty. You'll have to kick and bite with all your strength. I mean of course, it will be a difficult battle to win."

"I'm not going to fight alone," she said. "I know when to call in the necessary firepower."

"If it's who I think," Gild said as he glanced at the essay lying in front of her, "you're going to pay a high price. His kind of talent is very rare and just as expensive."

Dabny shrugged; she already knew that. "There comes a time," she said, "when the man on the mountaintop must take up a new challenge, because that is the kind of man he must be. Then, when the opportunity arises he will do what a man like him must do, because it's in his nature to do it."

"Then all I will do," Gild said as he rose to leave, "is say I don't doubt you'll attain what you want to attain. I'd have to be daft," he added with a canny tone, "to anticipate anything else." Then he leaned down to kiss her offered cheek. "One day soon," he said, "we'll meet again. At that time I'll reveal the mighty transformation which will create a world we're entitled to."

As the great man strolled out of the café, she watched him with eyes full of pure admiration. If she were a male, she'd want to be him. Yes, he was a genius and a creator of untold wealth and a leader in the business world. But she saw more than that. Jason Gild had soared into the rarified heights. He'd thwarted the quibblers and the government regulators and all those who'd bring him down to their mediocrity. His singular achievement awed her. She also knew there were others such as Jason Gild, younger people like her who were taking up the same battle and forging their own futures, preparing to rise above the submissive masses and the bureaucrats' heavy handed ordinances. Then, after taking a sip of wine she picked up the file and renewed reading the essay by Hondo Roache.

Remember, it is the very essence of a politician's nature to shirk his promise. Therefore, once the legislator commits never allow him the opportunity to renege. Instill in him the fear that if he fails to execute his commitment he will pay a heavy price. But, if a sufficiently sizable inducement is proffered (the word bribe will not be used here) then the legislator will do as he is told. Then he will most certainly ask for something in return (which is also in his nature), and you will dutifully provide that thing to him. This transaction will ingratiate you even deeper into his compromised soul, which you now possess.

The words in this essay, Dabny realized pointed to a sparkling fountainhead of new tactics, no, to an entirely new strategy which would ultimately bring her ownership of the airwaves. The most bothersome problem was her obstinate father. More and more he worried, too much she thought, about costs and not enough about the income side of the ledger. Of course, the bottom line is all important, but an investment in the future now will yield decades of greater revenues. But Jamesford Talbett, concerned about the loss of market share and the shrinkage of the company's cash reserves had devised a plan which was doomed to fail. Worse, he'd employed lobbyists who were not the highest caliber, though their fees were astronomical. Added to that, the funds the lobbyists required to 'lubricate the legislative logrolling' had cost Atlas many more unbudgeted millions.

"We can only afford what our cash flow allows," Jamesford admitted in secret to her. "Don't forget, we need to service the debt on our capital loans and we have a payroll to meet…the Hosts are demanding a big increase in their compensation and they want a retaining bonus, too…and we have to deliver our annual projection for the shareholders. Right now we have barely enough in our accounts to accomplish those tasks and remain in control of our finances."

There it was, her father's unnecessary concession of defeat. Indeed, he'd drawn an indelible line in the sand. She saw it clearly and understood a new reality had arrived. Yes, the time had finally come, which she both feared and had anxiously awaited. Ahead lay a new and untrodden path, one she had no choice but to trod upon. In the past she'd never gone against his wishes. She'd been the dutiful daughter, raised to defer to his considered judgment. For most of her life that was okay because she'd gotten everything she wanted. But now she wanted something else, something much greater than all the gifts Jamesford could give her. She wanted to own the nation's airwaves. Then, when her father inevitably retired or stepped down to become Chairman of the Board, she'd take over as CEO of Atlas.

Over the past few months the company's lagging earnings led to a drop in the value of its stock, from its high of $250 to its current price of $225. The profit margin had slipped too; it now languished at the breakeven point. Several Atlas Hosts had fled to the hated competition and the stockholders were getting nervous...well, to hell with them...so she couldn't deny Atlas was struggling. To her this was the perfect Opportunity to seize the reins and rise to a position of greater influence and power. That's right, she had to act now!

But no, within churned the foreboding she'd hurt the noble man who'd given her so much. Jamesford had nurtured and guided her on a trajectory to personal excellence and professional over achievement. He'd given her every possible advantage, the biggest home and the smartest tutors, the healthiest food and the finest education. And she adored him for it.

Suddenly, she felt a jagged anguish: she was scheming to betray the man who raised her. Oh, her conscience was acting up, was it? Well, she didn't have to listen to that worrisome voice.

In high school she'd read a great big book which espoused a theory she eagerly embraced. The theory stated the conscience is merely an illusion the ancient high priests conjured to keep their gullible followers under control. The theory had to be true. After all, she was an authentic individualist, intellectually gifted and impervious to the manipulations of the conniving high priests. She'd learned life's lessons from a master. Her father built Atlas by taking what he wanted and he never asked permission before he took it. And he never expressed any guilt about taking what he'd taken. Now she'd do as he had done.

Yet, she'd have to deceive him, for a second time. The first was not informing him that she'd 'adjusted' the number of Public Service Announcements their stations aired. Though not legally required to air any of the non-commercial messages, every radio station owner, to obtain a license to operate commits to air a customary amount of PSAs, generally one-third of a station's inventory. Dabny resented having to make that commitment. PSAs took time away from paid for advertising; they also annoyed the Hosts and irritated the listeners. So, five years ago she secretly ordered all Atlas General Managers to air half the customary amount. At W4, their most profitable station, she ordered the General Manager to air only one PSA per day. She knew she could get away with this drastic cutback. Jamesford hated the worthless notices as much as she and, since she was in charge of operations he never paid attention to them. Still, if he discovered her subterfuge he'd suffer the pain of a deceived parent, which would cause her a great deal of distress.

But she had no choice, did she? In order to take over the airwaves some deception was unavoidable. The question was: could she withstand the inevitable second guessing? Certainly, she would weather moments of nagging doubt and the pangs of inner turmoil. But when she gained the ultimate prize, her father would be so very proud of her. And more important than that, she'd possess a powerful entity, something no one else in the entire world could ever possess. And that would make her very happy, indeed. So it was settled: she'd take the necessary action, knowing sooner or later she'd have to ask his forgiveness. She expected Jamesford would give it. Her plan was set. To ultimately win the coming battle she'd wage a resolute and relentless attack, and enlist the most powerful gladiator in the arena.

We get the Lowdown on Rapid Roy

Raymond 'Fast Ray' Limerick was a star quarterback in high school and then for four years at Penn State, where he took his team to a national title. Then he played professionally for eight seasons during which he set many new records while leading his team to two world championships. All the while, Nancy Raye Hollis, his blond and lovely girlfriend shook her pompoms as well as her buttocks with the other blond and buttocks shaking cheerleaders on the sidelines of the gridiron. When Fast Ray retired from the game he took a job as a network play by play announcer and Nancy Raye, who was now his lovely wife, went on to host a daytime TV talk show. Both Fast Ray and Nancy Raye doted on their only child, their strong and handsome son they named Rapid Roy. He was expected to become a famous quarterback like his famous father, so he was given every possible preference and favor and break to insure his eventual success. But somewhere in his sophomore year at Penn State, Rapid Roy realized his life up to then had been more about his parents' dreams than a real life of his own. He'd followed their rules and directions and he'd crossed every goal line they'd set for him. But he was an individual, imperfect and needful like any other. His life was his to live the way he wanted, come whatever troubles that may rise up before him. He'd live the way he had to live; he'd take on his challenges like a man. Soon, he discovered he preferred over eating to sweating while doing push-ups, and over drinking and over drugging to sit-ups and pull-ups and those damn exhausting wind sprints. In the course of the following five years Rapid Roy was expelled from two colleges for sexual misconduct and public lewdness. But with the help of his famous father's name, he got a job with a local radio station as a sports commentator. It wasn't long before he turned his commentating to the world of partisan politics and soon enough, he had his own talk show with the Atlas Radio Company. In a few years he built a huge national audience and was making more money in a month than his famous father made in a year. Rapid Roy was the mainstay and brilliant star that made Atlas number one in Talk Radio and when other top Hosts left for CryCom he stayed in place because the Talbetts grudgingly paid the exorbitant compensation he demanded.

"Unquestioned loyalty to your family and to your employer," he told his listeners, "is the finest gift you can give them. Unquestioned loyalty to the cause of patriotism is the greatest gift of all. Now, why do I believe that? Because my friends, we're seeing how the lying, leftist Liberals are destroying our country's loyalty to its principles. I've told you about the concentration camps big government is building, right now, to throw all of us into. They want to throw us patriots into prison because we're standing up against the welfare state and the health insurance mandate and the Liberals' cruel death panels. They're trying to kill the free market, too. And why are they doing that? Because they know the free market does everything better than their lousy socialism. The leftists want you to believe

the personal accumulation of great wealth and unchecked political influence is bad, and that taxes are good for our patriotic job
creators. The Liberals want to take everything you've worked
for in your life. And worse than that, they'll steal your children's
dreams for a better country to live in. If I had more time today
I'd tell you what I'm personally going to do about it. But that
will have to wait until tomorrow. So in the meantime remember
this: your best friend Rapid Roy will tell you what you need to
know and I'll tell you in a way that you can easily understand.
I'll call the balls and strikes and the touchdowns the way I see
them and in a way that you can see them too. I'm the only man
standing between you and the lying Liberals and I promise to be
here when you need me. And that my friends is the very definition of loyalty. It's what I was born to do."

Chapter III
The Opposition Arises

In a modest, two story office building in the working class part of town, thirty-seven year old Rafe Nailer rolled up his shirt sleeves and let out an exhausted sigh. The former History teacher leaned over the messy desk, to gain more light on the document in his hands. Then, for yet another time the author of three books on the power of the People to rise up against corporate greed reread the letter's most important paragraphs.

In summary, the Public Cause Group urges the Federal Communications Council to immediately institute these measures:

1 Compel the Atlas Radio Company (ARC), without further delay, to initiate necessary changes in its operations. These measures must insure all ARC stations, from the commencement of their license period, will devote the radio industry's usual and customary amount of time to the broadcasting of Public Service Announcements (PSAs). These announcements will be broadcast throughout the day in as even a rotation as possible, and not lumped solely into the overnight daypart.

2 These PSAs are to be in the Peoples' interest and will be broadcast without charge. They will include messages from non-profit organizations and community charities and other such non-partial, unbiased, informative and

non-commercial material, designed to raise awareness and add to the public's knowledge of current issues and ongoing social matters.

3 If specific Atlas stations continue not to meet the current industry standard, and with the established rule of Law which states the broadcast airwaves belong to the People of the United States, and that the broadcast media is required to serve the Common Interest, then the Council will not renew the licenses of those Atlas radio stations. Furthermore, the Council must and will revoke the license of those ARC stations which do not comply with their commitment to air the customary amount of PSAs.

This petition, Rafe admitted to himself had little chance for success. PSAs weren't exactly a hot button issue with the Federal Communications Council. Its members paid little, if any attention to whether or not a radio station aired the customary number of the informative spots. And the absence of the messages doesn't enflame the People to rise up to confront the corporations that monopolize the broadcast industry. Still, History proves a minor issue can become the spark that lights the fuse which starts the revolution that brings down a mighty empire. It's the niggling, nagging details that finally damn the tyrant. The challenge lies however, in choosing the right niggling detail for a weapon. On a half dozen previous occasions he'd sent petitions to the Council; it routinely side stepped, or merely ignored those petitions. Of the council's five appointed members, the three Republicans fought against forcing any company to abide by the existing laws.

The modern day marketplace, those members wrote in their majority statement, *should be the overruling and ultimate*

authority on what and how a broadcast station operates. In this,
a Free Enterprise nation, the private owners of broadcast busi-
nesses must not be coerced to conform to outdated government
dictated requirements. The overriding principle must be under-
pinned by what the marketplace decides.

Rafe read that statement and was truly mystified. An imaginary thing can make a decision? He'd confront-ed that same magical thinking when he argued before the Communications Council. He heard Republicans in congress say the same thing, with straight faces no less, and he'd hear it uttered by corporate shills on the insufferable Pro and Con nattering partisan shows, those thirty minutes of wasted time when nothing is ever decided, not even the definition of what is a fact and what is not.

"This time we're going to win."

Vera Standfore walked up to Rafe's desk. "The Council has a new member and he's not in either party," she said. "That means he'll break up the majority. The Nation magazine de-scribes him as 'principled and non-partisan.'"

"Council members come and go."

Rafe was giving her a mischievous grin, the one that made her mischievously grin back. "But goofy ideas like 'the market makes decisions' will hold on for dear life," he said. "They're damn stubborn things, those goofy ideas. Hell, goofy ideas make a career for a lot of politicians."

Vera, tall and lean with short blond hair and vivid azure eyes, came closer to him. "I want my boss and future husband," she said, "to have all the luck he can get." Then she kissed him lightly on his lips.

"I'll expect more than that," he said, "to celebrate when the council does the right thing."

"What's the next step," she asked.

He picked up a thick binder. "The company's reports," he said, "show Atlas makes lots and lots of money, hundreds of millions every quarter. They make money hand over fist and like it's going out of style, like money is the only grease that lubricates every gear in every machine in the whole wide world."

Vera nodded solemnly as she elbowed him in the ribs.

"Atlas doesn't meet the PSA standard," he said. "So I'm making a license challenge to W4. It's their flagship station, with the highest ratings and biggest revenues...ninety-five million per year."

Starting three years ago, he and Public Cause volunteers spent painful hours monitoring the station's broadcasts. They documented the time given to programing—the rancorous Hosts took up most of it—and the time given to commercials and promotions, and the minutes allocated to PSAs. Their research revealed a revelatory fact: W4 aired an average of only one PSA per day, a 60-second announcement at 11:59:30 PM. No doubt, it was scheduled at that precise time so the official daily logs would show two dates with at least one PSA.

"Atlas shrugs off its promises," Rafe said, "the way a rattlesnake shrugs off its dead skin."

But Atlas crushed his previous challenges. The Talbetts pressured the Republican members to keep his petitions out of the official record. "The Atlas people think they're so damn big," he once said to Vera, "they can't see far enough down to notice me."

"What you need to do," she replied, "is take a bite out of their ankle bone."

"I'm getting to think," he said, "I should throw a few bricks through their windows." He looked at Vera who was giving him a cheerful scowl. "This time," he said, "I'll circumvent their lawyers and the politicians, the ones who take contributions from the Talbetts. Damn it, if I have to I'll kidnap the old bastard. I'll hold him hostage at knife point, no, at gun point, no at the business end of a blunderbuss until he agrees to obey the law. It might not be the nice progressive tactic to use, but at least I'll get his attention."

"Jamesford Talbett," Vera said, "will fight you like the devil."

"My intention," he replied, "is to fight like the devil, too. And then some."

When he had to, Rafe Nailer could indeed fight like the devil. He was a man driven to accomplish the unaccomplishable, set on the course of a seemingly unwinnable mission. For the past seven years the corporate media ignored his quixotic quest. His powerful adversaries, the good ol' boys in Big Oil and the Big Broadcast Network owners and the shameless banksters from the Too Big to Fail Banks did all they could to vilify him and soil his reputation, with little permanent effect. In board rooms across the country he was reviled as a self-serving do-gooder and overwrought fanatic. But in the smaller places where the common folks abide he was hailed as the People's Advocate. He suffered heartbreaking defeats and countless, bitter setbacks. Yet he kept fighting back, like a bloodied pugilist battling an intractable opponent.

"The more the big guys beat me up," he'd say, "the more exhausted they get. Sooner or later they'll be too weak to stand in the ring against me."

"The members of the council are still the referees," Vera cautioned. "They won't check to see if the Talbett's gloves have brass knuckles in them. Worse than that, when you're down on the mat the council will only count to five before they declare the Talbetts the winner."

Vera Standfore was Rafe's trusted confidante and relied upon comrade in arms. She did the daily grind work for the Public Cause Group because she believed in him and his mission. She stuffed envelopes and wrote articles for their press releases and she took a place in the first row in demonstration marches, right next to her fiancé. Vera stayed close to him and when she had to, she'd jump between him and an out of control cop. If the situation demanded she wasn't opposed to throwing a punch or two, even if he didn't join the fist fight. Now they were engaged to be married in a couple of months, and engaged as well in a looming battle with the herculean Atlas Radio Company.

"They don't acknowledge us yet," Rafe said, "so we need to get their attention. After that, I expect they'll come after us with everything they've got. I can't wait to get down in the dirt with them."

Chapter IV
Between the Ends, a Joining

Hondo Roache never backed down from a fight. He knew that if you show your opponent the slightest weakness then you've already lost the battle. He also knew that to gain the largest share of market a company must wield a forceful and convincing weapon. That's the work of effective lobbying.

"To prevail in today's over regulated environment," he'd advise his blue chip clients, "you must take a congressman by the hand and skillfully lead him to the place you want him to go."

The procedure is that simple, or so Hondo made it seem. "You don't need to pull too hard," he'd say to rapt audiences during his eagerly awaited appearances at corporate rallies. "You need to steer your legislator in the right direction and, most important of all you must obtain his commitment. Yes, the entire process hinges on the commitment you wrest from the fickle legislator. Think of his commitment as a heavy cudgel you hold to his head and if he ever wavers, never be afraid to club him with it."

As hundreds of eyes watched his every step, the champion of the self-made man would resolutely pace across the stage. His sandy hair and dollar green Armani suit were drenched in the spotlight's brilliance as he thrilled the audience of gratified CEOs and COOs and aspiring mid-level managers.

"The entrepreneurial business leader must reach out and grab," he declared, "for all his net worth, the thing he most hungers for in the world. The right to control our destinies," he said, "may not come from God above, and it certainly doesn't come from government, but it dwells deep down inside us…it's a true and lasting birthright. Remember, we have only those rights we're willing to fight and die for. It has to be that way. Otherwise we're merely slaves to the faceless bureaucrats who would make every man and every business equal to the next, and when that happens no one can rise to the top. And the top, of course, is where great producers are entitled to do their business."

This afternoon Hondo was driving his black Porsche Carrera to Café De' Le Aura to meet with Ms. Dabny Talbett. It's funny, he mused, only a couple weeks ago she and he crossed paths at a trendy West Side cocktail reception. It was a plushy soiree for a hot new artiste, a brash *wunderkind* who'd swept across the art scene like an unexpected fashion craze. Sure, the kid has some talent, Hondo conceded. But then it can't be too terribly difficult to splash some colored gel, the gaudy gold and crimsons and smarmy salmon pinks onto a defenseless sheet of canvas. Hell, supplied with an ample palette anyone, even a talentless hack can produce a popular piece of middling dreck. Still, if the cognoscenti of the Art World are happy to open their checkbooks, then fine, let the *Enfant Terrible* grab as much lucre as he can shove into his pockets. That's the way the marketplace works and the market is the ultimate, really it's the only true decider of value. Any and all values, that is.

"Miss Talbett is at her private table," the maître de informed Hondo. "She's been busy reading."

What she was reading, he realized, was one of his award winning essays. He'd written this particular piece five years ago and the passage of time only confirmed his thesis: lobbying is not only legal and legitimate, it's absolutely necessary for the continued operation of the economy. He went on to write, *lobbying is a highly productive method for the nation's leading lobbyists to inoculate their legislators against socially beneficial and ethically challenging issues.* Yes, Hondo absolutely believed what he'd written, and so did his admiring clients, especially when in conclusion he wrote, *Perhaps most important of all, effective lobbying will enable the country's farsighted job creators to obtain lower taxes for themselves, thus creating the vast wealth with which they can (but not necessarily will) use to create new jobs for the millions of out of work and over qualified American workers.*

"If I may say," he quipped as Dabny looked up from the essay, "that's a good way to impress me."

"Impressions don't mean a thing," she replied. "It's only the substance that matters."

Emitting an impressed laugh, Hondo took her hand. "When a woman as accomplished as you calls me," he said, "I assume she means business."

Yes, a call from Dabny Talbett meant serious business. After all, this was a midweek afternoon and a coming together of two of the country's most influential citizens. In a way, this was a perfect pairing of likeminded people. It's from unions like this that paradigm shifting ideas arise and spread across the continent, and then continent size paradigms are sure to be shifted.

"The time will come," she said in a conspiratorial tone, "when we'll look back at this meeting. It will be a time," she added, "when we've taken what we're rightfully entitled to take."

"And that would be something," he said, "which is above mere money?"

The word provoked her. She'd hoped, expected really that Hondo would grasp the true significance of this meeting. This, their first private conversation would provide each the opportunity to explore the other's capability. Perhaps more importantly, here each would assess the other's resolve to take whatever action was needed to ultimately prevail.

"Before there's money," she said, "there comes the struggle. But you and I both know before the struggle we must possess the knowledge of who we are and what we want, and what we deserve to possess."

"Self-knowledge," he said, "is the most important weapon in our arsenal. Without it we don't know what's actually at stake."

"And with our self-knowledge," she retorted, "we can never be defeated."

Her words rang with the finely wrought tone of time-tested veracity. Hearing it, Hondo sat down and studied her striking face. He noted the arrow straight line of her nose, the resolute shape of her jaw and most important of all, the fierce determination in her eyes. No, not mere determination. In the depths of those emerald irises roiled an icy ferocity that could never be subdued. Dabny's reputation was that of a brilliant yet stone cold competitor who never failed to achieve her objectives. Her reputation was well deserved and Hondo heartedly approved. To achieve great success a winner will pay the cost out of her finite emotional inventory. The more the winner wins, the more that inventory is depleted. It's a fair price to pay and Dabny had paid it willingly. Often, her name graced the headlines of the country's major magazines—not the vacuous celebrity rags— but the high end periodicals that examined issues in the financial and economic sectors. Her analysis was consistently spot on and she'd suggest actions that were sure to succeed, if only the moss-backs in Washington would follow her lead. Yes, here was an intelligent and noble woman. And this was, the lobbyist realized truly a moment he'd never forget.

"We'll begin," she said, "with me laying out the scenario."

"It's about the radio spectrum, isn't it," he replied. "I understand your efforts to privatize it have hit a snag."

She showed him her coy smile, the same as in her photos in those high end magazines. "I see you're up on the news," she said coyly. Of course, he'd be up on the news. This man dwelt in the vortex of congressional intrigue. He thrived in the murky corridors of political deal making. Certainly, he knew how to push the people who pulled the levers of legislative power. Hondo Roache inserted thoughts into the minds of high level decision makers and in a very real way, he swayed the leaning of the government. And government was the object she needed swayed to lean in precisely the way she wanted.

"My father intends to halt our lobbying efforts right when the tide is turning," she said. "Though I fully agree the CEO has the right to make that decision, I also believe Atlas needs to keep pushing. We're so close to winning it all now."

"Perhaps your father is choosing to fight other battles."

Hondo sought to evaluate her frankness which he expected would be candid and frank. "You need to keep the Hosts on Atlas," he said. "And Crystal ComCo is trying to take more of your market share."

"Frankly, Atlas needs our Hosts," she replied. "However, I believe they're our number two priority. When Atlas takes ownership of the spectrum we can establish new terms for all the radio companies, including CryCom."

"They're a dangerous opponent," Hondo countered. "Their Hosts get big ratings, and big comp packages."

"That's what I will change," she said. "I'll offer their Hosts a deal far in excess of what my opponent at CryCom can put on the table."

Her words, he thought might mean anything. It was a statement a crafty business leader would craftily employ: always be clear and always be ambiguous. When the anticipated opportunity arises, the anticipatory leader will execute the appropriate tactic and ultimately win the contest.

"At this juncture," he said, "you have a lot of work to do."

"My strategy is not unlike dominoes," she said. "Set them up in a nice, neat row. Make sure they'll all in the right position and, at the end set down the domino which has one more spot than the others. Then, when it's in the perfect place and the time is right, tap that one, leading domino. You know what will happen next."

Hondo marveled at the marvelous notion. It was a plan of action so utterly simple yet fraught with so much complexity. It exemplified the high stakes stratagem wielded by conquerors throughout history. Yes, Genghis Khan and Napoleon Bonaparte and Catherine the Great took on the world in a way lesser mortals never could. And now Dabny Talbett was wielding that same stratagem. At once, Hondo envisioned a sweeping victory, or a failure of historic proportions. And failure, historic or otherwise was the one thing he refused to accept, or be any part of.

"The devil," he murmured, "can win only if we concede to him."

"I've watched you take on the drudges in the capital," Dabny said. "And with your masterful lobbying congress passed a law, or repealed one. I know you're the perfect man for the job."

"The job can be accomplished," he said. "But to do so one must know the correct words to say and where to apply the right amount of pressure on the right legislator at precisely the perfect moment."

From a lifetime of experience, Hondo knew how to achieve the result his expectant clients sought and wrote seven figure checks to obtain. The lobbying process demands an abundance of patience and rock hard persistence and most important of all, a keen insight into those who pass the nation's laws.

"In a way," he'd joke to his colleagues, "the process is like studying a lower form of life. Legislators aren't like producers. Members of congress never create anything. Instead they tax the real producers for as much as they can get away with, and then they tell the voters the producers must be kept in line."

Growing up in southern Virginia, Hondo's days were split between society's elite and those much less elite, the coarser working people. His far-sighted father, who'd inherited a tobacco fortune from his father and his father before him demanded his son learn the value of real work. In his youth, Hondo took jobs as a fry cook in a greasy fast food joint, as a runner on the floor of a noisy commodities exchange and, during his college days at The Citadel he tended bar in a working man's tavern. During his long night shifts he learned how to use the sound of his voice—a soft inflection here and a vaguely threatening tone there—to produce the result he desired. He learned how to read the faces of his customers—the troublesome factory laborers, the tough as nails roofers and the rowdy construction workers—the sober and the drunk and the drunker, and he learned how talk an arrogant jock out of a booze induced fist fight. In college he also learned to use his sharp wit and smooth articulation to gain the contacts which would prove useful for his coming career. And the career he chose was in politics. He served one term in the Virginia state house and then three terms in the U. S. House of Representatives. There, he learned the rules and how to break them (and not get caught by the opposition) and he made the connections that would make him the most effective lobbyist working the halls of the capitol. His early jobs taught him the way a human thinks and considers the options and finally makes a commitment. He mastered the psychology of gentle and not so gentle persuasion and the positive results derived from monetary inducements.

"If I didn't truly believe you are the best," Dabny said, "I mean the top notch, no doubt about it best in the business, I wouldn't have called you."

"I wouldn't have come today," he replied, "if I weren't the very best."

It wasn't an empty boast and she expected to hear it. In fact, if she hadn't expected to hear it she wouldn't have called him in the first place. "So," she said, "what do think about my strategy?"

He was ready with his answer. "In order to enlist me in your cause, you'll have to commit, right now. I want ten percent of Atlas."

"I didn't think you'd ask for more than five," she said, frowning.

Hondo shrugged with mock deference. "I usually refrain," he said, "from trying to meet the expectations of others, especially when it involves a matter of business, and my revenues."

"I can offer seven," she said. "That's all I can do. It's coming out of my share of the company."

"Ten is an appropriate figure," he said. "After all, you approached me first."

She sat back to consider the prospect of giving this man part of her ownership in Atlas. It was a high price indeed. But in Hondo Roache she was getting the most talented talent in the entire country's talent pool. And she couldn't wait another day to take action. She sought the conviction in the lobbyist's convincing eyes. She tried to read his unreadable face. "You must agree," she said, "to the strictest confidence. My father must not find out until I have the spectrum in my hand."

"My silence comes with our agreement," he said. "A leak will hurt me as much as you."

The certainty of the man's pledge was quite certain; his cunning artifice couldn't be doubted. "So we're a team," she said. "Now, let's have a toast. Then we'll get to work. It's going to be a challenge but," she added, "we're more than equal to the task."

Now, we meet good ol' Ted Brundy

"Yes siree," the clever yokel Host drawled during his show on Atlas. "The cuckoo left wingers are at it again, good buddies. And I tell ya, this one's a great big ol' belly slapper."

Brundy grew up in Tulsa, Oklahoma, lived for ten years in a condo in downtown Little Rock, Arkansas and following that, eleven years in a subdivision outside Charleston, West Virginia. He'd perfected his countrified delivery in order to appeal to a targeted audience segment. From his experience as a commercial vermin exterminator he learned a down-home, folksy approach makes a certain kind of listener believe whatever you say to them. More importantly, his listeners trusted him and agreed with him and they kept their ears glued whenever his show was on the Atlas airwaves.

"This time the Democrats say it's up to you and me," he alerted the folks back home, "to pay the pensions of all those old, used up government employees. That's right, you're paying good money to those overpaid bureaucrat retirees who never did anything but push paper around all day while they sat on cushy chairs in air conditioned offices. And they drank coffee whenever they felt like it and had their own insurance plan! The big government boys aren't telling you the truth, so I have to. The reason America is in hock up to its big ol' donkey ears is because the leftists in Washington spent your money on welfare checks for a bunch of lazy do-nothings, and on food stamps for those same lazy do-nothings and on free medicine the lazy do-nothings sure aren't entitled to. And it's worse than that. They're giving your money to a bunch of lazy do-nothings in other countries! Your money is going over there to Africa and India, to people you'll never set eyes on. Think about it, good buddies. The leftists take your hard earned money and give it to a bunch of dirty, lazy, ignorant foreigners. Now I might not be the smartest schoolboy in the little red schoolhouse, but I know this is downright crazy. The leftists want one government for the whole world and we're getting squeezed out and stepped on. It's been their plan since that communist Roosevelt and the left wingers think they'll get away with it. So now that you know what they're after, don't you think we should do something about it?"

Chapter V
Wits are Matched, the Game is On

The early evening had cooled to a perfect temperature. The air held the right amount of moisture, not too humid, not too dry. The flowers in the garden, the rosy red rose bushes and gladiolas and the showy geraniums flaunted their opulent hues in the day's remaining rays of sunlight. Here, in the manicured grounds behind Leadership Place mansion walked Dabny and Jamesford Talbett.

"I'm not happy right now," he said in his cheerless voice. "God damn it, I didn't do all that hard work so I could be unhappy."

"It's not like I'm trying to cause it," she replied innocently. "I only want the best for both of us."

Jamesford, age sixty-seven, was wearing his usual double breasted navy blue blazer over a white silk shirt along with his trademark amber Ascot and summer woolen pants patterned in an understated hound's-tooth pattern. His posture was ramrod straight, his dark hair was swept heroically back from his brow and his coal black eyes simmered with their usual coal hard intensity.

"If we continue to pursue ownership of the airwaves," he chided his daughter, "it'll bleed our operating cash. Then we'll drain the last of our reserve funds. We've gone as far as we can. It's time to get out of the fight, and I damn well mean it."

"We can't give up now."

Dabny looked at him with concern mixed with defiance and more than a little wariness. Jamesford was powerfully built with broad shoulders and heavy arms and a chest made bullish strong from years of pumping iron under the guidance of his personal trainer, an ex-professional ballplayer. Sly and tough when he had to be, yet flexible and open to opposing views as well, Jamesford maintained an inner core of disciplined willfulness. He knew his daughter better than anyone; she rarely doubted or challenged him. Yet she had to keep pushing now, but not push so hard as to alert him to her secret intentions.

"Why shouldn't we own the airwaves?"

She spoke with the words of a fervent believer, one who believed fervently in the words she spoke. "Private companies own the railroad tracks that carry consumer goods from one coast to the other. Private business owns the cell towers that carry our phone calls and data. Private business operates schools and prisons, you know and who would have thought even twenty years ago that private companies would be spying for the NSA and fighting wars in those dirty places where congress doesn't want to send the Army."

"I'm well aware of that," Jamesford snapped.

His response only provoked her. "Private companies own the satellites and the cable that bring TV into our homes," she said, "and the programs which are produced by private companies. It only makes sense that in this new day, the private companies who broadcast radio signals should own the airwaves that carry those signals. Government needs to get out of the business of owning our bandwidth, or anything else for that matter. Government shouldn't tell us what we can and can't say on the air...the market should decide that. If listeners don't want to hear certain words they can simply push a button."

"I agree with you, of course," Jamesford said. "But I won't pay the price it will cost us."

Dabny knew not to quarrel with her father, not here, not now. As always, she contained her emotions, what few emotions she contained. She seldom exhibited the highs and lows... the sensations of anger or joy or lust...at least the kind of lust having to do with sex but occasionally she experienced the lust of well-earned avarice. Her thoughts controlled her heart and her thoughts were under strict control. Right now those thoughts were focused on her ultimate prize. She wouldn't allow herself the premature satisfaction of winning this single debate. Yet neither would she back down the way she had in the past. Still, she didn't want to make this conversation unnecessarily heated. Doing that would further provoke him. So she took a moment to adjust her tactics as she inhaled a rose's untainted scent. In her sleek white blouse, dark vest and black linen pants she looked exquisitely casual, as if in an oil portrait, casually posing next to the exquisite, red as the reddest of all rose blossoms.

"Father," she said, now with a soothing manner, "I've watched you over the years. I saw you work so very hard to create Atlas. I saw how you struggled when mother died...I was only seven years old...and I remember how you kept going every day to make your vision come to life. I know in my heart of hearts how much Atlas means to you."

"I believe your words," Jamesford said. "But I have to question the motive behind your words."

"Those days in the past," she went on, firmer now, "when you struggled to create a thing of great value...a unique and magnificent thing...are days that remain with us. I can't sit idly by and watch you let this opportunity slip away. We won't have this chance ever again."

Her words brought a frown to the frowning patriarch. "I built the company, damn it," he asserted. "I'll keep it profitable and safe."

"Profitable, yes," Dabny said, "but not as profitable as it can be. When we own the airwaves we'll control our destiny. We'll empower the Hosts to say anything we want them to say, without fearing the government. The bureaucrats will never again threaten us, or censor us. Atlas will do as we please."

"But there's too many who want to regulate us," Jamesford retorted. "If it's not the so called social watchdogs then it's those simpering Liberals in Washington. Damn it, why can't they see how wrong they are? You'd think they'd stop drinking that same old Kool-Aid. They should let us conduct our business the way we want to conduct it. Isn't that why we let them get into congress in the first place?"

His comment drew a stubborn shake of her head. "We won't give in to the parasites," she said. "If they try to steal our entitlements…if the government pulls us down to their level… then we'll fight back. And when we do," she added with conviction, "we'll win because we're smart and tough, and they are not."

"It's not as simple as that," he said. "You don't understand what's at stake."

She restrained a flippant reply. Taking a breath she watched a silent fire fly, the evening's early guest flicker bravely in the approaching evening. The little bug defied gravity as it winged its way past the roses and lifted itself upward, appearing for an instant like a promising beacon in the dusky sky. Dabny didn't believe in omens, but still, at this moment she appreciated the cosmos's magical power to portend the future with the actions of a lowly insect.

"We have this last chance," she finally said. "We'll free ourselves from government's damnable regulations. I won't quit the fight because I know I'm right."

"And if the fight bankrupts Atlas?"

Jamesford was looking at her with glinting eyes that glinted with inborn intransigence. "We need that money to keep the Hosts under contract," he said. "Even if we win the spectrum, if we run out of cash we'll lose our Hosts to that slippery lesbian at CryCom."

"Then," Dabny said, "we must change that situation."

Scowling, he turned his gaze westward, to the west. A growing plume of cumulous clouds was gathering on the horizon, framing the sun's final light in a blazing red and pink and sapphire display of Nature's grandest artistry. The sight, breathtaking and unique could be seen by millions in the region, the same millions who were controlled by an over regulating government, one that that kept a cruel chain drawn tightly across Atlas's shoulders. So yes, his headstrong daughter was correct: they were entitled to a Free Marketplace. They possessed the right to do as they wanted. And yet the cost, damn it the cost would surely end up destroying them.

"If you could do such a thing," Jamesford said, "the task would not be easy."

"Easy is for average people."

She tried not to sound overly zealous, yet she had to zealously voice her beliefs. "If a person is to create a thing of lasting worth, and if it's a worthwhile thing to do, then," she went on, "a worthy person will do what she must do. And that person...a smart and hard working person...will in the end succeed."

"You'd run into a lot of resistance," he said. "And you'd do more harm to Atlas than you know."

He sounded frustrated, she thought, or merely annoyed with her. But her determination could not be quelled. Sighing, she came closer to touch his arm. In the dimming light his worry shown in his eyes. Or, she wondered, was it more than mere worry? Perhaps Jamesford had become too cautious from the decades of battle to achieve success. For a considerable moment she considered her esteemed parent. In the past few years, and more so in the previous six months he wavered when making important decisions. He made mistakes, too, that he'd never made before. Recently he paid a vendor's excessive price for building materials needed to remodel their corporate suites. Another time Jamesford permitted a low level inspector, little more than a legalized flunky to view the company's proprietary operating equipment. In the past, the CEO would never allow that, not without a grueling legal fight. Yes, she thought with growing dismay, the once infallible Jamesford Talbett was losing his infallibility. Like anyone made of flesh and bone his powers were vulnerable and finite and worse, he was letting this opportunity escape, never to be recaptured.

"Father," she said quietly, "a smart leader knows when to press the fight, and when to hand the attack over to his second in command."

"You're implying I've lost my edge."

His voice reverberated with steely purposefulness, the voice of the purposeful ruler who'd subdued the radio industry with his steel hard notion of purpose. "Well by God," he said, "you'll have to prove it."

The words dismayed her. "You built a legacy that's honored by the people who make this country great. But I know you as my father. More than anything," she murmured, "I don't want to hurt you."

"First," he said, "I understand your feelings. You're young and smart and you know this to be true: one generation marches to the front and engages the enemy, head on. The battle is terrible and takes its awful toll. Then," he added, "the next generation must take up the sword. The circle turns in full, but the victory remains in doubt."

"I believe we'll be the victor in the battle," she countered. "And when we win, the whole world will be watching. In the days that follow other people like us will take up the fight. I plan to stay in that fight to the very end. My beliefs won't allow anything else."

Like a sacred pledge, her words hung in the air between them. For a silent moment they contemplated each other, father and daughter, wily mentor and willful student. Then Jamesford said, "if I didn't believe in you I would say so. You've got the guts and brains to achieve great things. But that's not all you need. You must learn when to press the attack and when to back off. Remember, take the other guy's gold when his back is turned and lie to get what you're entitled to, but never believe your own lies yet know other people will always lie to you. Most important of all, don't make a mistake that will ultimately defeat you. Those are the finer points of being a leader, which you must learn and understand."

Chapter VI
The Big Pitch

The bourbon was eighteen years old and the imbiber was fifty-seven. He was wearing a dark blue suit and starched white shirt. His tie was striped red, white and blue as was his American flag lapel pin. On his left hand was his college ring from Notre Dame and he was listening in a casual way to what Hondo Roache was saying, quietly so as not to be overheard by the fifteen other people in the hotel's event room. The cocktail reception was for...to Hondo it didn't matter. For him this was the perfect opportunity to chat in a not too overt yet not too subtle way with Senator Henry Gleason.

"This is a matter of fact," the lobbyist said. "The entire radio industry has undergone a massive and permanent change. Listeners listen online and from satellite services and podcasts. We're in an era congress didn't envision a hundred years ago. And as you know, the vision of congress is limited, but it's the only institution the voters depend upon to make fair and necessary laws."

"We say so anyway," Senator Gleason sighed. "But then, we say a lot of things in congress because we like to say them, especially in front of the C-SPAN cameras. And the voters expect us to say a lot of important sounding words. I guess all the talking makes everyone feel better about what's not getting accomplished."

The man's eyes were cigar tip red, Hondo guessed from the room's hazy cigar smoke and the effects of his fifth beverage. The senator wasn't yet drunk but he was nearing the condition that's ripe for deal-making and yes, commitment. The lobbyist raised his hand as a signal to the waiter: bring another bourbon for the senator.

"As you recall," Hondo said, "the last time we chatted you mentioned you sometimes listened to the Atlas Hosts. I remember you said you particularly enjoy Rapid Roy Limerick."

"I told you the man says some remarkable things," Senator Gleason replied. "Most of those things are out and out buffoonery."

"His fifteen million listeners think he's telling the gospel truth," Hondo said. "You know, mister Limerick is referred to as 'the conscience of the regular guy'. He can be very helpful to a politician, too. That is, if the politician believes what Rapid Roy believes in."

Senator Gleason laughed out loud. "God damn, Limerick has to be crazy to believe what he says to his fifteen million listeners. Last week he said the Liberals want to sterilize all our teenagers and the Democrats are conspiring with space aliens to take over the world."

"Rapid Roy sees himself foremost as an entertainer," Hondo said. "He doesn't necessarily deal with established facts."

Yes, Hondo knew that Rapid Roy Limerick, like all the other Talk Radio Hosts preferred imaginary facts—Rapid Roy called them 'yet to be established facts'—over the real kind of facts, the kind of facts that are in fact, factual. Imaginary facts are easier to find and much more convenient to use and more importantly, they're easier for his listeners to understand. Hondo also knew Rapid Roy took great pride in his ability to gain the unquestioning trust of his audience. Rapid Roy said just about anything he wanted to say, within and right up to the limits of the laws against slander and defamation of character and out and out lies ('yet to be established lies', he referred to them), and he was never called on by the press to explain himself. He once surmised the Democrats actually committed the heinous acts of 9/11 and the Gulf oil spill was intentionally caused by a cabal of rabid environmentalists who wanted to end all drilling, "because," he said, "those unwashed Greenies can't stand to see a corporation make one penny of well-earned profit."

"Rapid Roy Limerick," Senator Gleason growled, "isn't different from the other radio hacks, like that preachy ghoul Gary Bock and that viscous little shrew Anne Caldron. Two days ago she said the men in the Democratic Party have balls that are half the size of Republicans'. When I heard that," the senator added, "I asked myself how she could possibly know that."

"Ms. Caldron often uses metaphor to clarify her point," Hondo said. "Sometimes she'll use a double entrendre, even if she doesn't know what it means."

Senator Gleason swallowed some liquor and said, "what about that nitwit hick Ted Brundy? He said the Democrats are giving money to a clan of goat-headed island immigrants who live in a secret hollow in West by God Virginia. The man must be drunk on tobacco juice laced with hundred-proof moonshine."

"Mister Brundy is delivering a sizable audience for Atlas," Hondo calmly replied. "He's regarded as one of the country's leading social commentators. And by the way, he recently received the prestigious RightWay Talker of the Year Award from the neo-Confederates for a New Confederacy Confederation."

Hondo marveled at his ability to decorate an ugly truth with a plausible sounding rationale. And that's the work of a great lobbyist and he considered himself the greatest lobbyist of them all. Right now he had a job to do and he'd employ all his guiles to obtain the senator's final commitment to Atlas.

"So, what do you want, Hondo?"

Senator Gleason had swallowed the last of his bourbon and accepted a new one from the waiter. "Are you working on passing that tax deferment bill for PetroGasCo, or are you trolling for votes on the next bank bailout?"

"We're looking at a paradigm shift in the media world."

Hondo's tone reverberated with significance as he assessed the senator's condition. With his sixth drink now in hand and a look of bemused uncertainty on his face, the legislator indicated all the right indications: he was ready for the pitch. "The Atlas Radio Company," Hondo said, "can reinvent the radio industry in a way that's never before been possible. When the company brings the airwaves into the private sector it will create a vast new world, one where excellence is an everyday commodity and every voice can be heard."

"Sure, every voice *can* be heard," Senator Gleason said. "But the question is *will* it?"

"Atlas is committed to keeping the airwaves open and neutral," Hondo replied. "In the hands of the Talbetts the radio industry will undergo a wonderful rebirth."

Senator Gleason swallowed some liquor. "I hear the Talbetts might be having some problems," he said, "with their license renewal for W4. The new man on the council is rumored to be bringing in a brand new broom, you know, the kind of broom that sweeps everything clean."

"From what I've heard," Hondo countered, "the new man is more of a go along to get along kind of guy. I'm sure the renewal process will proceed in the usual problem free manner it usually does."

"This whole strange business," Senator Gleason said, now slurring slightly, "with giving the airwaves to Atlas is more complicated than I can think about right now. I can't see how it would help anyone but the Talbetts but who knows, it might not be a bad idea. Anyway, I need to look at it closer in the light of day."

Hondo knew what the senator meant because as an experienced lobbyist he understood a legislator's syntactically complex syntax. "The election is coming up next year," he said. "I'm sure you want to be prepared with a well-funded campaign chest."

"It's a god damn outrage," Senator Gleason groused, "what they want for TV and radio ad time. If the People own the broadcast spectrum how can those snaky corporations charge me so much to use it?"

"I'm sure Atlas will be happy to help you in that regard," Hondo said. "It will be in a very generous way."

Senator Henry Gleason swallowed more bourbon. "It's only fair," he sighed, "for me to consider the possibilities if we privatize the airwaves."

Gary Bock now appears, as if Foreordained

"This is the actual truth."

The popular Atlas Host spoke the truthful truth during his highly rated talk show. "Our country needs God more than ever before."

Bock was forty-six with crew cut blond hair and pale blue eyes. He'd grown up on a farm in western Kansas and went east to Bob Jones University expecting to get a college education. As it was, he came away with an Associate's degree in Corporate Communications. After leaving school, he worked as a college loan collector then as a teller for a too big to fail bank, and then as a used car salesman. One day he sold a third hand Ford Expo (with the odometer rolled back 100,000 miles) to the manager of the local radio station. Bock's agile speaking skills landed him a job behind the microphone. Once there, he knew that to succeed he needed to build a devoted but not necessarily a well-informed audience. Over the next five years he cultivated a reputation for knowing what's on God's mind and how He wants the country returned to a life of critically needed redemption. Soon, Bock had a show on Atlas and his ratings arose, growing as if predestined by the tens of thousands every month until his listenership was second only to Rapid Roy's. But Gary Bock's audience was number one in evangelical zeal.

"We've strayed, people."

He meant every word he said to his sometimes straying listeners. "Somewhere in the past, oh ten or twenty or maybe fifty years ago we allowed a virulent strain of godlessness to take hold in our government. This awful scourge uses our tax dollars to teach our children that God didn't invent the earth and heavens. It's a lie straight from the very pit of Hell. This scheme hides the truth of Noah's Great Flood and the wondrous Ark he built so the animals could live on God's green earth, after all that water went away. This education conspiracy even denies the undeniable facts about The Garden of Eden. It tells our kids we came from hairy monkeys with long wiggly tails that lived in banana trees in darkest Africa, and an invisible thing called

DNA makes us who we are and that God has nothing to do with anything. Now, I know we're living in a time when science has grown like a terrible cancer into all our lives. But we can abide science only to a certain point. When we hear scientists claim the cosmos is simply a collection of molecules and something they call 'elements', and there's no Great Maker, no intelligent designer then we must fight back, fight as hard and long as we can. We must elect the right people to our local and state school boards. We must see to it that our children's textbooks tell the proven facts, that evolution is an unproven and unprovable theory and a God hating one at that. We must take a stand, my good friends. Science is not the answer! Only our one God is the one and only true God and we must make our government responsible to Him. So please do this for me, and for our precious young ones. Elect members to your school boards who'll put God back into our kids' textbooks. This is what all of us must do, the most important thing that will keep our religion and our government one and the same. We must make sure the United States of America remains the greatest God fearing country in the entire world, which scientists claim is round like Eve's apple but is in fact flat like Adam's fig leaf, but not quite so leafy shaped."

Chapter VII
Dabny Plans her Attack

"Pull!"

At the command, Dabny released the coiled spring which sprung a gray and yellow disc from its captivity. It sprang through the air in a perfect, frantic arc, for a moment weightless, flying unfettered through the morning light. Then in a split second, at its apogee it exploded into a dusty cloud, vaporized by invisible lead pellets.

"That's nine in a row," she exclaimed. "Damn it, you beat me again."

"We'll go one more time."

Rapid Roy Limerick lowered his long barreled gun. "The wager will be doubled," he said. "If I win you'll send me another case of that tasty Black Sea caviar, delivered to my opulent beachside villa and billed to Atlas, of course."

Now relaxed after this round of shooting, they walked off the firing line to reload their weapons. In the day's crisp air, the remote area served as the perfect meeting place for them to discuss in secrecy their mutual and promising future.

"With a shotgun I can do many things," she said, picking up a box of shells. "For instance, I can stand on the firing line and massacre, one by one an entire air force of inanimate objects. Sure, it takes a little practice, but anyone can learn how to shoot skeet."

"It's still not easy," Rapid Roy replied. "And you can't do it with any old shotgun."

"With the right ammunition," she said holding up a shell, "I can go into the wilds and track down a crafty wild bird, say a long necked turkey and, with my sharpshooter's prowess I can bag that big ol' bird and take it home for the family's Christmas dinner."

Rapid Roy laughed, a little too loudly. "Like in a Dickens novel. But," he added, "Scrooge caved in to his own pathetic self-doubts."

As the two prepared for another round, they took a moment to view the pristine setting. To the north, beyond the shooting range lay two thousand acres of untrammeled woodlands, alive with curious mammals and resplendent birds and shy, green reptiles. The old growth forest, off limits to the People was owned by the Talbett family, like the land to the east, five square miles of restricted grassland with gently rolling hills that sloped leisurely down to the sand and dunes of a private beach, on the edge of what was currently a calm and silvery ocean. On this unspoiled morning, Dabny was wearing a tan shooting vest over a red plaid shirt. She had on dark brown pants and stylish ostrich skin boots.

"In the next round," she declared in her airy way, "I'll show you what real shooting is."

Rapid Roy, short and flabby in the middle, age fifty-five, wore a shooting vest too and a red turtle neck sweater, dark gray pants and giraffe hide western boots. They created the impression he was two inches taller and twenty pounds lighter, he liked to think.

"I'll match you," he replied, "shot for shot."

"The trick is," she retorted, "think of them as real birds, and not clay pigeons. When I shoot I tell myself this: if it flies it dies."

A long brimmed cap covered her hair, which was drawn into a pretty ponytail that shone in the new sunlight. Rapid Roy wore a white Stetson on his pink, balding head. Without that protection his sensitive scalp would sunburn in a few minutes. Currently he was enjoying a larger than average cheroot, skillfully hand wrapped by the hands of fully skilled wrappers in Havana, Cuba. Dabny had never smoked.

"Speaking of clay pigeons," he said as he exhaled a stream of smoke into the clean, clear air, "when will CryCom give up trying to steal W4's license?"

"They can't win and they know it," she replied. "The council won't let them get their hands on our number one dial position. We'll keep the license, don't worry."

"By the way," he said, "I heard an interesting bit of gossip. It seems that nosey troublemaker Rafe Nailer is on his way to D.C. It's possible the new council member might be open to what the so-called People's Advocate has to say."

She'd heard the rumor too and indifferently shrugged it off with a shrug of indifference. "Nailer has never been a problem and I don't expect him to be. The council won't bend over because some asinine left-winger asks them to do something they've never done before."

"If the new guy joins the two Democrats," Rapid Roy cautioned, "you'll have a new problem on your hands."

"From what I know about the new guy," she said, "he's a career paper-shuffler. Apparently he's a non-partisan, spineless bureaucrat who can't get anyone's attention, not even if he murdered his own mother and father, and the judge and prosecutor, and all twelve members of the jury."

"You never know," Rapid Roy said, laughing at her joke. "The man might've grown a pair of balls since he joined the council."

To Dabny, the prospect of the new member turning the council against Atlas was not realistic, not plausible and not even possible. Over the previous thirty years the council never took up a challenge to one of Atlas's licenses, let alone not renewed it. "I need to focus on the immediate situation," she said. "We need to turn two votes in the senate. One requires a sizeable campaign contribution and the other calls for some very special lobbying. I'm in the process of making that happen. Then," she added with an excited tone, "I'll own the airwaves!"

"Don't forget," Rapid Roy said, "the ratings books will come out in two weeks. If the Hosts numbers are up, they'll demand a big bump in their compensation. They'll be negotiating a new contract over at Crystal ComCo."

"This is what I want you to do," she said. "Tell those Hosts my checkbook is bigger than Abby Watsamore's. She may run CryCom, but she doesn't have the juice to beat Atlas, or enough money to stand up to me."

Money made Talk Radio talk. With lots of money, both Atlas and Crystal ComCo employed the nationally famous talk show Hosts. They were the medium's top draw and biggest names. They commanded the broadcast heights: prime daytime slots which demand the highest advertising rates. Every day of the week, tens of millions of Americans tuned in to listen to the imperious, peevish Hosts: a cadre of uncompromising white men and a handful of harpy tongued females, also white and just as uncompromising as the men. These dogged bloviators electrified the airwaves with vociferous vocal volleys vilifying their adversaries on the Left, notably blue state congressmen and women, especially the women.

"Everyone is fair game," big talker Rapid Roy ranted on his number one rated broadcasts. "That includes those loud-mouthed femmy-goons with their braless sagging boobs, and the wishy-washy moderates and overeducated Liberals and worst of all, the noxious east coast intellectuals, those egghead Progressives who are turning good American values into stinking, dirty, disgusting sewage."

Words like those, Dabny knew are neither polite nor savory and they were never used in the company's board room. But those words delivered big ratings for Atlas. And once the airwaves were privatized, the Talk Radio Hosts would become shriller and harsher and they'd blast out baseless lies ("Lies don't hurt people," she would say, "only people can do that.") and the ratings would grow even bigger. And then the Hosts' rantings would become louder and shriller and ever more lurid ("We won't know the limits," she'd also say, "until we break the old ones."). Certainly, the definition of free speech would be in for a serious overhaul.

"The Hosts' words are often crude and unpleasant," she admitted to a meeting of the directors. "But every one of Rapid Roy's tirades brings another half million to our bottom line, which keeps our revenue bigger than CryCom's."

"You know," Rapid Roy said as he shoved another round into his shotgun's magazine, "I don't particularly care for CryCom. That woman who runs it, Abby Whatshername is a god damned big ol' bull dyke. Personally, I'd never work for a god damned bull dyke."

"Don't worry about her," Dabny said, enjoying the insult to her reviled competitor. "Abby may not like it, but when I call her bluff she'll give up and let the Hosts come back to my open arms."

Hearing that, Rapid Roy expelled a contented sigh and looked over the shooting grounds. Littering the earth were the remnants from the shattered targets, plaster discs blown to bits by high powered weaponry. Like dismembered corpses strewn across a battlefield, the shards bespoke a terrible truth about the realities of Human Nature: if he is to attain his goals in life a man must destroy things. The notion confused the young Rapid Roy. He recalled the day his father found the book of poetry he'd been reading, the one his seventh grade English teacher had urged him to explore. Rapid Roy read the first three poems and though he didn't fully understand them he enjoyed the way the words fit together. Words, he realized can be more forceful than a quarterback's throwing arm. But Fast Ray told him a quarterback's arm will get more money and adoring girls than any line of pretty words. A game winning touchdown pass, his father pointed out, will get you laid every night of the week while fancy-dandy poetry is for limp wristed faggots and out and out losers. Ashamed and angry, Rapid Roy threw away the poetry books and dutifully pulled on his helmet and shoulder pads. But he never forgot the power of words. In the years that followed he secretly read more poetry and he practiced the skill of speaking words in the most effective way possible. His practice paid off when he finally threw away the helmet and shoulder pads and sat down at the microphone. Then his words became the most powerful things flying through the air.

"From what I've heard on the gossip grapevine," Dabny said to him, "the Hosts who left us for CryCom are having second thoughts."

"The grass is not always greener," he replied. "Nor is any man an island and some roads are never taken, not even the roads that go through the woods. You see, once they got there our Hosts discovered CryCom's production studios are way out of date and the equipment isn't as good as ours. They're going to demand better facilities before they sign the next contract."

Dabny knew that, too. Crystal ComCo had gone without upgrading its physical plant in order to have the money to hire the Hosts away from Atlas. She also knew Rapid Roy stayed in close contact with his former work mates, even though they currently competed against him for audience share. But the millions of Talk Radio listeners would switch stations with their favorite Hosts. If she rehired those who'd strayed to CryCom, she'd regain their loyal audiences, too.

"If anyone can bring them back," she said, "it's you, Roy. I want you to talk to them, in absolute secrecy. Tell them I'll add twenty percent to anything *my friend* Abby Watsamore has to offer."

"You're talking about a large bump," he said. "Only a very large bump will bring back the big two timers."

The big two timers were Brilly O'Neal and Anne Caldron. Together, from morning drive time through the midday period the CryCom duo delivered an incessant stream of stiletto sharp chatter, and their avid listeners kept tuning in to replenish their spite and fear of everyone left of center.

"They won't come back without an incentive," Rapid Roy said. "That's a bigger pay check and a bigger benefits package."

"Atlas is good for it," Dabny replied. "Persuade them to come back to us."

The money to rehire the erring Hosts, she'd calculated would be recouped with higher ad rates. In addition to that, she'd have more time to sell when her stations no longer had to air those inane PSAs, for free. Already, she'd begun her secret campaign to air half the standard amount. Still, across nine hundred seventy three stations the PSAs that did air cost Atlas hundreds of thousands of lost revenue, every day. At W4, which aired only one PSA per day, gross revenues had soared far beyond the brightest projections, which elated the board of directors. Those huge profits also convinced Dabny she'd accomplished a shrewdly shrewd maneuver. Whenever she heard a PSA, say a message from a neighborhood art co-op, or from a local homeless shelter or one those sappy requests from the community food pantry she grit her teeth. As soon as she took control of the airwaves, all PSAs would be history. That was what Hondo Roache was working on in D.C. So for now, she needed to address the other half of her plan, before the big two timers signed a multi-year contract with CryCom.

"Get them to come back to Atlas," she said to Rapid Roy. "For your efforts, I'll give you a thirty per cent lift in your comp package. Keep that between you and me."

"I'll start next week," he said. "I'm having a night out with O'Neal and some of the boys. Brilly doesn't know when he's too drunk to stop talking and best of all, he doesn't have a loyal bone in his oversized torso."

Dabny knew that about the tough talking Host. She also knew Brilly O'Neal was a habitual liar and a temperamental prima donna. The very way he spoke on air—his monotonal sermonizing against anyone even vaguely liberal—could be construed as the mumblings of a sanctimonious sociopath. His self-important style was cunningly concocted to mesmerize his less than keen witted audience. However, Dabny didn't care if the man was a bloated egomaniac; he brought in millions of listeners, and they brought in the advertisers who wrote great, big checks to the radio company.

"Once you get O'Neal to jump ship," she said, "Anne Caldron will be quick to follow, like the next domino."

"It's going to be fun to get the whole gang back together at Atlas," Rapid Roy said. "It'll be like a family reunion, even if it's an extremely dysfunctional family."

That reunion and owning the airwaves, Dabny was thinking would make Atlas impervious to its competitors and the detested government regulators. Then she'd remake the entire radio industry. Still, Jamesford had to be kept unaware of her activities until she'd taken what was hers to take. But to do that, she'd have to rely on Rapid Roy Limerick. It was a risky gambit. The big talker wasn't famous for his ability to keep a secret and his loyalties were in question. But no one else could do the job so Dabny would have to take the risk. This was, she realized, the second time she'd have to trust a man to help her make her dream come true. To her, the words 'Dream' and 'Man' usually didn't go together in the same sentence.

"You and I are going to make history," she said to Rapid Roy. "The bureaucrats will wonder what hit them, but it'll be too late. Now, let's get back to the firing line and kill another batch of pigeons."

All about Brilly O'Neal

When Brilly O'Neal turned seventeen his juvenile record was permanently sealed by the district judge in Camden. No one, and especially personal injury attorneys and snooping reporters would ever learn about the alleged window peeping and the animal abuse and the deferred adjudication for the molestation of his twelve year old neighbor. Brilly quickly learned the Law is open to interpretation. With that knowledge he moved on with his life. In his twenties he worked behind the counter in an adult video store and then he took a job with a local radio station as a courier, driving his unmarked van around town picking up advertisers' commercial tapes and ad copy. One day the on-air jock jokingly asked Brilly to join him behind the microphone. That's when he first said in his droning style, "it's a well-known fact too many perverts and left-wingers get elected to congress. Then we wonder why everything has gotten so incredibly screwed up. Really people, what are you thinking? If you want to live in a country you can be proud of then you have to get rid of the trouble making Liberals. They're the ones who're destroying the very foundations of this great nation, and that's something you should be ashamed of."

Not long after that he came to Atlas as the Host of his own commentary program. Over the next ten years he developed his verbal skills and devised a style of delivery that was described as 'down to earth' and 'monotonous but effective'. Brilly soon built a huge local, then national audience and then two years ago, along with Anne Caldron he went to work for Crystal ComCo. Now he was that network's biggest talking talker.

Presently Brilly was looking up at the studio clock. Five minutes remained in the hour. Then his show would be over for the day. He took a sip of water to refresh his tired vocal chords. He glanced at his notes as he listened to the last words in the commercial break. Then, when the director cued him he spoke into the microphone with his usual monotonal tone.

"As I was saying before the break," he reminded his listeners, "Conservatives are better people than Liberals. Isn't it obvious? Conservatives are better at everything like making sensible laws and caring for our families and for grooming our pets and for doing the right thing when the right thing needs to be done. So this is the problem: big government Liberals are trying to silence me. They're trying to keep me from telling you the real truth about what's going on in Washington. But I won't be silenced. I'm the Liberals' biggest nightmare because I'm on the air every day. The Liberals are telling us that we have to compromise with them. They say we have to accept the immigrants who are stealing our jobs, and the scroungy occupiers who are disrupting traffic in our busy streets and the monstrous marijuana abuse that's tearing at the very fabric of our society. But you know in your heart that we don't have to compromise. Nor should we. We have the power, yes you and I have the power to change the direction the leftists want to drag us. We can take back this country and make it the way we want it to be...the way we're entitled to have it. And the Liberals won't be able to stop us. They're wrong and we're in the right and we've always known it. And the right way is the way we right thinking folks will always rightfully fight for."

Chapter VIII
Another Line is drawn in the Sand

Half a mile from the White House, the office window looked out to Pennsylvania Avenue. As always, the thoroughfare teemed with lumbering tour buses, taxi cabs and the ever present police cruisers. Like regal livery, black limousines with dark tinted windows ferried the Lawmakers of the Land to their destination, the capitol and its labyrinth of behind closed door deal-making. Every day and night, the activity proceeded; the never ending demands of Government and the faceless, furtive people who make it work, about half of the time.

"It took a damn miracle of bureaucratic mail delivery, but that petition found its way to the right person."

The words were spoken by Leonard Kilroy, newest member of the Federal Communications Council. Standing at the window, the stooped forty-four year old was gazing at the harried D.C. scene like a weary traffic cop. "I can use the petition to make some needed changes," he added. "It's about time Atlas obeyed the law."

"Jamesford Talbett will fight us," the visitor said, "like an irate war lord."

"Even an irate war lord." Kilroy replied, "can trip over his own sword."

"And that will make an irate off war lord," the visitor said, "all the more irate."

Kilroy shrugged his agreement. He had an academic's long face and bushy eyebrows and rimless eyeglasses rimmed his glassy eyes. He was wearing a wrinkled shirt and blue tie, loosened at the neck. His cheeks wore two days of stubble and his graying hair needed a trim. He turned from the window and walked to his desk. Sitting down, he gazed at the man sitting across from him.

"This is the first time," Rafe Nailer said, "a council member has spoken with me in his office. I almost feel welcome."

Kilroy kept from smiling. This was a new experience for him, as well. Up to the last month he'd served as an assistant in the SEC and FTC and EPA. Before that, with his Master's degree fresh in his hands he'd entered government service with the noble, if not starry-eyed notion he could make a positive difference for the country. So far, his efforts produced only the country's abject indifference, and more disappointment than personal satisfaction. Still, he pressed on and, in a move that surprised the Democrats and Republicans as well as Kilroy himself, the president appointed him to the open position on the Communications Council. That post had been vacated by a Republican who died in an auto-erotic asphyxiation incident. The position on the council was the very opportunity the non-partisan Kilroy had been seeking.

"Your timing is excellent," he said to Rafe. "W4's license period will expire next week. Apparently, the people at Atlas assume the council will merely rubber stamp the renewal like it's usually done."

"W4 hasn't produced the daily logs for the council," Rafe said. "Atlas has to prove they aired the number of PSAs they promised."

Like they'd done for every license renewal, the Atlas lawyers had submitted the minimum paperwork, and not W4's attested logs. The Communications Council never demanded to examine those logs, like the law specified. This relaxed process was comfortable for all concerned, smoothly transacted and effortlessly concluded. And no challenges were ever accepted or acted upon.

"The council chairperson says accommodation is more important than the law," Kilroy said. "In his mind the marketplace should make the decision."

"I'm at a loss to understand that," Rafe said. "But you would know better than I."

Kilroy blinked and said, "actually, I don't."

"I've read the reports," Rafe said. "Crystal ComCo is after W4's license."

"That's common knowledge," Kilroy said. "What's not common knowledge is I'm not going to let Atlas shrug off the law like it has in the past. The Talbetts expect nothing will change. They're wrong about that, I think. Then again, they could be right. It's not unthinkable they're right. But no, I'm positive about it: they're quite wrong."

He took a moment to gather his thoughts. He had to remind himself he was now speaking as a member of the Communications Council to an outsider, a partisan outsider at that. "The Talbetts believe they're special because they're running the number one radio company. To get there they used illegal tactics," Kilroy said. "The police reports show how the Talbetts' competitors experience a lot of odd technical problems, like short circuited transmitters and broken...or should I say severed...transmission lines and broadcast antennas that mysteriously melt down, which make the stations go off the air for weeks at a time. When that happens their listeners switch over to the Hosts on Atlas. I admit the method is quite effective. I also read about the alleged kickbacks to the research companies that conduct the rating surveys. Though the companies deny any misconduct, the ratings show Atlas's audiences tripled in one week while their competitors' ratings were cut in half. Statistically that's impossible. But for Jamesford Talbett impossible isn't impossible, especially when it comes to ratings, or the law."

"He's damn good at what he does," Rafe conceded.

"Talbett overlooked a simple fact," Kilroy replied. "Whether we like it or not—and no one really does, I certainly don't—government is the only thing that can make and enforce the law."

Rafe shrugged; he knew that too. "It's the 'enforcement' part," he said, "that's been lacking."

"Let's face it," Kilroy said. "The Hosts, or more likely the people who pay them, use the airwaves to ridicule people they don't like, politicians and ballplayers and east coast economists. No one likes having dirt thrown at their favorite idol."

"But it's so much fun to throw the dirt," Rafe replied, "at someone else's idol."

Kilroy agreed with him. He also hoped he could rely on this activist. Committed citizens like Rafe Nailer are sometimes the government's most effective instrument of positive change. Or they can mightily screw things up. Kilroy had to decide which was most likely, and he did. "I want you to act as my unofficial emissary to the Talbetts," he said. "Take them this message: the Communications Council is going to enforce every regulation on the books."

"That's a short message," Rafe said. "I need more words to throw at them."

"Also tell the Talbetts this," Kilroy went on. "When Atlas loses the license for W4 it will be only the beginning. Inform them the new man on the council is ready to take the necessary action. I think I am, anyway. Usually what I think is right, too. That is, most of the time I'm right. But sometimes I'm not right, that is I'm wrong once in a while. But yes, I'm sure of it. This time I'm in the right."

Rafe had to believe Kilroy. Trusting him was another matter and relying on him demanded more faith than Rafe had to give in good faith. Still, his options were limited and that's when faith has its advantages.

"I wouldn't tell you this if I hadn't spoken with two of my colleagues."

Kilroy knew this was important, or it should be. "They've promised the votes which will make a majority. Then again, they might change their minds and this whole thing will blow up in my face. Then it will blow up in yours."

"If something is going to blow up," Rafe replied, "it's the top of Talbett's head when he hears what I tell him. The son of a bitch thinks he's entitled to take anything he wants to take."

Years earlier, Jamesford wanted to run his daddy's seven radio stations, which he did when pater suddenly expired on his sixty-seventh birthday. Broadcasting in the country's largest cities, the stations were the crown jewel in the patriarch's treasure chest. Beauesford Sanford Hansford Talbett, a cultured and patrician gentleman, used the stations to bring classical music and news from the world of the Fine Arts to the common listener, and not as a means to add to his enormous fortune which he'd inherited from his father who'd made that fortune selling the ingredients of high explosives to Germany right before WWII began. Jamesford realized the undervalued value of those seven valuable radio stations. A day after his father passed into the medium of dead air, he killed Ludwig and Amadeus and that brash upstart Leonard Bernstein and though it pained him to do so, in the musical geniuses place he programmed Barry Manilow, The Osmonds and Ted Nugent. Dreck of the top forty variety drew a big audience and to the top forty dreck Jamesford added high pitched disc jockey hype and big money contests and never ending promotions. Jamesford hated the awful noise and he hated those gimmicky gimmicks but those gimmicky gimmicks brought in the hundreds of thousands of new listeners he needed to build his envisioned empire. Then, using his immense inheritance he attacked his competitors with a blitz of even more promotions and high dollar contests and he underpriced his air time. The tactic forced the other stations to match his artificially low prices, which over time lost them hundreds of millions in ad revenues. Some of those stations went into the red and Jamesford hired away their on-air talent. Then he acquired the failing stations and fired all the employees he'd just hired. After that, he operated the stations using tape machines and mass produced programs that played the same pap pop music and even bigger dollar contests. Then in the late eighties, a day after his pal President Reagan gleefully killed the Fairness Doctrine (he always detested the word 'fair'), Jamesford gleefully axed all his remaining on-air employees. He threw away the pap pop music, too. In its place he unleashed a shockwave of Talk Radio Hosts. Over the next twenty-five years the Hosts attracted a multitude of leader seeking listeners and Atlas became the leading leader of the radio business. And Jamesford Talbett amassed a fortune more immense than the fortune he inherited. He also amassed the political power to ignore the laws that other, not as fortunately inherited radio operators had to obey.

"If anything, the name Talbett means 'arrogant,'" Rafe said. "Or 'stubborn', or both."

"Before he can change his ways," Kilroy said, "he has to know what's coming at him."

Rafe didn't expect Jamesford Talbett would change his ways or change anything else for that matter. "Hell, he'll probably shoot me before I step through the front door," he said, raising to leave. "That is if he lets me come in that way."

"I'll send an official message ahead of you," Kilroy said. "It will say you're bringing critical information from the Federal Communications Council, intended only for Jamesford Talbett."

At the desk, the two shook hands as they looked each other in the eye. "Convince the Talbetts I'll do what I say I will do," Kilroy said, blinking. "I'm going to do it, too. Yes, I am, I promise I will. Really, I will. The Talbetts will be smart to listen to you, and they'll send those logs to the council."

"In any case," Rafe said, "we shouldn't expect any valentines from them next year."

After exiting Kilroy's office Rafe walked down a brightly lit hallway. The corridor held portraits of departed presidents and rugged, wartime heroes: America's glorified canon of venerated and deceased cannon fodder. Rafe knew all about them. Idols are only idols to the gullible and naïve. He wondered what little quirks each of them indulged in. From his pocket he pulled out the latest acquisition he'd liberated from Kilroy's desk: a shiny 24K Noteworthy ink pen. The gold instrument felt heavy and solid in his hand, like an expensive writing implement should feel. Tiffany's was only place that sold them and he wondered how Kilroy came to own his, which wasn't Kilroy's anymore.

"Taxi!"

When the vehicle pulled over Rafe jumped in. "National Airport," he told the driver. "Please hurry, my plane leaves in forty minutes."

"You're as good as there, buddy."

The shaven headed driver accelerated away from the curb. Traffic was heavy but the cabbie bullied his way into the jumble of buses and other taxis. Soon they were changing lanes and passing more cautious drivers. It was then Rafe recognized the voice on the radio: Gary Bock, one of Atlas' most popular Hosts.

"It's outrageous," Bock bristled in his bristly way. "It's outrageous, I say how the government can order schools to teach our little ones History that's just plain wrong, like the country once belonged to the red skinned Indians and America has started illegal wars and there's supposed to be some kind of wall between our churches and the government. How can they get away with those lies? Our kids deserve to know the real truth. We must get rid of the godless Department of Education and take our kids' learning back to the parochial level, to the tested and true ways of home schooling. We must teach our kids respect for our ancient beliefs and our sacred religion and for all the blessings God gave us…our unquestioned faith in our faithful ministers and in our fathers and their fathers and all the unquestioning fathers before them. We have to go back to the time when this country was proud of itself, because it is and always will be the only country God sheds his grace upon, and twice on Sunday."

The cab driver guffawed. "I tell ya," he said over his shoulder to Rafe, "I get a good laugh listening to that clown. You'd have to be a fool to think he's not joking."

"Some jokes are hard to understand," Rafe replied. "I gave up trying."

He ignored the Host and peered through the auto's smudged window. He noted the ever-present flags, all that red, white and blue flying like victory from towering poles. It's colorful, even if it's only window dressing. Rafe looked at the heroic statues and the granite buildings of state, seen by most of the People only in movies and TV newscasts. As he gazed at the chiseled masonry, Rafe thought of his youthful years when he learned about the world beyond his small town's boundary.

He grew up the third of five children in a Midwestern middle class family. Living in a machine shop and family farming town, in a two bedroom house with one small bathroom, Rafe grudgingly learned the necessity of sharing. He didn't like to share and sometimes he hid his toys from his grabby siblings. But they'd find his hiding place. It was a lesson Rafe took to heart: one might as well share his wealth because sooner or later the other guys will take their portion. Some people embraced that thinking, others refused to accept it. Sure, everyone has the right to pursue his own happiness but with that right comes the hard reality that life is never fair. Life treats most of us like useless flotsam. We're not equal in height and muscles and brainpower, and certainly most of us aren't born into wealth but damn it, we've got to have a fair chance at the good things the world has to offer. That's why he took up the struggle to change what he could, even as he knew his struggle would never end. Sometimes he thought of himself as a laughable idealist bent on a fool's errand, but most of the time he refused to allow that thought to enter his head.

"It's the fault of the lecherous, licentious Liberals."

Gary Bock was fuming now, fulminating on one of his most fulminatable topics. "The lecherous Liberals want to take us down to their smutty level, where dirty, unnatural homosex is acceptable and there's no such thing as sin and nobody believes the facts in the Bible. My friends, God is not uninvolved in our lives! We have to take back our schools and kick out the licentious liberal teachers who are teaching our kids those disgusting lies about bodily functions and the evils of godless evolution. We have to make our country clean again and God fearing and safe for the next generation and for all the generations of fearful Americans yet to come."

The cabbie laughed out loud. "Lordy," he said to his passenger, "this Bock guy doesn't have a clue about the generations yet to come."

The generations yet to come, Rafe was thinking, are screwed before they're born. They inherit a world trashed out by their parents and their parent's parents, and all the parents and tribes and clans who've ever skulked or lurked or dragged their knuckles over the earth. And from their twisted chromosomes came the slave traders and generations of inbred bluebloods and the venal Robber Barons and a host of liars and gilded takers who took whatever they wanted to take because it was there for them to take. Why were they entitled to fuck everything up? Somewhere, somehow someone has to draw the line and say, "not another dime, prick." Greed may or may not be good, but there sure the hell is a lot of it festering inside of some particularly over entitled people. If anything, the generations yet to come should be plenty pissed off the second they slide out of the womb and see the god-awful mess they arrived in. It's no wonder the first thing we do is bawl our heads off.

"History is made every day," Rafe would say to his students. "So let's ask ourselves if this is the best our lives can be. And when we see all piggishness and waste and downright boneheaded thinking going on around us, we damn well should get pissed off. And then we'll make some real progress happen."

Once inside the terminal, Rafe hurried through the hustling, harried crowd and made his way to the security bottleneck. Fortunately the line was short and the TSA officers didn't impede, for too long the travelers' forward movement. After slipping his shoes back on, he located the correct gate and jogged down the corridor and arrived at an area that teemed with passengers waiting to embark. He had enough time to call his fiancée.

"You sound happy," Vera said. "You must've gotten what you wanted."

"My collection has a new piece," he said with a satisfied grin. "Now I'm going to see Jamesford Talbett. He's never recognized the Public Cause Group but the bastard knows better than to keep out an appointed messenger of the law."

Chapter IX
Strong Enough To Count

After she finished the call with Rafe, Vera took a last hit from a joint and flicked the stub out the Charger's window. She remembered her college days when she'd use a roach clip to take that last, good hit. She didn't have to do that now; three more fat joints were stashed in her pocket. A big benefit of being a political activist is unlimited access to the very best weed.

At the next corner she pulled into the parking lot of a convenient Quick 'n Easy store. She didn't bother to lock the doors as she hurried inside, into a brightly lit corporate owned place she ordinarily wouldn't patronize. But today time was at a premium. She had to buy enough coffee, the kind that's already ground in a can to brew for the two dozen members of the Public Cause Group's Lancer team. An hour from now they were going to picket in front of a too big to fail bank and Vera was going with them. In fact, she was going to lead the demonstration and a part of her was hoping one of the bank's ethically challenged VPs might happen to come her way. Oh no, she wouldn't slap the corporate stooge, or punch the stooge in the face, that is unless the stooge made a false move, like looking around for help.

"That'll be thirteen fifty-two, dear," said the clerk behind the cluttered counter. She was middle-aged with gray hair and a too wrinkled face and she had a husky build which matched her husky voice, which was huskified and made harshly hoarse from way too many years of smoking way too many cigarettes, the pretty white sticks of death that rot the lungs and stain the teeth and make the smoker's voice sound like a husky, cancerous death rattle.

"Do you want to try some beef jerky, honey? It's on sale, three for three dollars."

"I'll pass, thanks," Vera replied. "I'd rather chew on my brogans. At least I know what they're made of and where they've been and who they've been with."

"You don't know what you're missing, sweetie," the clerk said with a husky, hacking cough as she rang up the sale.

Standing behind Vera was a young man with blondish hair and ordinary brown eyes. He had a flat nose and a wispy, thin mustache that made him look bland and ineffectual. His face was more oval than round and what passed as a chin was more round than square. His frame appeared solid and he was wearing a lime green t-shirt with a pro sports team logo—it looked like a cross between a mountain goat and a leprechaun. He was holding a twelve pack of domestic beer and he had a smell on him that attested to his lack of taste in after shave. Perhaps he lacked a sense of smell along with his lack of taste in beer.

"That jerky is really great," he said eagerly to Vera. "You should try it."

"The thing is," she said, "I prefer to eat real food."

"You sound like you think you're better than me," he said. "You're not, you know."

Vera picked up her change and dropped the coins into her jacket's side pocket. Then she picked up her purchase and turned to leave. "I'm not better than you," she said, as sweetly as she could. "But I don't eat crap food from crap companies who don't care if they poison their customers because there's always someone ignorant enough to eat the crap they keep making and selling to their ignorant customers."

"It so happens," the man replied, "I write copy for the agency that creates their ads. As a matter of fact," he added with a proud grin, "I came up with the tag line, 'The jerky that makes your mouth glad you bit into it.'"

"It's catchy," Vera said as she made her way to the door. "But it doesn't catch me."

The jerky loving man stepped in front of her. His breath reeked of beer and semi digested jerky. "You know what turns me on," he said. "It's a woman who doesn't take BS from any guy, not even from me."

"I'm delighted you shared that information," she replied. "Knowing it makes my life perfect." Then she tried to walk around him.

At that moment a new customer walked into the store. He was wearing a dark gray business suit and a clean white shirt with a necktie that was gold and yellow and red. His dark hair was perfectly trimmed and shaped exactly for his roundish face, which indicated an age in his early forties. His eyes were a pale, pale shade of gray and at this moment they were aimed at the two young people, who seemed to be engaged in some kind of humorous lover's quarrel.

"Let's take this twelve pack and go over to my place," jerky man said to Vera. "You'll really like my new flat screen. It's got sixty-four diagonal inches of pure, high-def video, which is great when you see the hard core porn I'll play for you. I bet you like the rough stuff, don't you? Then, if you're a very good girl, I'll give you a taste of my big ol' jerky."

"I'm sure it's very tender," she said. "Unfortunately, I've got work to do."

Suit man had stopped and was listening to the conversation as jerky man said to her, "you got a way that makes me want to see more of you."

"You've seen plenty of me."

Vera sought to walk around him. "And honestly, I've seen more of you than I care to."

Suit man chuckled and kept watching.

"You're not going to walk away so easy," jerky man said. "When I meet a woman like you I don't let her get away, not without getting her number first."

"One," Vera said. "That's the number of punches I need to put you down."

Suit man chuckled, out loud this time.

Jerky man leered and said, "I want to get you like you've never got it before."

"Perhaps another time."

She'd reached the door and was trying to push it open but jerky man blocked her path. "You can't walk away from me like that," he said. "I think it's very impolite."

"I'll have to remember that the next time we meet," she said, "which I dearly hope will be never."

Suit man laughed again, louder. The clerk behind the counter looked over and chuckled as well. Young lovers are an entertaining break in the day's tedium.

"You've got a snarkiness about you," jerky man said. "It's the kind of snarkiness that'll get you into trouble. And I'm the trouble you're getting yourself into."

"It's been fun."

Vera tried to push him aside. "But it hasn't been a lot of fun," she said. "Honest to God, I've got to run away now."

Jerky man grabbed her arm and yanked her toward him. "I'm going to make you a real woman," he jeered, "the kind that learns to like what I'm going to make you take."

"If it's not my way out of here," she said, "you might not be glad you tried."

"I think you're a grubby bitch," jerky man hissed. "A tramping, filthy bitch like the kind of tramping, filthy whore Michelle Fang talks about on the radio."

"So it must be true."

Vera grabbed his hand and jerked his thumb as far back as it could go, and then she jerked the jerk's thumb even further, all the way back, extremely and excruciatingly past his jerking wrist.

Jerky man gasped in pain. Suit man guffawed. The clerk looked on in surprise and worry. This altercation might result in a lawsuit.

"We do what we can," Vera said lightly. "And by the way, boys like you don't want what I've got. It makes them hurt where they don't like to hurt. And then it gets worse, much, much worse. But if you don't believe me, try putting that hand on me again."

"Damn you," jerky man said as he held is injured hand. "You're nothing but a dirty, stinking tramp." He drew away and still holding his hand, walked away muttering, back to the checkout counter.

Suit man laughed again. Vera walked over to him. "It's a great relief to know," she said breezily, "there are still some good old fashioned gentlemen around, the kind who'll help a lady in distress."

"It wasn't any of my business," he stammered. "I saw no reason to help you."

"Then I can only assume," Vera said to him, "that you're a too big to fail bank vice president."

He flushed crimson and said, "how did you know that?"

"How could I not?"

Then, clutching the coffee can, she walked out of the Quick 'n Easy, jumped into her 2001 candy apple red Dodge Charger and burned rubber out of the parking lot.

Rapid Roy is the Protector of our Religious Freedom

In the Atlas on-air studio, the big talker sat in his over-sized, padded chair and after clearing his throat, spoke into the microphone. His words reached out to the millions of his alarmed listeners, who listened to those words with growing alarm. "We've got an alarming problem, folks. I've heard the rumor that the leftist Liberals plan to impose their corrupt income tax on our churches and our pastors. It's outrageous! Why, this is the nightmare we've all feared. It's as if our churches were engaged in a money making business! And mark my words, the cities with the leftist mayors, and the seedy public school districts run by the leftist Liberals are planning to assess a property tax on the mega churches where we meet and share our good fellowship. The leftists want to tax the millions of acres of parkland our churches own, and even the parking lots owned by our churches and that includes, my God people the government will tax our lavish church parsonages and rectories and chapels and all the magnificently landscaped grounds they rest on. Then they'll tax our church owned dormitories and apartment buildings and the hangers and the Gulfstreams our devoted pastors fly to reach out to our needy brethren in needful lands like Las Vegas. The Liberals will tax our daycare centers and our tennis and basketball courts and our handball and squash courts and our gyms and saunas and recreation centers where we exercise our bodies, yes the finely crafted bodies God crafted for us, and they'll tax our vineyards and wineries and our cafeterias and meditation centers and our conference halls and our auditoriums and our soft ball and soccer fields and our vans and tour buses and stretch limousines. I mean it, they'll even tax our croquet lawns and our badminton courts and our beautiful church owned woodlands and our souvenir stores and gift shops and our fully equipped camp grounds we use for our annual retreats when we commune with all of Nature, even when we commune with God Himself. And what do the Liberals want to do with our tax money? They'll give it to a bunch of dirty, homeless beggars and to shiftless vagrants and for food stamps for the losers who can't even get a job. You must write to your congressman! Tell him to stop the radical left before they take away our churches' tax deferments. We can't allow the Liberals to steal from us that way. Call your congressman; demand he keeps our sacred Christian churches tax free forever and ever, because they're entitled to always be free from taxes!"

Chapter X
The Strong and the Stronger, Together

"So far, everything is going as planned."

Dabny was wearing a white cotton blouse and gray linen jacket. Sitting in a corner booth, she was partially hidden in the shadows in Delade's Parisian Bistro. The modest café, nestled on an unpretentious side street on the east side of town, was nearly vacant of patrons and the lighting was subdued, which was why she chose this locale. Here, she wasn't known and wouldn't be recognized, and neither would her collaborator.

"Rapid Roy is on board with us, now."

She stealthily spoke in a stealthy voice, the quiet voice she spoke when she didn't want to be overheard. "I don't think Abby Watsamore, my not so lovable counterpart knows what's happening behind her back."

Dabny hoped Rapid Roy would do as they'd agreed. He claimed to be a man of unquestioned integrity. She'd have to trust him, but not without question. That's what a great business leader sometimes has to do: trust their not so trustworthy minions. She sipped from a glass of iced Perrier, accented with a slice of yellow lemon. The chilled beverage refreshed her and helped focus her thoughts.

"I don't have a doubt Rapid Roy will do the job."

She was thinking how much her life would change once Atlas owned the airwaves. First, her father would be shocked and angry she'd deceived him. But after he finished venting, she'd stroke his hand and talk earnestly to him and soon he'd concede his shrewd daughter had shrewdly done what she was entitled to do. Then, with the spectrum in her possession she'd control every dial position in the country. She'd decide which corporation would broadcast on those dial positions and she'd compel broadcasters to follow her programming rules. The Hosts on Atlas such as Rapid Roy as well as those on CryCom would be free to say whatever they wanted to say, as long as she approved. And what would she do with Hondo Roache as a partner? She wasn't sure yet, but the possibilities intrigued and worried her.

"How are you coming along with the Senators?"

"Gleason is a question," answered the lobbyist. "So far, he won't commit one way or the other. I assumed he'd take that position. He doesn't say it in so many words but he might be swayed if a contribution, a generous one finds its way to his campaign fund."

She hoped to hear that. "So, that makes him number fifty," she said with an air of finality. "That leaves Brumble to get us to fifty-one, right?"

"He's something of an odd bird," Hondo said. "It must come from growing up in the mountains."

She didn't laugh, assuming Hondo wasn't joking. "When we close him," she said, "the majority leader will bring the bill up for a vote. I want Brumble's commitment right away."

"He's not running for office again, and won't accept our contribution," Hondo said. "I need to get inside him and understand him at a gut level. Once I figure out what drives the man, then I'll work on his vulnerabilities."

"Dig up some dirt from his past," she told him. "Find out if there's a pissed off mistress sulking in a love nest on

Fifth Avenue. Or maybe there's a cabin cruiser another lobbyist bought for him, you know, an embarrassing skeleton the press would love to know about."

Those were the typical lawmaker's foibles and a good lobbyist would know of their existence, and use to his advantage. "I've looked into Brumble's lifestyle," Hondo said. "I didn't find any unusual appetites or compulsions, or unpaid balances I can use as leverage."

"It's not right."

Dabny was gazing thoughtfully at her colleague. "We're on the verge of taking a giant step for Atlas, no, for the entire broadcast industry. I can control the airwaves but stubborn old men, politicians from a political party that I don't like are holding me back. I hate having to wait for those old bastards to commit to us."

"Beside the other forty-nine senators already in our pocket," Hondo replied. "And remember, we wouldn't have gotten this far if the Republicans didn't have a majority in the House. They want to privatize everything the government owns, or should I say that's owned by the People, the so-called Commons. I can't understand why they're entitled to own something we can use to make a profit."

"We're only as free as a congressman's vote," she sighed. "The Supreme Court decides what we can and can't say on the air, or anywhere else for that matter. The state of affairs has to change."

The state of affairs will change big time, Hondo knew, after he acquired the votes from the two remaining senators. "After they commit," he said, "you'll own the radio spectrum. That's a lot of capacity."

"Atlas is big enough to carry it."

Dabny had calculated the numbers and the numbers added up to incalculable new wealth. "We'll make the industry leaner and more profitable," she said. "We'll lease out dial positions to companies that will generate the biggest revenues. A corporation like Atlas will own ten or fifteen or even more stations in a big metro area. Probably, one or two companies will operate all the stations. And I'll cut the number of stations any city can have. Really, the common people don't need so many signals. I'll lease the unused bandwidth to cell companies and create a brand new revenue stream."

It was the vision that fired her imagination, a magnificent vision she was about to see as a reality.

"I'm designing a franchise fee schedule," she went on. "It'll be scaled for all city sizes. Any company who wants to keep broadcasting will lease that franchise from us. If no one can meet the cost, then that dial position will simply go silent. If half a dozen stations go off the air only a few people will care. Even if a lot of them complain it won't matter to me. I'll own the bandwidth and I'll do with it as I please. In fact, I might turn off the spectrum in an entire city, to prove that I can do it. That'll show the bureaucrats who's got the real juice in this country."

"Don't be surprised when your opponents fight back," Hondo said. "They don't like it when someone of stature, one with brains and willpower seeks to rise above them."

Hearing that, her lips broke into a guileful smile. "You're an expert in these matters," she murmured. "We both know what the ultimate goal is."

Yes, focus on the ultimate goal. He took a swallow of his sweetened iced tea; the sugary taste appealed to him. Sipping it, he felt a strange kinship with the sensation it evoked. It was a sensation which in the past had served him well. Once that first pulse of pleasure overtakes the prey the next stage is an eagerness to take another sip. Then, in no time inevitably comes the following stage, agreement and then finally the ultimate goal: commitment. That's when victory tastes the very sweetest.

"When Brumble and I sit down, I'll ask about his favorite charity," Hondo said. "The senator might commit if Atlas promises to fund an addition to his hometown hospital."

"I'll agree to that."

Dabny was calculating the cost of such an investment. "But it has to be a one-time payment. I'm not in the business of long term health care."

The quip evoked a laugh from the lobbyist. "I'll be sure your name is on a plaque in the lobby," he said. "We'll send a news release to the media. It never hurts to look like a hero to the masses. They want to believe people like you care about them."

"I care that they listen to my radio stations," she said. "I care that they hear our commercials. I care even more if they have a ratings diary and they write down our call letters, without any errors."

She paused to gaze at the manly face of the man named Hondo Roache. Here was a man who made a real difference in the world. The fortunes of corporations and entire industries rose or fell with the result of his expert lobbying. He persuaded legislators to vote for bills which entitled corporations to spew millions of tons of toxic waste into the People's air and waterways, and he convinced lawmakers to make laws that gave billions in subsidies to the too big to fail banks and the venal banksters who run them. Hondo didn't experience self-doubt or the fear of failure, or relented to his foes. Nothing intimidated him, not even the threat of utter defeat; he'd never experienced it. Yes, here was a steadfast and reliable man, a man she could steadfastly rely on. As she studied the masculine crease in his left cheek, she wondered how many other women had placed their trust in him. In the past she never trusted any man other than her trustworthy father. He'd been the standard by which she judged all other men and so far she'd never met one who could stand in Jamesford's overpowering shadow. Yet at this moment, in a subconscious part of her consciousness there rustled the tiniest sensation. She wasn't sure what it was, admiration perhaps or simple fondness or something more unsettling, an incipient yearning, the desire to be desired and to desire the one who desired her. It wasn't a terrible feeling, unusual yes, but it wasn't unpleasant, not at all.

"It's vitally important we keep your activities a secret," she said. "Father mustn't hear even a hint about it."

"I'll have the votes in hand," Hondo said, "before the rumors make their rounds in the capitol. The gossip will get back to Jamesford," he added, "but not until it's too late."

That's what she expected to hear. "I plan to tell him I've made Atlas invincible," she said. "He and I will control the radio industry and no one will be able to take it away from us."

Rapid Roy knows the Real Facts about Climate Change

"Lying is wrong," he told his believing listeners. "It doesn't matter who does the lying, either. And the worst lies come from the lying liars in big government. You know what I'm talking about: the lies the lying Liberals tell about the so-called climate change and that the ocean is getting too dirty for the fish to live in. Really, they want us to believe that nonsense? Have you ever seen the ocean? It's so big you can't see across it. It's got more water than we can count. It's time we wake up to the lies, my friends. So, with that settled I'll take a call from one of my faithful listeners in the great Hoosier state."

"Rapid Roy, you're doing God's work, man. I may be only one guy out here in the heartland but I gotta tell you I'm a true believer, one of your biggest Me Too-ers. There's millions of us out here and we believe every word you say. So keep up the great job and know we're all behind you!"

"There, that's what I'm talking about; another voice speaks for all you Me Too-ers. So listen closely when the leftists tell even more lies. They say we have to stop drilling for oil because the air is getting dirty. Ha! It's an established fact that oil comes from under the ground and the air is *above* the ground. And the two don't mix! So how can oil make the air get dirty? Don't you see what those freaky Greenies are trying to do? They want us to believe the world is getting hotter because we heat our homes with gas and oil. Here's the real truth: the leftists own stock in companies that make those big wind mills and those glassy things they want to force us to buy and put on our roofs. It's a big, fat lefty conspiracy, that's what it is. If we start believing them we're going to get ourselves into a big, stinking pile of Leftist pooh-pooh. That's a fact you need to know in order to walk around it."

Chapter XI
Man on Earth / Man to Man

Approaching the imposing portico and massive front door of Leadership Place, Rafe took a moment to appraise the immense structure. Never before had he entered such a private residence. Really, this mansion was a palace. To Rafe, any home need not exceed a couple thousand square feet, okay, three thousand square feet was acceptable. He couldn't guess this manse's dimensions except, damn, did these people even know the word, 'enough'?

"Mister Talbett is in his library."

The housekeeper peered suspiciously at him when she opened the door. With graying gray hair she was meanly middle aged, dressed in a dark skirt and a light blue blouse under a starched, white apron. She held herself perfectly erect; her somewhat scary face wore too much reddish blush and too little hospitality.

"I'll inform him you're here."

She led Rafe off the main hallway to a snug side room. The handsome space contained two leather easy chairs and a deep couch and a set of wide, high windows. They looked out to the rolling lawn and further down the recently mowed hill, to a shimmering pond upon which a family of mallards cruised across the surface, creating a perfect V-shaped wake. Taking in the scene, Rafe enjoyed the moment. Why not? This may be his opponents' home turf, but it was also a comfortable space, nicely appointed, a perfect place to spend a few minutes to ready himself for the coming confrontation.

In a way, he began preparing for this meeting five years ago. That was when he discovered Atlas stations aired only half the customary amount of PSAs. At W4, only one per day was broadcast, at midnight. Atlas was breaking its agreement; in effect, Atlas was breaking the law. Yet the company gained renewals on its licenses. Atlas bought up weaker stations, thus silencing more innovative broadcasters. That kept fresh ideas and Progressive opinions and alternative programming off the city's airwaves. As Rafe learned more, the more he realized how one corporation can dominate an entire region's radio spectrum, and ultimately control what the People can and can't hear on the airwaves they own. And that pissed him off.

"I'll take you in now, sir."

The housekeeper's voice brought him back to the present. He followed her down a marble floor hallway, passing the busts of watchful Roman gods. He detected the scent of fresh cut roses and recently oiled mahogany furniture. And he sensed something intangible, an environment that bespoke the residents' self-satisfied contentment. Lucky them. Contentment is priceless, even when it's rightfully earned and it's never on sale at the market. The housekeeper opened the library door and he stepped inside the stuffy room.

"Ah, Mister Nailer."

Jamesford Talbett set down a manila folder. His solemn face wore a look of deep solemnity. He was wearing a black turtleneck and black pants. He rose from his desk and walked around it, carrying himself in a dignified manner like a grave dignitary, or a dignified grave digger about to shove his unsuspecting visitor into a deep, dark, undignified grave.

"You must feel like you're entering the lion's den."

He neither smiled nor offered his hand.

Not offended, Rafe replied, "if there's a nasty animal around I'll know it right away. I can detect the stink of a used litter box."

Jamesford frowned. "As I understand it," he said as he indicated a chair for Rafe, "you've come as a flag-bearer for the government and not," he added as if spitting out the words, "as the leader of a so-called public interest group."

Rafe waited as Jamesford returned to his chair. This media titan acted too distinguished for a man famed for his dirty tactics and illegal acts against his competitors. Still, such a distinguished man can willfully push a button that sets off the ton of dynamite hidden under a schoolhouse. Distinguished men had caused plenty of damage in the world and this particular distinguished man wouldn't hesitate to cause Rafe damage of the professional, or personal or even the physical kind. Chances were good that in his desk's top drawer waited a cold, black Croaker, cocked and loaded with hollow point bullets, ready to shoot an unruly guest who got out of line.

"I'm one of your least favorite people and you're a very unpleasant old man," Rafe said. "I don't like what you do and you want to step on me like an insect. So, with the niceties out of the way, I have a message you need to hear."

Jamesford scowled. Rafe thought he looked like an aging movie star whose best features were behind him. The head of Atlas sat erect and haughty; he emitted the cloying aroma of French cologne mixed with the smell of a recently smoked cigar, and did he also exude a whiff of old man smell?

"In the past I've heard nothing from Washington," Jamesford said, "which could benefit me in any way. So, now you say you want to help me?"

Rafe tamped down a laugh. "If you burst into flames I'll agree to hand you a bucket of water," he said. "But I'm here to inform you about the license renewal status, for your station W4. You may not be aware you're about to lose that license."

"Am I supposed to believe you?"

Jamesford spoke as if to an insignificant serf. "None of my stations has ever lost its license. Why, it's ridiculous to think it could happen. The lawyers who do the paperwork would've informed me long ago."

"Maybe you didn't hear them."

Rafe tried his best to sound helpful. "Maybe your lawyers are so busy with the paperwork for all your stations that they didn't follow the necessary procedures. They haven't responded to the Council's request to produce W4's daily logs. It's one of those bothersome little laws that can get overlooked, even by over-paid lawyers, for five years."

"Those incompetent, half-witted suck ups," Jamesford huffed. "In the past we've submitted the usual forms and in a month or two, we get the renewed license. The council never makes me do any silly dog and pony shows."

The claim didn't surprise Rafe. Over the years the Communications Council had become partisan riven and ossi-fied like a petrified tibia, exactly the condition its Republican members (obeying their corporate overlords) had worked like slavish grave diggers to achieve.

"The law is a pesky thing," Rafe said. "Your promise to follow the law can become a pesky problem, especially if you don't do what the law says you have to do."

"You're blowing a lot of smoke up my ass."

Jamesford was scowling again. "The council won't dare deny my license renewal. It's crazy to think it could happen. I've made sure the majority is on my side for every vote."

That didn't surprise Rafe, either. "Call your people in Washington." He noted the expression on Jamesford's face: resistance, of course, and anger and yet there was the realization that what he was hearing might be true.

"I'll be happy to wait outside," Rafe said. "Go ahead and make that call."

He got out of his seat and walked to the door. Before he reached it, Jamesford said, "this won't take long."

Rafe closed the door behind him. Now in a long hallway, he walked to the far window. Reaching it, he gazed out to the bright sunshine and a glistening swimming pool, at least seventy feet long, anchored in a mooring of cream colored concrete. Surrounding it were a dozen sea green umbrellas and wrought iron chairs and a dramatic stone oven and eight sumptuous chaise lounges. At the pool's far end a woman, early thirties Rafe guessed, was climbing the ladder of a high diving tower. She was wearing a black, one piece swim suit which enhanced her sexy figure. She walked to the edge of the high board and threw herself into the air, executed a perfect jackknife then sliced like a blade into the water. After a moment she reappeared, her raven hair a shining mass and with several strong strokes arrived at the pool's edge where, glistening with shining rivulets she casually lifted herself onto the concrete. The woman was not only attractive, but she was a skilled and powerful athlete, like his fiancée. But the swimmer was shorter and more muscular than Vera, and no doubt not nearly as likeable.

"Get in here!"

Jamesford was shouting at him from down the hallway. "This is impossible," he seethed. "It's the handiwork of morons and paper shuffling meatheads."

Rafe saw a new expression on the man's now seething face. Definitely, here was an individual who might strangle him, or pull out his Croaker and shoot him dead. Yes, this was the real Jamesford Talbett, the intractable oligarch who loathed the government and roared in defiance at it.

"You and those bloodless cowards don't know what I'm capable of," he sputtered. "I won't let them steal my license."

"They can't steal what they own," Rafe said and enjoyed saying it.

Jamesford flushed a shade of red redder than an apoplexy flush, redder than the reddest red of a beet red seizure blush, redder even than a pair of bright red buttocks being thrashed with a long handled scouring brush. "I can broadcast whatever I want. And not you or those greasy worms in D. C. can make me do otherwise. I have my rightful rights. I'm entitled to do as I damn well please."

"You need to hand over the logs," Rafe said, now freshly flush with confidence. "Otherwise, you might lose your other licenses, too."

"His threats don't frighten us, do they father?"

The woman with wet hair had entered the room. She was wrapped in a white beach towel and fine leather slippers protected her feet's soles. Her soul, if she had one needed a different kind of protection. In the interior light her face with its prominent cheeks and strong jaw was distinctly distinct and at this moment, she was distinctly irritated. Her burning green eyes burned like an emerald cutting torch.

"I know who you are," she said with a knowing tone. "It seems you're out of your depth here, Mister Nailer."

"Just in case, I brought my life preserver," he replied. "I even brought shark repellant."

Jamesford snapped, "I can't stand zealots like you."

"Sometimes a zealot can make more trouble than you want to deal with."

"I'm Dabny Talbett," she said. "I will not allow you to come to our home and speak to my father and me in this manner."

Rafe knew who she was, but he didn't care to say so. "It's all the same to me," he said, shrugging an offhand kind of shrug, a shrug that implied the problem couldn't be handed off onto his eminently shruggable shoulders. "I'm sure you'll send W4's logs to the council right away, like the law requires."

"Father, don't let this man upset you," Dabny said. "He's merely a mere messenger boy."

"This is extortion, that's what it is," Jamesford fumed. "I won't stand for these threats, not by the government or by an empty-suit flunky. Furthermore, I will see to it that Atlas is kept free from the bureaucrats' coercion."

"You don't have to obey the law," Rafe said. "But it can make you miserable if you don't."

Dabny was staring with cold ferocity. "You'll forgive me," she said, sounding coldly ferocious, "but I must ask you to leave now. We'll consider your message in due course."

"If you need any answers," Rafe said, "I'll be delighted to hear your questions."

She stepped aside and motioned to the door. "Leave your card," she told him. "We'll be sure to get back to you."

Rapid Roy knows all about his Right to Pursue Happiness

He'd read the Preamble to the Constitution in his high school civics class, which was later changed to Social Studies whose curriculum didn't include learning about the Constitution. Besides that, Rapid Roy didn't get through Article One. But he instinctively knew what the founding Founders intended.

"Here's a fact you should never forget," he said to his sometimes forgetful listeners. "The Constitution, that's right the law of this great big land guarantees us the right to pursue our happiness in any way we choose. We're entitled to do what we want, whenever we want and wherever we want to do it. Read the Constitution, the words are there to see! It's all about our guaranteed rights, isn't it? It's true and it's a fact. The Founders intended us to have the absolute right to say and do as we please in whatever way that pleases us. Now that I've made that indisputably clear and true let's hear from another one of you, a rightfully entitled caller from the great Cowboy State of Wyoming."

"Rapid Roy, I'm a proud Me Too-er from freedom loving Laramie. I called to say how much we admire your courage in standing up to the lying left wingers. If it weren't for you I don't know who we'd follow, and we have to follow someone, don't we? So hang in there! We've got your backside, big guy!"

"Hear that? The caller proves my point. It's a fact America is the most important country on the planet and it's a fact we are the most important people on the planet because the Founders gave us the freedom to do whatever we want. If you don't agree then you don't know the facts. Maybe you should look them up. Then you'll know the true facts and we'll all get on with our lives the way the Founders wanted and the way I want because I only want what's best for all you Me Too-ers. And that too my friends, is an absolute, undeniable true fact of life."

Chapter XII
Parking Pause

The Public Cause Group's office was on the second floor of an aging stucco building. Behind the structure was a black-top lot in need of a new layer of asphalt and it contained only two rows of poorly marked parking places, none of which were reserved. Employees in the building had a hard time finding an available slot to park their car, which was the case today. Vera had circled the lot for ten minutes—losing valuable time before she'd lead the Lancer team in the bank demonstration—and she hadn't seen any movement, no back up lights turning on and no car pulling out. Damn it, why couldn't one person get in their car and drive off? But then, right there! A gray green Toyota Celica was cautiously backing out, but on the far side of the row where she was slowly trawling in a line with three other cars. If she timed her approach exactly right, and she didn't sideswipe a parked car she'd get the space before someone else and yes, yes, she made it in time and switched on her blinker to claim the spot as hers. But she had to wait; she even had to put the Charger in reverse as the Toyota backed up into her lane before driving away and while that was happening a black C-50 pick-up truck swerved around the Toyota and, with the driver smirking at Vera, slipped into the space, right in front of her frustrated eyes.

"Damn you!"

She flung herself out of her Charger and charged over to the pick-up whose driver was stepping out of the truck. The man was broad shouldered and plaid-shirted with rolled up sleeves and his forearms were thick like an oak tree with a blue tattoo on his right arm of a smoking Croaker on the muscle below the elbow. From inside the cab growled the growling voice of Rapid Roy Limerick.

"Remember this fact," he growled. "As an American you're entitled to pursue whatever happiness you want. You don't have to worry if you disturb other people. If they don't like what you do then it's their problem not yours."

"I wouldn't care, really I wouldn't," Vera said to the man, who had longish dark blond hair and a pudgy baby face which needed a shave. "I've got an important meeting and I'd appreciate it if you let me have this spot, since it was already mine."

Leaning against the truck the man popped open a can of domestic beer (the lite kind) and took a long slug. Then, after belching out a booming burp he said, "I've got a right to this space. I don't care if you don't like it."

"Please," she said. "I need to…could you turn down the radio so we can talk?"

"I don't think so."

His face worn an aggravating grin intended to aggravate her, which it did, aggravatingly.

Rapid Roy said, "you have the absolute right to all the freedom you can put your hands on and if that means crossing a line, then go ahead and cross it. You're entitled to do it. And it's your right to do it and don't forget, your rights are more rightful than the rights of other people. Remember, you're entitled to more rights than anyone else."

"Please."

Vera raised her voice over the big talker. "I'm in a jam for time. I'll give you ten bucks, that's all I've got."

"My rights can't be bought off."

The pick-up driver took another swig. "Besides, I seen the sticker on your bumper. What does it mean, People Rise over Corporate Lies? You're a god damned lefty troublemaker, ain't you?"

"I'm only asking you to give a girl some consideration," she said. "Please, I'd really appreciate it if you helped me out."

The man grinned bigger and said, "you're not as smart as you think you are, Missy. People can't rise over lies. It don't make sense."

"I don't have time to chat today," she said. "How about it, ten bucks?"

He grunted a laugh and reached inside the cab, bringing out a handful of rags and a can of car polish. "This place is exactly what I need," he said. "The sunlight is perfect and I can get this baby all shined up real good, just like new and I can listen to my main man Rapid Roy while I set to work."

Vera sagged. This jerk wasn't going to show her any mercy, not even the consideration one might show a homeless orphan. "I hope an aneurism hits you right now," she told him. "I hope it destroys that tiny lump of a brain inside your Troglodyte skull and you die in horrible, excruciating, searing agony."

"Hey!"

The man called out as she walked to her car. "Hey, do you know what? Rapid Roy says the Constitution gives me the right to seek my happiness and do you know what else? Right now I'm real happy."

Vera spun around and walked back, right into his face. "I can be happy too," she said more coolly than she thought she could speak. "The Constitution gives me the absolute right to break an over entitled prick's nose and if that makes me happy then it's your damn problem, not mine."

"I'd like to see you try it," jeered the man as he brought up his fists.

For one second she assumed a fighter's crouch and moved toward him. Then, from twenty feet away came the sound of a car door slamming and a motor coughing and turning over and then she was at the steering wheel, deftly driving to where a blue Nissan's back up lights were glowing bright white like a homing beacon, creating a coveted vacancy for the charging Charger's short term parking, which for Vera was free of charge.

The Notable Lady makes her Long Awaited Appearance

Michelle Fang was part Filipino, part Mongolian, part Chinese and all American. She took an online degree in Advertising from the University of Phoenix while pursuing an extracurricular affair with the school's CEO, himself a graduate of that same advertising curriculum. After 'graduation', she slept her way through an Oklahoma oil man, a cow girl who ran a dude ranch in the Texas Panhandle, a Louisiana life insurance executive and an exotic dancer from Atlanta, Georgia. That last lover was also intimate with Rapid Roy. One day she sent the big talker an intriguing photo…one that would abash his abashable listeners if they ever saw it. The picture showed him handcuffed to an unmade bed, in itself not such a terribly terrible image. Except while he was handcuffed to the bed his deeply dimpled derriere was being briskly beaten to a bright reddish shade of red, by a long handled scouring brush held by the exotic dancer, in a room at the Hold 'em Down There Motel (with reasonable hourly rates). The abashing photo persuaded the seldom abashed big talker to pull the necessary strings with the Talbetts. Soon thereafter Michelle got her very own talk show with the Atlas Radio Company.

"The lack of morals in this nation's women has gotten so bad," she apprised her moral listeners, "every one of them, even the young girls and teenagers think she has to look like those trashy 'take me now' lingerie models in shopping mall advertising posters. This is shameful to all women, especially to those of us who take pride in the alluring body God created for us. We must tell our legislators to ban contraception because it allows women to believe sex is merely another way to have fun, like eating chocolate cake and they can have as much sex as they want and have no bad results. We have to ban birth control because it makes women want more sex than they need. Women should have sex only when it means something good and pure and perfect. Sex is our most treasured gift and it's about more than feeling good and satisfying your husband. Sex should lead to pregnancy and to the birth of our lovely children. That's why we must ban contraception. Even the word sounds unnatural and evil. Sex is a woman's greatest treasure so remember this ladies: spend your treasure wisely."

Chapter XIII
Nobility in Crises, Two Minds Meld

"Mister Rafe Nailer," Dabny muttered, "must think very highly of himself. But I can't see a reason why he should."

Her words produced a distressful look on Hondo's usually distress free face. "It wouldn't be wise to underestimate the man," he said. "From what I've heard, he's taken some hard body blows and returned each one with greater force."

The muggy evening enveloped them like an envelope as they walked alongside the reflecting pool. At this time of night, the National Mall didn't seem grandiose. But Dabny never thought it was so grand, and certainly not awe inspiring. The middleclass lawn, she often called it was where the radicals and rabble rousers and their parasitic followers would gather, with their silly banners and hand painted signs, in the tens of thousands to make a dreary spectacle of their unified inferiority. These grounds contain little more than rank propaganda in marble; a collection of gaudy buildings that housed a bunch of cartoonish statuary intended to edify the common crowd. In particular, the Jefferson Memorial tries too hard to deify a man who thought the rabble should be equal to the nation's true leaders.

He actually believed that nonsense, she once wrote in a term paper. *The masses should rise up and take power away from the producers. In truth, Thomas Jefferson was a danger to the country's elite business class, the only people who really matter. If he had his way, there'd be a revolution every month and fighting in the streets every year. And if that happens the mob won't care about some radical, slave bedding president who died hundreds of years ago.*

Earlier today she'd taken the Atlas corporate jet to this unplanned meeting. She didn't want to see Hondo in his office, or meet him at a café for fear of being seen together. Then the rumor mill would fly into action. Here, in the Mall's shadowy shadows they could discuss the troubling new development. As they followed a course that would take them across the length of the Mall, Hondo considered the dismaying news with growing dismay. "We have to take Nailer seriously," he said. "He's making headway with the new member of the council."

"It's ridiculous," she replied. "I've got to kowtow to the council to keep W4's license. It galls me to have to stoop to their pedestrian level."

"This will be the last time you'll have to go through the procedure," Hondo said. "When Atlas owns the spectrum, the licensing process will go the way of the Passenger Pigeon."

Yes, she thought giddily, like the once ubiquitous bird the regulations that held Atlas down would soon go extinct. And, like the Passenger Pigeon extinction would come by way of human action, in this case a true producer's deliberate action. "We have a dozen other stations that are up for renewal this year," she said. "We need to get our bill passed immediately."

"I can nudge the majority leader only so far," Hondo said. "He has rules to follow, too. I suggest we follow our original game plan."

"I'm not going to wait," she said. "Nailer can cause more trouble. The best defense against him is an all-out attack."

Hondo raised an eyebrow. Here was Dabny Talbett revealing her usually unrevealed self. In an odd way he thrilled at seeing her reveal her true persona, fiery and determined and taking the offensive.

"You should consider the possibility of unintended consequences," he counseled.

"If I did that every time I took action," she replied, "I'd never accomplish a thing."

"What do you have in mind?"

She responded. "I own nine hundred and seventy three radio stations in one hundred and twenty-two cities. I control the big time Hosts who have a weekly audience of thirty million listeners. Those listeners talk to their friends and families," she said. "They get together in their bars and churches and they write blogs and letters to the newspapers. Some of them tweet every day to thousands of readers and some operate their own websites. That many people can turn the slightest hint of impropriety into a national outrage. Beginning tomorrow," she went on, "my Hosts can tell those listeners some recently discovered facts about the so-called People's Advocate. We'll make up some dirty little secret which we'll broadcast to the whole world."

"I'm not sure that's the right tactic," Hondo cautioned. "You're so close to getting what you want in congress. Declaring war on a public citizen, even if he's obnoxious and self-serving might work against your ultimate goal."

"Nailer has to be brought to heel," she snapped. "Even when we own the spectrum, he can cause problems. I need to take him out now."

They arrived at the Lincoln Memorial, now dramatically lit as if it were the setting in a dramatic TV drama. Taking in the sight was a collection of individual tourists. Some were gazing at the statue with reverent reverence, speaking in reverential voices about the much revered Republican log splitter from Illinois. Others sat on the steps and gazed out toward the Mall, at the other monuments to the nation's fabled history and its grandly proclaimed ideals.

"We're entitled to enjoy the fruit of our labor," Dabny declared. "If I don't nail Nailer now then I'm conceding to him. God damn it, I can't stomach the thought of it."

Her voice resounded with the Talbetts' noted combativeness. Jamesford Talbett never fled from combat and neither would his combative daughter. In her throat's throaty timbre rang the certainty of a leader who refused to surrender her certitude. This great country became the greatest country on the earth because daring people dared to fight for what they were entitled to. They struggled and suffered and fought to attain their magnificent dreams—dreams not dreamt by the common lot. And from those suffering struggles arose this one indispensable nation, exceptionally exceptional in every possible way without exception, prosperous and powerful far beyond anything humanity had ever seen or could ever foresee, even if humanity could see into the unforeseeable future. In Dabny Talbett a willing champion was emerging. She was an emergent and willful woman and yes, she was darkly beautiful in a way that darkness is beautiful in a woman. Her charisma evoked a keen yearning and her physical nearness provoked a keener feeling, a need to be closer to her as if a man could absorb her vital life force and so become one with her. Now, in the nighttime's cloying closeness, Hondo felt the stirring of that yearnful yearning. Yet, he needed to keep his thoughts focused and give her his honest advice.

"I suggest you hold your fire for another day," he said to her. "I should have Brumble's commitment by then."

"I'll think about it."

They reached the perimeter of the Mall and were walking in the direction of the Capitol. The evening was cooler now but was still humidly humid, a kind of humidity that felt like vapor in the air. Hondo recalled his favorite place: the high desert of the Southwest. There the air is crisp and dry and the colors of the earth are earthy and rich and the rugged landscape evokes a mysterious power, the kind that mysteriously provokes a man's secret powers and passions.

"Let me suggest we relax this weekend," he suggested. "I want to take you to a different place."

Surprised and curious, she stopped and stared at him. "Am I to understand you're inviting me on a pleasure trip?"

"I want to get to know the Dabny Talbett," he answered, "who lives inside the driven woman I'm looking at right now. I bet there's another woman in there, one who has a woman's drives and needs, one who'll give all she has to give to a man who'll rightfully accept it."

"This is unexpected," she murmured. "But not unwanted."

Then he saw her face open up, as if she were allowing him a first glimpse into her inner being…a little peek now… with perhaps more to come. "Outside of Taos," he said, "there's a dirt road that goes five miles to a majestic mountain. On the far side of that mountain is a lodge with the most spectacular view anyone can see. I own that majestic mountain. I also own that lodge and I own that spectacular view. I want to show all of it to you."

"It sounds marvelous," she said. "And very provocative."

"When you see the landscape," he said, "you'll want to reach out and take it in your arms, like it's a prized possession… a prize you're rightfully entitled to possess."

She looked into his eyes. She saw his bottomless self-confidence and the dedication to his beliefs. She'd respected and admired this admirable man but now she experienced a new sensation. A feeling like veneration rushed through her. She'd connected with the brilliant Hondo Roache in a way that was perhaps inevitable yet was wonderful, even joyful in its surrender, an emotion she'd never felt before. Maybe now was her time. Maybe this was the man.

"Yes, I want to see it," she whispered. "I want to see it with you by my side."

"We'll learn things about each other," he said, "that we only think we know."

Then he gathered her in his arms. And then they kissed.

At last, we get the Skinny on Anne Caldron

At Crystal ComCo, the female Hosts were not playfully referred to as the split-tongued harpies. The phrase didn't offend Anne Caldron. In fact it pleased her.

Now a straight haired blonde, but earlier in her life a mousey brunette she had a long face and thin lips that, at the corners of her mouth curled upward into a pointy point that some people described as pointedly cruel and mean spirited. Childless after two legal abortions, Anne had married a hedge fund manager but he divorced her for 'cruelty and mean spiritedness and physical abuse to bodily parts both above and below the waist line'. In response, Anne sued him for 'allegedly harboring covert Democratic tendencies' and then she agreed to pay an undisclosed settlement to end her ex-husband's counter suit. Meanwhile, she talked her back door lover, a sports radio talk show Host named Timmy 'Big Talker' Thompson into letting her talk on his live program. In no time her incisive commentary built a big listenership and soon she was talking in a very big way for Atlas. Now, after leaving it for a big check and bigger perks she was the leading harpy Host talking on the Crystal ComCo network.

"Where is the outrage?"

An outraged Anne was speaking to her outragable listeners. "Where is the justified offense and the justifiable anger, people? There's a huge swamp in Washington and it's called the U.S. Congress. It's filled with whiney leftists who hate America and we have to get rid of them. We have to drain the swamp people, but I can't do it alone. We have to expose the liars and the cheats. You know who I mean: it's those gutless, simpering little men who are so small and flaccid they don't deserve to enter into congress. Who let them slip their slippery way in there? I'll tell you who, it was the lying liberal media...the gutless left wing press who joined the lazy, wimpy Liberals in the government. I ask you, where are the real men? Where are the hard chested men who've got the muscles to take hold of this country and pull it back to the right side? I want to see those big, calloused hands; the hands of hard working men grab us and take us back to the way that makes us want to stand up, erect and proud to be an American. So this is what I say, no, this is what I demand: let the strongest men arise and do with us as they will, because Republican men know what's best for all of us."

Chapter XIV
Filling in the Dots, One at a Time

The office was hardly larger than Kilroy's. Like his, this room had the usual book shelves overburdened with tomes on constitutional law and government regulations and congressional records and precedents. On one wall hung a photo of an older man, the occupant of this office and his still young looking wife as they posed before the Washington Monument. Another photograph showed three freckled faced children, their faces alit with youthful energy as they pulled the arm of their beaming grandfather. Next to that, two American flags framed a window that looked out to the capitol steps. In front of that window was a desk piled with file folders and writing pads and notebooks. Behind the desk, wearing a starched white shirt and dark blue tie sat white haired Senator Kenneth Brumble. He looked across the desk, with dismay at his two dismaying visitors.

"If I were to confide my intentions to anyone," he said, "it would not be to either of you."

"We'll respect your confidence," Leonard Kilroy replied. "We only want to know if there is a move to renew Atlas's take-over of the radio spectrum."

Senator Brumble shook his head. "This is a matter that I'm not at liberty to discuss."

"Tell us if a certain lobbyist is working the Senate," Rafe Nailer said. "Is he trying to get you to commit to vote a certain way?"

"Indeed," Senator Brumble sighed, "the capitol is awash in rumors. I can't confirm or deny them, otherwise that's all I'd have time for. My constituents expect more than that from me."

Two days earlier Kilroy got wind of Hondo Roache's activities. At first the rumor seemed like a flashback of a bad trip, one that Kilroy thought had been laid to rest. The radio spectrum remained free from a corporate take-over. But no, as he made phone calls and button-holed legislators and aides the fearsome facts emerged. The Talbetts were still at work, using the relentless Hondo Roache in secret, determined to wrest control of the airwaves away from the People.

"Damn it," Kilroy had said to Rafe, "while I was looking at one specific license, the Talbetts were busy stealing the whole spectrum. I thought being non-partisan freed me from the tired old ways the council conducts its business, but in fact I was leaned over backassward looking at the wrong spot. And that particular spot ain't very pretty."

"Hondo Roache is still working the senator," Rafe said. "That means he hasn't closed the deal."

The deal wasn't yet a done deal but Hondo Roache was nearly finished with his task. When he gained a commitment from Senators Gleason and Brumble the bill would go to the full body. When it passed, the Talbetts would own the radio airwaves. The terrible possibility terrified Kilroy and Nailer.

"Next a television network will lobby to own all the TV channels," Rafe said to Kilroy. "Another corporation will try to take over the internet and another will try to privatize all the cell frequencies and another will want to own the interstate highways."

"Roache will keep up the pressure on Brumble," Kilroy said. "I don't know if the senator is capable of resisting, that is if he even wants to. Then again, I could be wrong, but I don't think I am, not this time. I could be right, too. Yes, I'm sure of it. I'm not wrong about this."

"From what I know of him," Rafe replied, "Senator Brumble is the kind of man who'll consider all the available facts before he makes his decision. Either that, or he won't."

Rafe had researched Senator Kenneth Brumble. The second of six siblings he grew up in an isolated village in the Northeast, in a tucked away hollow inside rolling, tree covered mountains. Flowing down that mountain was a cold water river which, a hundred years earlier supplied the power to a run a small but profitable textile mill. That mill employed Brumble's father and his mother before the babies began to arrive. As a kid, little Kenneth went to the only grade school and then the only high school in the surrounding thirty miles. He was a bright and curious boy and he asked a lot of questions, to which his parents could only answer, 'look it up in the encyclopedia.' The only one of those in town was in a weathered frame building that functioned as the town's underfunded library. Behind it, amongst the trees and rocks on the edge of the village nestled a ramshackle radio station and next to that was a five hundred foot tower. That tower broadcast the only signals not blocked by the surrounding mountains. During the years of Brumble's youth, before he went away to the state university this was the most reliable source of news about the world beyond those mountains. Kenneth realized the power of the broadcast signal and the critical information it provided to the people in town. When he entered the United States Senate he took a seat on the powerful Telecom Committee. The position gave him access to information known by only a few insiders, as well as the power to change the existing laws.

"I don't envy Brumble," Kilroy said. "If he votes 'no' he'll be accused of taking free speech away from Atlas. If he votes 'yes' he'll turn over the airwaves to a corporation that will broadcast anything to make a profit."

It wasn't that simple, Senator Brumble thought as he gazed across his desk at the two resolute men. They resolutely saw the issue in black and white. The senator knew better. The way Hondo Roache explained it, when Atlas took over the airwaves the entire creaky system would be streamlined and modernized. Frequencies now licensed to second rate broadcasters, those who lacked the resources to fully utilize their dial position would have to cede that dial position to companies with greater finances and talent, like Atlas. All the second tier operations, especially community supported stations would simply be turned off, thus clearing the spectrum of unpopular clutter and static. Professionally produced material would air on every dial position with more disc jockey chatter and more celebrity chit-chat and more sports news and more sports coverage and more sports talk programs and more interviews with ballplayers and coaches and managers and team owners and call in shows with rabid sports fans who'd sound off on past and current sports stats and sporty sports gossip from smart sports announcers and sports related commentary and the always all-important sports fan trivia. Material that bothered listeners like the depressing news from D.C. and boring analysis by brainiac analysts wouldn't be allowed on the airwaves. Who wants to hear that dreary stuff anyway? More importantly, the talkative Talk Radio Hosts would be talking on the air, all the time. And of course, Hondo had pointed out all radio broadcasts would still be free of charge to the listener. This would be accomplished by ridding the airwaves of tiresome PSAs and replacing them with paid for commercials.

The average listener Honda added, doesn't know the difference between a rectal cancer PSA or a spot for Anti-Leakage and Fungal Protection Suppositories, nor does the average listener care. Better still, tax money spent on regulating the industry would be put to better use, or those taxes could be eliminated. And after all, everyone wants to eliminate their taxes.

"If I were to confirm such a lobbying effort is underway," Senator Brumble said, "the information would have to remain in this room."

"So the lobbying effort is focused on two senators?" Rafe surmised. "The only two," he added, "who have not committed their votes?"

Senator Brumble shrugged.

"It's come down to Gleason," Kilroy said, "and to you. Right?"

"As I told you," Senator Brumble replied, "if such a move were underway then I'm not at liberty to confirm it. But," he added, "I'm not at liberty to deny it, either."

The senator's non-denial denial, Rafe realized, was intended to be tacitly understood, or at least to dodge the issue or to confuse him, which it did. "Would I be mistaken," he asked, "to assume you've made your decision?"

"I can't say and I won't say," Senator Brumble managed to say. "You may be mistaken, or you might not be mistaken."

He paused and looked first at Kilroy then at Nailer. "But I will definitely say this," the senator said, shrugging indefinitely. "I'm not going to make a decision based solely on what an activist tells me, or on the promise of a lobbyist. I will only say I won't say anything until I'm good and ready to say what it is that I have to say. Then I'll say what it is that I have to say because the time has arrived for me to say it."

Rapid Roy knows his Statistics, for a Fact

The mighty Host had a headache and the four aspirin he'd swallowed weren't working the way they're supposed to work. Still, he had a shift to work and a working professional goes to work when he has work he has to go to. After all, he had a calling to answer and millions of his avid listeners were avidly waiting to hear his avowedly avid voice.

"Here's a fact you need to know."

He paused to let his significant tone of voice express the significance of the words he was about to give voice to. "More than seventy-five per cent of all Democrats think America is no longer the greatest country in the world. That's right, seventy five percent of all Democrats hate America. And there's more, and it's even worse. Eighty-three per cent of all Democrats believe a woman should get paid the same as her male co-workers! Now if you don't already know let me tell you this fact: if women get paid the same as men then our job creating corporations will have to close their clothing factories and fast food restaurants. They simply don't make enough profit to pay women what the Democrats are demanding. And it gets even worse. Eighty-seven per cent of all Democrats want to raise the minimum wage again! I ask you, how will our small businessmen be able to pay that? Remember this fact: maid services and manicure providers are the country's biggest job creators. But if they're forced to pay women a higher minimum wage then they'll go out of business. An employer's meager profits will go to their female employees who, let's face it, don't work as hard as men. Sure, it might sound all equal and nice and fair, but what happens when men can't get jobs because women are stealing money right out of their pockets? I ask you this: which gender will bring home more bacon? But the Democrats want it that way and I can't stand for that, and neither should you. I know what I'm talking about because I know the true facts. And that's a true fact, too, a fact nobody can deny because I know more facts than anyone."

Chapter XV
Dabny Plans to Prey on her Prey

The morning sun filled Leadership Place with golden luminosity, as if wondrous King Midas had graced the mansion with his gentle touch. The marble veined white veiny marble, quarried from out the heart of Italy gave off its eternal luster, obdurate and invincible. The hallway statues, Jupiter, Apollo and Mars silently looked on as Jamesford and Dabny Talbett walked by as they had for many years, on their way to their weekly breakfast together.

"If we let Nailer get away with his threats," she said, "we'll have to fight him forever."

"He's a damn, dirty zealot," Jamesford said. "I can't stand to be in the same room with him. You know, he has a look about him, like he crawled out of a rat infested landfill. After he left I realized the son of a bitch stole my gold Noteworthy pen, the one you gave me for Christmas last year. He must think it it's some kind of trophy, the pathetic fool."

They arrived in the casual dining room, an intimate space with peach hued walls and pastels on canvas and a French oak table. Here they took their coffee and croissants and eggs soft boiled to the exact texture Jamesford demanded. Dabny, fresh from only a few hours of slumber sat across from her father. "This morning, when I woke up," she said, "I hoped we can agree on a new strategy."

"Sometimes a first thought is mistaken," he replied. "Sleep can make you dull witted and groggy. It has that effect on me. Some nights I can't sleep at all. That makes me tired. Oh, I hate getting old like some common man. It's not fair to me."

"We have to move aggressively," she urged. "I want the Hosts to tear the bastard apart."

Jamesford shook his head. "We have to save W4," he said. "Otherwise I might go along with you. I'd like to see Nailer's organs ripped out of his body and nailed to the kitchen door. That's right. I'd like to see him tortured to unbearable pain, then drawn and quartered in horrible torment and his innards fed to the swine. But we've got to shoulder the burden, as much as I hate it and give the council what they want."

"We need to attack now," she countered. "We'll force the council to back off. The Democrat members will see what the Hosts can do and at least one of them will fold like the cowards they really are. We'll get the renewal easily enough, you'll see."

She recalled an incident, three years ago when she'd unleashed the Atlas Hosts against a woman named Sandra Lowell. The twenty-three year old grad student—one of those insufferable femmy-goons as Rapid Roy called them—had testified before a congressional committee how the wealthiest four Americans possess more money than one hundred forty million of their fellow citizens.

"Every day we suffer," she said to the committee. "Millions of us, our grandparents and parents, our brothers and sisters and our babies are struggling to survive, as if this is a third world country. Our families suffer from homelessness and malnutrition and the lack of medical care…the care they desperately need and deserve by the simple virtue that we're all in this life, at this place and in this time together." A tiny tax increase of one tenth of one percent on the mega-billionaires, she testified, "will bring in enough revenue so we can care for our nation's sick and hungry. Then we'll attain the standard of living of most European countries."

"That woman is a poor excuse for an American."

Rapid Roy patriotically proclaimed this fact on his talk show. "If she thinks rotten old Europe is better than us then she should go over there to live! We'll be better off without her dirty lies and femmy-goon nagging."

Rapid Roy's sentiments were echoed by Gary Bock who exhorted on his show, "Sandra Lowell makes me ashamed to be a human because God made all of us and He's very angry right now. Sandra Lowell is a sinner and a liar. She's obviously deluded and probably retarded and she needs to be locked away in a mental ward. I will pray to God to make it so." Michelle Fang, on her talk show asserted, "Sandra Lowell was a teen-age hooker and an alcoholic and a meth addict and now she's tramping like a filthy whore for the bleeding heart Liberals. It's no wonder there's so many lazy sluts in this country. It's all because women like her think the world owes them a favor. She needs to learn the real facts of life! She needs to get a high paying job like I did."

Such was the influence of the Hosts that the tiny tax on mega-billionaires that Sandra Lowell had championed was killed by the Republicans, who voted in lock step as always.

"That new man Kilroy worries me," Jamesford said. "I thought he's nothing but a weak-spined pencil pusher who's afraid to stand with a political party. But god damn it, he turned into a nasty, yellow toothed ferret. We've got a problem with him."

Perhaps they did. Last night, on her way back from meeting Hondo, Dabny had studied the file on councilmember

Leonard Kilroy. His early years were markedly unremarkable, with his childhood in a middleclass Baltimore neighborhood. A second son of a foreman in a unionized steel wool factory, Kilroy went to public schools and to a state university. His grades were slightly better than average and he graduated slightly above the middle of his class.

"He's as dynamic as a bowl of cold oatmeal," she'd said to herself. "He can't be a real threat to us." Then she read the next file.

The former low level assistant, when he took his seat on the Communications Council, vowed to 'insure the People's airwaves remain neutral and open'. Dabny wasn't sure what that meant. In the past two decades other council members had made similar politically correct statements but they'd never refused a license renewal. Atlas never faced an actual threat from any of those pointy headed drudges in D.C. But if Kilroy joined forces with Rafe Nailer, then Dabny had to act now. Waiting wasn't her way to conduct business, or to attack an enemy.

"I'll call Rapid Roy this morning," she said to her father. "By noon Nailer's name will be linked to a room full of child pornography and poisoned heroin. He'll be a national pariah. The press will crucify him. Better yet, the council won't allow him into the building."

"We must remain calm," Jamesford said reprovingly. "We can still salvage the license for W4. I've instructed W4's General Manager to supply the council with all the necessary paperwork, including those god damn logs for the past five years."

The news stunned her. Those logs—the attested and notarized record of everything W4 had actually broadcast—would prove the station aired only one PSA per day, a fact her father still didn't know. That in itself was bad (really, why was it so important?) but the problem was repairable. However, six months ago she'd sat before the Senate Telcom Committee and testified under oath.

"I need you to respond to my question."

Senator Brumble made the query as clear as he could. "Simply answer yes or no. Does the Atlas Radio Company air the industry standard amount of PSAs, as you promised in order to obtain the license...the license your company uses to profit from the People's airways?"

"It might not be incorrect for me to say Atlas doesn't follow the standard," Dabny answered, "as we promised in order to obtain the license. I can tell you in all good faith that Atlas would never break our promise if there's a way for us to gainfully conduct our business without breaking our promise."

The senator let out an exasperated sigh. "Now then, Ms. Talbett, please answer yes or no to this: does the station in question, W4 you call it, does it air the customary and standard amount of Public Service Announcements?"

"I will tell you truthfully," she said, "as I know the truth to be that yes, W4 airs the standard number of PSAs. Please know Atlas is eager to obey all laws and adhere to all our promises and I might add, we are grateful to use the People's airwaves in our endeavor to entertain and distract the masses. If the case were otherwise I would certainly say so. And isn't that what I'm here to say to you, here today?"

Remembering that episode, she realized that lying to a federal committee could be construed by some overzealous people as perjury. She wasn't sure if she'd sufficiently obfuscated her answers.

"I'll call our friends on the council," she said to her father. "The chairperson always supports us and the other Republican will too. All we need is to convince one of the other three to come to our side. We can settle with them later…a new car for their kid or a college scholarship."

"That's not going to work this time," Jamesford countered. "We have to let the process follow its course, whether we like it or not. And god damn it, I don't like it one bit."

Outwardly Dabny remained calm, but inside she roiled. This day had started badly. "I'm going to call the chairperson," she said. "I'll demand a continuance. I need time to revise my plans."

"Your plans?"

Her father gazed at her with eyes filling with confusion and anger. "You haven't told me about any plans, young lady. If you have plans you damn well better share them, right now."

"It's merely routine," she said, rising from the table. "Before we give the council the logs I want to be sure what's in them. That way I'll be able to answer any questions that might be asked." She left the room and called the council chairperson in D. C. Then, after she instructed him to suspend the renewal process she returned to the table. Jamesford was looking at her with a deep row of furrows furrowing his already furrowed brow.

"We've promised to be truthful with each other," he said. "I think you're hiding something and you better stop it."

If he intended to provoke her he succeeded, but only a little. "Father," she said with an unprovoked tone, "we have each other's blood, and the years of trust between us. There've been times when we had to rely on each other and times when we had our doubts, but in the end we joined together and we came out on top."

"This business with the logs," he snapped, "is not a problem, I hope."

"There's no such thing as a problem," she replied. "There are only opportunities. And I won't let an opportunity go unanswered."

Her words reverberated with her undaunted spirit, there, in that warm room, their private family space where for years they'd meet for their morning meal. This was their sacred place where they told each other the real truth. Here Dabny once confessed to bribing an Economics professor with a ten thousand dollar grant during a short lived college fling. Jamesford admitted a wayward affair with a gullible pop music diva. That was a year before his wife was killed, drunken driving her yellow Lamborghini on a crowded suburban freeway, zigzagging around and past sedans and semis and slow moving pick-up trucks. The minivan she smashed into contained a family of four who were on vacation from Schenectady. All of them were killed as well.

Yes, those were the bleak days, a desperate time like a fateful plague that might descend upon the manse of a royal family. Certainly, such a disaster could not be foreseen. Perhaps it could've been avoided, though, if Jamesford had taken away his wife's car keys after her driver's license had been revoked following her third DUI conviction. But Jamesford rose to his sudden single parenthood to comfort his seven year old daughter. And Dabny, in her bewildered shock and grief—this kind of thing couldn't happen to a perfect family like hers—immediately realized Jamesford was now her sole benefactor. From that day on the two of them grew closer than most fathers and daughters. Only during the last few days had that bond been tested to a critical point.

"I don't want to discover you've taken action without my knowing, or approval," he warned her. "You're not in the

CEO's chair yet, and I don't plan to let you sit in it anytime soon. Frankly, I think it's still too big for you."

"We must keep Atlas free from the ghouls in D. C," she said. "If we act now we'll retain the license for W4 and we'll get rid of Nailer for good."

To Jamesford his daughter's intentions were too head-strong, too bullish, too soon. In the past Atlas easily obtained the renewal and they remained flush with cash, as well as the political wherewithal to remain an unbowed colossus. The veteran CEO saw no reason to panic. But his observant daughter might see the situation more clearly. Perhaps caution blurred his vision and his famous instincts were infamously betraying him. Maybe, Dabny was right. Perhaps they needed to go on the attack. They could crush Rafe Nailer easily enough. But no, Atlas thrived because he made the right choices, especially when he dealt with the bloodsuckers in government.

"We're going to take the smart course," he told her. "It will insure Atlas remains on solid ground. This silly business with the logs will be cleared up in no time."

"We both want Atlas to remain strong," she said. "I've never defied you and it's not my intention to start now."

Her subdued manner had its effect. Jamesford reached over and patted her hand. "You'll see, my child," he said. "There's great wisdom in following my way. We'll keep the license and move on. After all, we still have our powerful Hosts and the highest ratings and largest market share in the industry. I intend Atlas will last forever…and by God we will."

"I've never stopped believing in you, father," she murmured. "You know what's best for us."

"What's best for us," he reminded her, "is acquiring everything we're entitled to acquire and we're entitled to acquire anything we want. After all, what good is it to be entitled if you can't acquire whatever there is to acquire? So remember my child: it's never wrong to acquire the thing you want. And if the bureaucrats say it's illegal to acquire that thing, claim your entitlement to acquire it supersedes the law because you're entitled to do so. But don't forget this: be sure the thing you acquire is the same thing you want to acquire. Then when you have no doubt and no one is watching, go ahead and acquire the thing you want."

A valuable lesson for life from Rapid Roy

When he told his audience to 'know your enemies' the big talker intended to educate them to an important fact of life. "Know your enemies," he said, "because an enemy defines the man. Really, it's that simple. If the bad guys don't like you that makes you a good guy. If the collectivists don't like you that makes you an individualist. So be forewarned: the nattering, naysaying regulators will try to bring us down. They'll use their worst weapons, their income taxes and their regulations to try to destroy us. It's an undeniable fact they desperately want to be as good as us but they never can be. So, with that cleared up and laid to rest without any doubt, I'll take a call from one of my very favorite places on the planet, the Big D, Dallas."

"Hey ya'll from the Lone Star state! I'm one of your biggest Me Too-ers. You sure got me thinking how we've got to believe in you Rapid Roy, because we don't listen to nothin' else. I mean it, too. The leftys are out to steal everything they can so we've got to fight back. Personally, I'm not going to pay my income tax and I'm signing every petition for secession. I say 'Remember the Alamo!' Those boys were real heroes, the kind that fight till they're dead, firing their muskets at all those illegal foreigners. So keep up the great work, big man. Us Texans sure do love hearin' whatever you tell us!"

"There you have it. You Me Too-ers are the great people who make this great country what it is and if I had my way, we'd live in a world that's free from the spineless collectivists. I promise you that one day, great men like us will take what's ours to take and then we'll have a country we deserve to live in. That's why I say 'know your enemies' because sooner or later you'll have to destroy them."

Chapter XVI
Drawing Closer, Together Again

The day was turning into evening while she waited for
him. She'd taken the last toke from her third joint of the day and
she was feeling better now, having dashed through the jumble of
taxis and smoke belching buses and muscled her muscle car to
an open spot at the curb as he walked out of the terminal. Rafe
jumped in and Vera stepped on the gas.

"You covered a lot of ground," she said. "Are the government guys any saner than the Talbetts?"

"Saner yes," he replied. "But just as shifty. The guys who
have to make a decision will keep from making that decision for
as long as they can. I heard a lot of equivocations and hedging
and round about evasions wrapped in vague elusions and they're
all tied up with a great, big question mark."

Vera pulled a fresh joint from her pocket and handed it to
Rafe. He lit it and took a deep drag.

"The next move is up to the Talbetts."

He expelled a smoking stream of smoke from his deep
in his lungs, up through his windpipe and out his rounded lips,
expelling a smoky smoke ring into the charging Charger's air
conditioned air.

"I bet they'll try something sneaky."

Vera jerked the Charger into the mass of traffic that was
snaking its way out of the airport's confines. She began to tail-
gate a white minivan heading toward the toll booth. She was

having a good time; it was fun picking Rafe up. Each time he jumped into her car it was a reunion of sorts. She enjoyed reunions, even when she reunited with her uptight family.

The Standfore family, of which Vera was the third of four children, was the Standfores of the Standfore Manufacturing Company. The family dynasty went back to pre-Revolutionary days when some men wore waistcoats and powdered wigs and others wore leather aprons and worked with the skill of their hands. For over two centuries the Standfores were a leader in creating jobs for thousands of hard working Americans. Now, with highly productive factories in seven states and a payroll with eighty-five thousand employees, Standfore Manufacturing produced high end machine parts and farm tractors and a line of exceptionally efficient firefighting pumper trucks. Vera's two older siblings, blond Nolan and red haired Nigel took positions in the home office working directly under their father, Nathan. Her younger brother, sandy haired Neil also went to work with them, after he graduated from Yale, as did his older brothers. Vera attended Oberlin where she majored in English Lit. and minored in Western History and Thought, and she graduated summa cum laude. During her student days she refused to join a sorority though several had invited her. She made friends easily and participated in many extracurricular activities like the intercollegiate chess match and the Philosopher's Inner Circle. She maintained a regime of rigorous exercise and was captain of the mixed gender Mixed Martial Arts squad where she mastered the tactics of frontal attack and the most effective ways to incapacitate her opponent. One time she fractured a competitor's sternum—in two places—and another time she socked an opponent's right eyeball right out of its eye socket, to which she shrugged and said, "he should have ducked sooner." Over the course of four years she won all but two of her bouts and twice led the team to a conference title. In her senior year she humbly accepted the college's Best Sportsperson on Campus award. She also joined GreenSpace and the Union for the People's Democracy. She wrote press releases and managed the phone banks and accomplished any task that needed accomplishing. She marched in pro union demonstrations, usually the non-violent kind but not always; sometimes to prove her point she had to punch out a security guard or other corporate lackey. She sat in sit-ins and carried signs and distributed leaflets outside non-union shops and factories, even one owned by her father. That got her disowned, but only for a year. When she graduated, however, she didn't continue her activism. Instead, she took an entry level job at an independently owned New York publishing firm. There, she worked as an assistant to the chief editor. One day she came across a poorly typed manuscript authored by an ex-History teacher turned political activist. After reading the man's inspiring words, her lost inspiration returned. She quit her job and drove her charging Charger across six state lines and one time zone to meet the author in person.

"If you wrote that inspirational book," she said in the interview, "then I want to work for you. The Public Cause Group is my kind of organization."

"There's only one available position," Rafe had replied. "It's Assistant to the guy who sometimes doesn't know what he's doing."

Hearing that, she leaned over the desk and said, "let's not know what we're doing together."

After that they were inseparable.

"The demonstration went great yesterday," she said excitedly as she steered the Charger around the minivan. "We had thirty five members of the Lancer team marching in front of the bank and at least another fifty volunteers, and there must have been five hundred more people, occupiers and onlookers. Most of them were cheering for us, too." She tromped the accelerator; the Charger blew past a slow moving bus. "I got in the face of one of the bank's VPs, a creepy guy with a blond mustache and a nasty sneer and thin lips, like he didn't have any lips at all."

"I hope you didn't slug him," Rafe said.

"I only kneed him the groin," she said. "I told him to grow a bigger pair of balls and to get the hell out of the banking business. Frankly, I don't believe his balls can get bigger, that is after the swelling's gone down. I think creeps like him are made in a test tube in a laboratory in the basement of an investment bank. They're bred to steal from community pension plans and screw elderly widows out of their social security."

Rafe was relieved his fiancée hadn't gotten into a fist fight, not this time. He took another drag from the joint and tried to relax, which was tough to do with Vera's hands on the wheel and her foot stomping the pedal.

"There were hundreds of cops, rows and rows of 'em with their shields and helmets and billy clubs," she continued. "There were plenty of other cops in plainclothes trying to incite a riot but the Lancers didn't fall for that trick. The cops rolled in a tank-mounted water cannon and they started spraying us like we were on fire. A cop helicopter was hovering overhead and a bunch of newspaper reporters were there, and a couple from a TV station with their video equipment. But they didn't get a picture of me when I started a fire in a trash can. Then I threw it into the bank's lobby. That got the sprinklers going and water was squirting everywhere and there was lots of smoke and people were screaming and crying and climbing over each other to escape the building and then the fire trucks roared up with all their sirens blasting and then the cops rushed at us. They broke through the blockade we made with stolen grocery carts and they started tasing us. I didn't get hit or arrested, but Mark and Maddy did. So did Cristina and Daniel. The whole thing went down like a really cool movie and the news crew filmed most of it. My interview will be on the news tonight. I can't wait to see myself on TV."

"Jesus," Rafe exclaimed. "The demonstration was supposed to be non-violent."

Vera cut around a delivery van and swerved to miss an oncoming school bus. "I like it when things get exciting," she said. "It's like a party and you know what they say about that: a party ain't really a party 'til the cops come to break it up. Anyway, I broke free from the cordon of cops and the giant cloud of teargas and after that I sent our legal flacks to the jail. They got our guys bailed out within two hours."

"I'm glad we've got good lawyers," Rafe said. "They know what they're doing and better yet, they work pro bono."

Vera zipped around another slow moving bus and stomped on the accelerator. "You wouldn't believe," she said as they were leaving the airport behind, "what I was listening to before I picked you up."

"I've warned you about that," Rafe said. "That stuff can rot your brain."

She giggled out loud, enjoying having him back. "Don't worry," she said. "I don't see how anyone can think the woman really believes what she says. She can't be that obscenely nutso."

With that, Vera clicked on the radio. "The lying sluts and the Liberals are at it again," Michelle Fang groused. "Listen to this: they want every woman in this country to have free birth control pills! And not only that, they want the filthy tramps to get free morning after pills! And it's even worse: they want every female who does manage to get pregnant…the way God and Nature intend it…to get an abortion, for free! The dirty minded Liberals want to use your tax money to pay for all the raunchy sex those trashy women are indulging in. The radical leftists are turning our country's women into dirty, filthy whores."

At the wheel, Vera laughed. "Damn," she said to Rafe, "it's the slutty Liberals who're having all that torrid sex. I hope you're faithful to me, my love."

"It's not a matter of faith," Rafe said. "I don't have the time to be unfaithful, to you or anybody else."

"It's outrageous," Michelle Fang rasped. "Some women will drop everything and open their legs. If I didn't know better, I'd think they enjoy it. Please, people. We have to stop it right now, before all our women are sleeping around like filthy, street tramping, filthy, filthy whores."

"Before we buy a new house," Rafe said to Vera, "let's find out who the neighbors are."

"We're not even married yet," she said as she switched Michelle off. "And you're worried about what the neighbors are doing behind their curtains."

He shook his head. "I don't want the neighbors," he said, "to see what going on behind *our* curtains."

They were on the freeway now, careening into the city. Traffic had thinned and Vera had the Charger going eighty-five, charging past Ford vans and Chevy sedans and airport shuttle buses. Flashing by were fast food joints and gas stations with shining logo signs and dry cleaners and pet supply stores and more fast food joints and then came a mile long stretch of car dealerships whose lots contained rows of stylish foreign made autos. Vera gunned the motor to ninety five.

"I've got to get a tune up," she said. "The mechanic said this ol' Charger needs new spark plugs and its injectors should be cleaned out. Then it'll perform better than new."

"I can't wait," Rafe said as his knuckles turned white from grasping the armrest.

They barreled onto the overpass that belted the city's commercial area where brightly illuminated office buildings rose into the evening sky. They flew by restaurants and women's fashion stores and office supply stores and stores that sold high end electronics. They sped by joggers and groups of young people wearing the trendiest cloths. And they passed people wearing clothes that weren't so fashionable or clean, the kind of people the Chamber of Commerce doesn't want visiting conventioneers to see on the city's streets.

"Remind me to pack up your old suits for the Good Will," Vera said. "Also, when we get home I need to sew a button on your blue dress shirt. It's the one that goes so well with your pin stripped suit. You know, the one you never wear."

"I'll try to set up an interview," he said, "where I'll need to look sincere. Sincerity plays well on TV. The problem is I have to find an interviewer who'll agree to interview me. "

They exited the freeway and came to the edge of a residential area. They drove by high rise condos and newly built apartment buildings designed in the Art Deco style and then they passed large homes with wide green lawns. They came to a section where the homes were more modest. Vera yanked the Charger onto the street where they lived, still three blocks away. She slowed to ten MPH over the limit. That's when Rafe's cell buzzed. He looked at the ID, which didn't identify the caller.

"Who could it be," he said, "at this ungodly time of night?"

"This is Dabny Talbett."

Her tone was like an earnest phone solicitor's, offering the opportunity of a lifetime to this call's lucky recipient. "I've been thinking about your visit," she said. "It was impolite of me to act the way I did, especially since you were a guest in our humble home. So, I want us to meet again. I have something important to discuss with you. I only ask that you keep our meeting a secret."

Ted Brundy sees Trouble Ahead

"America is the land of the free," the folksy Host informed the mostly uninformed folks in his audience. "So good buddies we have to make sure we stay free. And we do that by keeping the government's paws off our guns and their dirty claws away from our hard earned money. Now I might not be the pointiest pick ax in the ol' wood shed out back, but I know one thing for darn sure: we've got a big, bad government that wants to take away our guns because that's how we'll defend ourselfs when they come to get us. We've to stop 'em before they put a tax on us so we can't afford to buy our Croakers and high capacity magazines and our ammo belts of steel jacket bullets. They think we're not watching 'em, but we are, aren't we? Right now they're making laws that will force us to surrender our guns. I know because I talked to a man who seen it in the papers. Now, I may not be the sharpest razor blade in good ol' Floyd's barbershop but I know trouble when I see it and I see it coming our way, big time. Yes sir, we got a whole lot of fightin' to do. I know you're up to the task because you're all good Americans and that makes you darn good marksmen, and that's all you have to be to fight 'em till they run for cover."

Chapter XVII
Metal Woods and Tricky Traps

"Oh, the things I do for Atlas."

Rapid Roy swallowed the last drop of a spicy bloody mary and blearily gazed out at the long stretch of green, green grass. To his right arose a stand of blue spruce trees, each trimmed to a perfect pyramid shape, in a straight row that bordered the length of the number one fairway. To his left, holding a three wood just now used in the day's first tee shot, was a frowning Dabny Talbett.

"If you get out of the cart," she chided, "you can take your swing now."

"Playing with a lady is harder than with a guy," he grunted. "If I can't talk the way I normally do my whole game will be ruined."

Not laughing, she walked to other side of the cart and, after sliding the club into the bag strapped in the carrying compartment, sat down on the seat. "You can't say anything," she scoffed, "that I haven't heard a hundred times before."

"It's not the words so much as the way I say them."

"That's why you're on the radio," she replied, trying to relax. "You're one of the most famous people in the country. I wish I had your name recognition."

She didn't mean to sound envious, he knew. "You have something that's better than fame," he replied. "You've got a god damn corporation." After that he pulled out his metal wood with a famous trademark on the oversized head. He lumbered to the tee box. After plugging the tee into the soft earth he set up his ball and then, with an effortless swing gained from years of repetition, sent the ball three hundred and ten yards straight down the fairway.

"Now then," he said as he returned to the cart, "I can report my meeting with Brilly O'Neal is set for Thursday, next week. I'm sure he'll be eager to consider making the move back to Atlas."

She wanted to hear that. "Remember, you have to persuade him to commit."

Rapid Roy pressed the pedal. The cart moved down the path to Dabny's ball, lying like a pearl in the fairway, maintained to exact standards by the country club's expert greens keepers. Details like that pleased her. She selected a seven iron and with a graceful motion struck her ball. It arced high in the air and landed five yards short of the green. Then it rolled onto the edge of the short grass, fifteen feet from the flag.

"That's birdie territory," she exclaimed. "And on the first hole!"

"I should never have spotted you five strokes," Rapid Roy muttered. "I think you tricked me."

They drove to his ball and, with a smoothness that defied his bulk he hit a shot that landed on the green, ten feet from the pin. "They call that a money shot," he crowed. "In the game of golf, that is."

"Am I to think," Dabny said, "O'Neal will want more than the twenty per cent I offered?"

"He's not a greedy man," Rapid Roy answered. "But he is a cautious one. Brilly might move back if you guarantee the money for at least three years."

They arrived on the green. She studied her ball's position and the slight depression in the surface, slanting away from the hole. Then, after taking a practice swing she tapped the ball in a perfect route to the target, but it stopped a foot and a half short.

"I'll have to settle for par," she sighed. "Par is for average golfers and I can't stand the thought of being average, at anything."

"O'Neal will want to be sure."

Rapid Roy was walking to his ball. "He'll want to be satisfied you and Atlas will be around in three years. I expect he'll say there's a rumor about a cash squeeze in your bank account."

"Atlas is as flush as ever."

She was annoyed yet concerned by Rapid Roy's impertinence. Okay, she was worried, but only a little. In the past two days she'd spent several million on retaining bonuses for the Atlas Hosts to keep them with the company, and away from CryCom. And she couldn't forget the ten percent of Atlas she'd transferred to Hondo Roache. That was a far greater financial outlay than she'd planned. Atlas stock was down to $215 and the boys on Wall Street were starting to question that price.

Worse, Jamesford's aborted attempt to privatize the spectrum had depleted their operating budget. The quarterly dividend checks were going out to the shareholders and a balloon payment was due to their lending bank. And oh yes, a preset compensation package had to be paid to the board of directors. Atlas's coffers were nearly empty. Well okay, she was more than a little worried, but she'd regain market share when the errant Hosts returned to Atlas. Then the revenues would start flowing in again. She couldn't let her father find out about her activities, not yet. She was relieved he'd entrusted her with Atlas's finances. She had to keep the situation a secret until Hondo gained the commitments from those damn stubborn senators. Why couldn't he close them?

"The rumors about our cash flow are only that," she said to Rapid Roy. "No doubt they're being spread by my *lovely* competitor Abby Watsamore. I'll have to speak to her about that."

Rapid Roy had reached his ball and was calculating the necessary speed to the pin. He leaned over and, with a movement as smooth as a tiger's tail tapped the ball the perfect distance and the ball clicked into the cup, for the first birdie of the day.

"Abby Whatshername, the big ol' diesel dyke," he said, "is one nasty broad. O' Neal says she rides her Harley to work every day, even if it's raining and she brings a bag of road kill to the office for lunch, along with a bottle of hundred fifty proof sour mash."

They moved to the number two tee box. The hole was a par five, dog-leg right, pocked with a half dozen sand traps and a water hazard on the left. "You need to watch out," Rapid Roy said as he studied the long expanse. "You'll get into trouble if you don't go straight."

"What's it going to take," Dabny said, "to bring O'Neal back to Atlas?"

"A signing bonus I expect," Rapid Roy answered. "That'll probably be necessary with Miss Caldron, as well." He set up his ball then drove it in a towering arc, slicing neatly with the curve of the fairway. It landed out of sight, probably set up for his approach shot.

"I can meet their demands."

Dabny didn't like even saying it. "But I won't wait for them to play some stupid game of hide and seek." She peered down the fairway, noting the sand traps and the overhang of trees on the right, then took her swing. The ball sailed in a straight trajectory, but hit the one branch she'd tried to avoid. Frustratingly, the ball dropped short of her intended target.

"You can make up the difference," Rapid Roy said, "between what they want and what you'll pay with a Christmas bonus. They'll agree to that," he said. "O'Neal will, anyway. It's hard to say what Anne Caldron will do; sometimes she's not totally rational."

Dabny shook her head. "Actually, I wouldn't care if Caldron stayed at CryCom. Her show is dropping in the ratings and I only want her because she's part of the two timer package. If anything," she added, "Caldron manages to stay in the business by basking in the halo of the other Hosts."

Dabny knew the ratings and demographics, the audience research based on age and gender, and the more salient facts such as the income and education and religious affiliation of the Hosts' audiences. For example, Brilly O'Neal's listeners were mostly middle-aged, white males with a high school education. They worked in blue collar jobs and drove American made cars that were on average four and a half years old. They spent approximately one hour and fifteen minutes a day listening to their favorite Hosts, usually in their cars on their way to work and after the day was over, to their favorite tavern. There they drank domestic beer, usually three bottles per night along with two shots of off brand whiskey and, after making their way home they ate a meal of potato chips and hamburger on three day old sesame seed buns or pre-cooked egg noodles (the wide kind) with canned (non Dolphin safe) tuna fish (or leftover fried chicken on Monday night, wings and legs only) with mashed potatoes and white cream gravy followed by a dessert of three scoops of neapolitan ice cream piled atop two Twinkies, or two giant dollops of Cream Whip slathered over a pair of Ding Dongs, each cut in half, diagonally.

On the other hand, research showed Anne Caldron's followers were a cultural mixed bag (the mongrel audience Dabny called them). They were low wage men and women with less than a high school education, living in a two bedroom household with six family members. They ate at least five meals a week at fast food joints (once a week at a national brand pizza place where they ordered the extra-large pie with double cheese toppings and deluxe hamburger crumbles) and they watched TV seven and a half hours a day, mostly professional wrestling and reality programs. They went to a Protestant church (usually one of the Baptist brands) two times a year, not counting Easter but including Christmas Eve and roughly a quarter of them were on Medicaid and / or Food Stamps. Their quality of life hovered at the poverty level and yet, inexplicably, if they ever bothered to vote, they usually voted Republican.

"They're not the Grade A audience component," Dabny conceded. "However, they pump up the national ratings. The ad agencies want big numbers for their clients, so every listener counts."

"If you play it right," Rapid Roy said to her, "you can cut the corner and hit the fairway around the dog-leg. You'll have an open shot to the green."

They pulled up at her ball and, using an eight iron she punched the ball a hundred yards. It landed in the fringe on the far side of the fairway. "I can hit the green from there," she said as she returned to the cart. "I can still make birdie."

"It's not going to be easy," Rapid Roy said, "if you lose W4."

"I won't let it happen," she retorted. "You can tell the Hosts at Crystal ComCo that. And you can also tell them Atlas will grow more powerful. I'm going to make a big announcement in a few days."

Rapid Roy arrived at his ball. He assessed the distance to the flag and chose his nine iron. The ball traced a perfect line across the cloud dappled cloud-filled sky and fell to earth, kicking up its own cloud in a sandy sand trap on the right side of the green.

"It's doable," he sighed, "if it's got a good lie."

"I'm telling you the truth," Dabny snapped. "Right now I've got a man, the best there is, making sure Atlas will continue to own the biggest share of audience. Tell the CryCom Hosts our future is absolutely golden."

"That's what I want to talk about, our mutual golden future."

Rapid Roy steered the cart to Dabny's ball and watched as she determiningly pulled out her trusty niblick. "Not enough club," he offered as unrequested advice.

Ignoring him, she set up for her shot, which bounced maddeningly over the turf and stopped ten yards short of the green.

"I can still make par," she said, sounding as determined as ever.

"If you think you're going to be the big dog for a long time to come," Rapid Roy said, "then I want to be in your kennel."

She laughed scornfully with a scornful laugh. "The Atlas kennel," she said, "is for pure breeds only."

He hit the brake. "Sure, you don't care for mutts," he said. "But it's mutts, millions of 'em that Atlas is standing on. I'm not offended because I know you didn't mean to insult me. But," he said, "if you want me to roll over for you then you're going to let me in into the owner's house."

"Please Roy," she said, with her most pleasing voice. "I'll raise my offer to a fifty per cent lift in your comp package. Plus I'll throw in two more vacation weeks."

"That's still employee benefits," he huffed. "I want a chair at the table. I want five percent."

The demand surprised, and angered her. Atlas belonged to Jamesford and her, and now to Hondo Roache. The company was a family edifice, a generational estate. It must remain within the clan, possessors of the same genetically pure genes. Yes, the Talbetts had incorporated, selling the stock they needed to finance Atlas's mighty growth. But the family still held the majority of shares. She couldn't part with anymore of her portion; that would leave her without the leverage to keep the board of directors under Talbett control. More important than that, she loathed the idea of allowing a crude man like Rapid Roy to enter her family's intimate domain.

"I'll consider your request," she said, trying not to sound inconsiderate.

"I've earned a stake in the company."

He'd stopped the cart near the green. "Without me Atlas can't hold up the price of one damn share."

She kept her cool. This was not the time to open a rift with Rapid Roy. Atlas needed him now, as much as she hated to admit it. But she wouldn't give in to this blackmail. A Talbett never conceded like that.

"I've got a tough shot here," she said. "But I can make it."

She climbed out of the cart and, taking her pitching wedge and putter walked to her ball. "I'll make this in two," she said. "Shots like this win the game." Using the wedge, she bounced the ball onto the green, where it rolled over a slight indentation and came to a stop, six feet from the pin.

"That's for par," Rapid Roy said. "If you can sink it."

"We're not done yet," she replied. "You still have to dig yourself out of the trap."

His lie was on the uphill side, which is the way he wanted, but the ball was buried in the sand. He had to take an unbalanced stance as he swung and struck the powdery stuff an inch behind the ball. Thrust up from the explosion, the ball arced over the green and after landing in a shower of sand, rolled only two more feet.

"Good enough," he said. "From there I can get my birdie."

"You're not in the hole yet."

She watched as Rapid Roy, who was farthest from the pin assess the distance he still had to go. "Be careful," she said. "Your lie is trickier than it looks."

He glanced over at her. "The trick is to know how hard to push it."

Then he set himself over the ball. His putter moved like clockwork and lightly tapped the ball, which followed the exact line but passed the cup and kept rolling for another three feet.

"Sometimes," she said, "you can push things too hard."

Then, with a scowling Rapid Roy watching she took position above her ball, which she tapped with the perfect speed. Like a well-trained animal the ball rolled along the anticipated route, dipping an inch toward the pin, then dropped into the cup.

"There," she said, "I saved my par. That's as good as you can do, if you can do it at all."

The Country needs to Man Up, so says Anne Caldron

"Nanny, nanny, nanny."

Some people, not all of them her fans, likened her voice to the snarling sound a vicious alley cat makes as it intimidates its weaker prey. The simile pleased her.

"The cowering Liberals," she hissed, "want us to live in their prissy little nanny state and be forced to obey their prissy rules and regulations, like not allowing us to text when we drive and taking away our super-sized sodas. The Liberals hate the real stuff in life. And they don't have the balls to run this country. They're nothing but finicky little boys who can't stand up to real men. The prissy, goody-goody two shoes don't want to hurt anyone's feelings. Oh, no! They're afraid to say something that might be politically incorrect, it might insult someone's so-called 'heritage' or 'ethnicity' or 'racial character', and you know what I mean by *that*. The nanny, nanny boys want to make everybody be like them, persnickety and sissified little children who're afraid of their own shadows. Now I ask you, is that the kind of people who should be making our laws? I'll tell you one thing: prissy boys don't do the work of real Republican men, and that's who we need right now in congress."

Chapter XVIII
Picking the Brain, Luring the Prey

When he arrived at the designated spot, by a towering water fountain, Rafe took in the sight. On either side arose a wall of glass. Ten feet high, it stretched down a wide corridor for what seemed like a half mile. He noted the smell: the aromatic aroma of the darkest dark chocolate...the expensive kind made in Belgium...mixed with the scent of new suede leather added to the smell of perfume school girls wear to weekend raves. Beneath the high ceiling the air rippled with a ripply, unnaturally muted, unnatural light; it drained everything of color, making the locale colorless and in a way, uncolorful. The hum of unintelligible conversation mixed with saccharine pop music created a constant drone, like inside an insentient human hive. Around him an endless stream of shoppers, mostly well-dressed females—teens in pairs and middle-age ladies and slow walking blue haired matrons— streamed by carrying oversized bags stuffed with the latest fashions and stylish feminine footwear.

He never came into places like this; he never had the need or felt the inclination. What is it he wondered, that draws people here? Of course, the answer is simple: this place is the perfect convergence of convenience and consumption; a seductive gathering locus for social interaction, to see and to be seen, and to covet the attractively displayed products that one can easily live without. And yet, every day thousands came to look and dream and make their purchases and carry away the object of their fondest and temporary desires.

"It's a good place to meet."

Dabny walked up to him. "Especially if you want to get lost in the crowd."

"I try to stay away from crowds," Rafe replied. "I might not be heard above the chatter."

On her way here, she'd pulled a floppy hat over her hair and was wearing an inconspicuous beige jacket, a white pullover and dark pants. Wearing this, she could be any of a hundred women who were walking through the mall. "I bet you were surprised," she said, "to hear from me."

"You wouldn't call me," he replied, "if you weren't worried about W4."

"Smart people know how to work out their differences," she said. "I don't doubt you and I can reach an understanding." She nodded in the opposite direction she'd come and they began to move within the parade of consumers, looking like a normally consuming couple on the usual shopping expedition.

"You've got me at a disadvantage. This is foreign territory."

He'd stopped outside a store window that featured a foldable massage table and a big leather chair that vibrated with massage like effects, and a string of massage beads and an assortment of massage oils and next to that was a small black machine called a massage oil warmer.

"The customers here must have a lot of aches and pains," he said. "Apparently they lead very hard lives."

"The market brings us everything we're entitled to," she replied. "The consumer has the right to choose from hundreds of choices."

This place intrigued Rafe. Store window after store window displayed colorful shirts and blouses and sweaters and shawls and scarfs, coats and jackets and parkas, raincoats and hats and caps and hoodies, and shoes and boots and sandals and more pants and skirts and dresses than he thought could ever be needed or worn. But those things would be bought and worn—perhaps once or twice—then tossed aside to make room for the next season's newest styles. Yes, the market brings consumers everything they want. Most people assume this lifestyle will go on forever. Perhaps it will.

"We both know W4 will get the renewal."

Dabny had prepared for meeting; she had to get him to commit. "And we both know Atlas will remain the strongest radio company in the country. I can't see the sense in fighting with you. We both know it's a waste of our time and money."

"The reason we fight battles," Rafe replied, "is to change the way things are, or to keep the way things are from changing. You and I each have one of those reasons and we both know which ones...and who is doing what."

Quelling a flippant reply, she glanced at his face. With his dark eyes and sharp features he wasn't bad looking. In another place and time, and if she had a different opinion of him she might even find him somewhat attractive, or at least less repugnant. She wanted to think he was reasonable and open to compromise. That's the way superior people work out their differences. But in Rafe Nailer she was dealing with a close minded zealot, one who'd never be content until he'd taken all the true producers down to the lowest common denominator.

"Let me propose a solution," she said. "You aren't against hearing me out, are you?"

"I'm still here," he replied.

He didn't sound unreasonable, but he also didn't sound interested. Still she'd decided, forced herself really, to make this overture. For the last few days all she could think to do was to attack him with every weapon in her arsenal. It wouldn't take long before Nailer's name had been so sullied he'd be tossed into the dust bin of ignominious failures. But then she recalled Hondo's caution about unintended consequences. There might be, she realized a more effective course of action, a strategy which would produce the most beneficial result. She would take the enemy into her arms (figuratively, of course) and show the Communications Council how the Talbetts were above the rancor of the common crowd. She would show the world that no enemy, no matter how venial or deceitful, could sully the name of Atlas.

"First," she said, "I understand you want to be sure Atlas conforms to the pertinent laws and that we follow all the regulations."

"In a perfect world," he replied, "we wouldn't need those laws. But alas…"

He didn't make her angry. She wouldn't allow herself an emotional response; feelings like that are self-destructive. "You're a smart man, Mister Nailer," she said. "You know when a proper solution presents itself. I'm willing to bet you're also a man," she added with as positive a tone she could manage, "who'll agree to that solution and not get all self-righteous if the other side proposes it."

"Some solutions can upset a person's ego," he said. "But if the solution solves the problem then I'd say the problem is solved sufficiently. "

If he was attempting to goad her into an argument she wouldn't fall into his trap. She'd seen him use that tactic on other opponents. One of those was an oil company CEO. On a

Sunday morning talking heads show the man from Big Oil allowed Nailer to play the role of noble hero battling a heartless corporation. Nailer baited the CEO who came off looking sullen and mean spirited. After that the company's stock lost half its value. That kind of loss, she vowed, would not happen to her.

"You have a golden opportunity here," she said to him. "It will give you what you want; a way to insure Atlas holds up its promises."

"I'm still listening."

She thought he'd say that, too. He wasn't about to reveal his thoughts and she had to keep to her plan. "I hope you'll be thrilled to accept it," she said it the way she'd practiced but the words still tasted awful, "if I were to offer you a seat on the board of directors."

There, she'd voiced the awful words. This was the most painful thing she'd ever done. But like a needed surgery, the result would benefit her for years to come. That's what she'd convinced herself of, anyway.

"This is a surprise," he said. "It can't be an easy decision for you."

"You'll make your concerns known to the other members," she said. "You'll have a real say in the way Atlas conducts its business."

He kept walking, not straying off course. "It's an intriguing offer."

"Things will change once you're on the board," she went on. "You can make recommendations on how Atlas manages its properties, which ones we sell, and what metro areas we buy stations and what kind of benefit packages we offer to our employees."

"It's a lot to consider," he said.

She couldn't read him and that distressed her. But she had to keep going. She had to get him to commit. "In the months to come," she continued, "you'll have a say in the way Atlas approaches the Communications Council. You'll represent us in Congressional hearings and in interviews with the press." She paused to emphasize her next statement. "You'll become the public face of Atlas."

"I never imagined such a thing."

"Don't forget," she added, "there will also be your compensation package...call it an honorarium if you like...which will be in the seven figure range, annually. If you choose, it can be donated to your favorite charity, even to your little Public Cause Group, if that's what you think is proper."

Rafe kept walking. The prospect of taking a seat on the Atlas Board of Directors challenged his assumptions. Yet here was a chance to shake up the compliant directors. Once he took the seat he'd address all the issues that needed to be addressed. He could influence and maybe nudge Atlas in a new direction.

"You'll have a vote, too," Dabny said. "You'll be equal to the other six members."

"The part that appeals to me," he said, "is that I could make a real difference."

She thought he was leaning the right way, teetering and about to commit. "You can take your seat at the next meeting, which is in one week," she said. "I'll make the arrangements tomorrow. We'll all be thrilled when you join us."

"I'll give you my answer," he said, "when I have an answer to give to you."

Enemies are bad, so says Rapid Roy

"Know your enemies," he told his wary listeners, "because they'll look you in the eye and they'll lie through their teeth. They know you're stronger than they are, and you're smarter and you're going to fight them with all your might. And that's what your enemies fear because they know you will defeat them. We smart people know the time has arrived. We have the money and the brains to make our own rules, and that's what we should do right now. I mean it! We need to build a huge wall between us and them; we need to build bigger gates for our gated communities and more armed guards to protect our property. That's why you must know your enemies because they're out to get you…they're in the liberal media and the corrupt court system and in our shabby public schools, waiting to steal from us. Remember, know who they are and never turn your back because you can never trust your enemy."

Chapter XIX
A Majestic Mountain Nesting, Feelings are Felt

"Who knows, he might take it, and when he does one of my problems will be solved."

Dabny looked over to Hondo as he manfully manhandled the Land Rover over the bumping bumps of the bumpy washboard trail. Five miles back they'd pulled off the blacktop and followed a private drive, kicking up a dusty cloud of dust as they passed the scraggy pinion pines and the pretty prickly pear cactus, their fragile petals all red and pink and perky, quivering like little petals in the arid breeze. Soon they reached the rock strewn rocky foothills and then they drove onto a series of switchbacks, taking them higher through Ponderosa Pine on their way to the very top, up to Hondo's lodge on the crest of a majestic mountain, which he'd cleverly dubbed, 'My Majestic Mountain Nest.'

"Nailer will hold off giving you his answer," he said, "until it suits him."

"I can leak it to the press the offer has been made," she said. "That will compromise him even if he doesn't accept."

"The problem with that is," Hondo replied, "it might compromise you as well."

Indeed, the risks were highly risky. She knew that when she made the offer. She hoped Nailer would commit, but wasn't surprised he didn't. Still, it was a shrewdly shrewd maneuver: it pushed the activist off balance, giving her time to complete her plan. If he accepted, Nailer would gain a seat on the board of directors—a symbolic position without real power—and he'd lose credibility with the media and the public. And if he lost them then his actions against her wouldn't be credible. Atlas would be freed from the troublesome troublemaker and Dabny could concentrate on her looming ownership of the air-waves. In a real sense she and Atlas were carrying the world into a sunny future, the kind of future that lies in the sun filled days ahead.

"When we get to the lodge," Hondo said, "I'll call Brumble and prod him a bit. It shouldn't be much longer until he commits. Maybe he'll commit to me today."

"That would make this trip all the more perfect," she said. "I hope you keep some bubbly in the fridge. Or do you call it an ice box up here?"

Hondo steered the Land Rover around a final curve and a last stand of piney pines. They arrived at a two story building made of hand hewn stone, hewn by the hands of hardy, local artisans at half the price of the hand hewing artisans back east. A covered veranda looked out to a vividly vivid vista. From there Dabny viewed a vast view of the high desert, a chromatic land-scape of deep reddish reds and the whitest of whites, the arroyos carved into the ground by the windy winds and the limestone hoodoos and angular buttes that arose from the earth like beau-tiful fortresses, all contained in a panorama as wide as the far horizon. And above the scene a lone eagle was floating on the rising thermals as it stealthily stalked its prey on the earthy earth below. Of all the birds that flew in the air, the eagle most amazed and transfixed her. It symbolized cunning and power and the ability to take what it wants and to live by its own rules. But no, Dabny realized the soaring bird might instead be a scavenger buzzard, seeking its already dead meal on the hard scrabble ground. Either way, it was a bird and it was big and really, that's all that mattered.

"I hoped your lodge would be like this," she exclaimed. "I can see for a hundred miles!"

"That's King Ferdinand peak."

Hondo was pointing to the north, northward at a purple mountain majestically rising over two less majestic peaks. "And over there is Devil's Delight," he said pointing farther out, to the west. "Legend says a company of Conquistadors hid a cask of gold coins somewhere on that peak. They planned to retrieve it one day but they all died from thirst. Their bones are still out there, scattered in all directions and sometimes when you're hiking you come across an ossified leg bone, a tibia I think. It's like seeing the remains of ancient history lying at your feet."

"I love stories about lost treasures," she said. "They're so romantic."

Romance was the reason she'd come, the chance of finding it anyway. Dabny was both curious and thrilled when, while they were on the National Mall he'd had asked her to join him on this weekend retreat. Since then she'd imagined what kind of time was in store for them. She normally kept her feelings close, like a secret only she knew and would never divulge, not until she met the one right man. She still wasn't sure if Hondo Roache was that one right man but she was willing to explore the possibilities. After all, they were superior people, the rarest kind of rare individuals who recognize the opportunity for a perfect pairing, especially when a pair of perfect people recognizes it.

Hondo unloaded the Rover and Dabny helped. They carried their bags into the lodge and in no time had settled in, tired from the long journey but excited at having arrived. Dabny began

to fumble around in the kitchen as if she knew what she was doing. Perhaps the filet mignon needed a marinade and the lobsters
needed to be boiled. They did get boiled to death, right, or did you
kill them first? If so, exactly how did one do the killing? While
pondering that imponderable problem, she overheard Hondo on
the phone to Senator Brumble. She couldn't tell from the tone of
his voice if Hondo was happy about what he was hearing.

"We're still on course."

He'd finished the call and joined her in the kitchen.
"Brumble is leaning, but he's not ready to commit. I'll wait another day and then I'll give him that last push over the edge.
After that I'll talk to the majority leader and have him put our bill
on the Senate's agenda. Within a week we'll own the spectrum."

"It's ours to have," she cheered as she came to him and
kissed his lips, first lightly as if in celebration then more force-
fully, thrusting herself against him and pulling him to her.

"I wanted to do that all day," she whispered. "But I didn't
want to cause an accident on the road."

He chuckled knowingly. "I knew this trip would give us
a chance to get to know each other." He gazed at her beguiling
face and was beguiled by her guileful visage. Yes, this was a
rare woman, one who never feared to test herself against whatever obstacle that rose up before her. She never retreated. She
never stopped nor wavered. She kept pushing and striving, willfully grasping her sought for prize, the kind of prize she'd prize
for rest of her life, or at least until she found another prize she
wanted to grasp for.

"I want to take what's mine for the taking," she whispered
to him. "But I have to be sure the time is right for me to take it."

"Time is our ally and our enemy," he said. "But today, we
deserve our time together, every moment of it."

And, every moment during the next two days would bring a new discovery, a favorite color or cherished song, a fond memory from their youth. Dabny recalled a childhood prank that wasn't quite as funny as she'd expected: her nanny drank a cup of what she thought was Chamomile tea but was in fact a mixture of dish detergent and scalding bleach water Dabny had slyly concocted. It took thirty minutes for the stricken nanny to recover. All the while Dabny was eating from a forbidden bag of chocolate chip cookies. She relished every bite. Hondo reminisced about the time (he was only eleven) he and a friend took his father's bolt action .22 and shot a wayward daschund who'd stupidly wondered onto the grounds of the family's estate. The shot wounded the animal in its hindquarters and it howled in pain. It wasn't as funny as Hondo expected, but still it was kind of funny to watch the silly looking beast limp away like a rightfully punished trespasser. Dabny confided that she loved great, big brownies and vanilla ice cream but when she ate them, she ate them sparingly. Hondo admitted to a craving for peanut brittle and bourbon laced eggnog, and an occasional yearning for cheesy hominy grits. They discovered their childhoods had been very different from each other's. But in those years of learning and growing they realized their lives wouldn't be the same as those around them. For Dabny and Hondo only the highest height of fulfillment could ever satisfy them, if they could be satisfied at all.

"Before she died," Dabny said, "my mother would say her little princess was going to grow up to be a queenly queen, one with the power to make the world bow down to her."

"She was a remarkable woman," Hondo remarked. "I'd like to have known her."

Dabny touched his hand and said, "mother taught me that only the strong will prevail in life. It's funny how right she was. Whenever I look at the world I see two kinds of people: those who dare to take what's theirs...the kind of people who don't fear failure because they know that in the end they will succeed. And then there are all the others, the rabble who'll accept whatever is available and never try to climb out of their humdrum lives."

"It's only the few of us," he said, "who have the will to risk it all. I know because I feel it, like a churning deep inside me. I must go forward, every day. And every day I see the vast possibilities, the great fortune that's waiting to be taken by a man who's entitled to take it."

"Yes," she said, "oh yes, I know it too, the sense that in all the world only a special man and woman, oh there's so very, very few of us who'll climb to the highest place. And waiting there is a treasure for us and for us only. We'll be together as one, on the crest of the most majestic of all the majestic mountains, anywhere on the map of the United States."

Her words touched him like an immutable truth, the utterance of a self-willed woman, her, Dabny Talbett who stood so close to him like a stainless idol, one who'd come to life in this unstained moment for them to discover a love that was so utterly pure and stain free. And that's the way people like them must have it...love isn't love unless it celebrates the greatest of all values: the immeasurable value of true self-love. Love must surpass the common sentiments, it's driven by the mind's ultimate power over the body's baser bodily cravings, yet it melds the two together in a sanctified wholeness...wholly whole in its sanctity...a doubtless and eternal knowing.

"We have it within us," she murmured, "to come together in a perfect union, like the way an idea joins with our convictions. We'll find a meaningful new meaning in our touching of each other, an expression of our beliefs that I thought I'd only find in an abstract way, not with a real, flesh and blood man like you. But with you, Hondo, I can feel what I think. Oh! It's the embodiment of my most cherished principles."

"Yes, we'll find a new meaning in our words."

He was stroking her sinewy hand and delighted in touching each and every sinew. "We'll learn new words to speak to each other, as if we're creating our own secret language. I hoped," he said as he marveled at her face, so proud and sublime and flaw free like the face of an unflawed Roman statue, "that one day my life would be complete when I found a flawless female like you."

She gazed wonderingly into his eyes. "Oh, yes," she whispered breathlessly. "Yes, I know exactly what you mean! We're more alike than even I knew, at least at first. Then I wasn't sure, because to be sure is to forget all doubt. And doubting makes us who we are and who we are is who we must be, and I have no doubt about that. Yet now… it's doubtless and it's true and yes, it's so exciting…I can feel my feelings!"

Chapter XX
Deliberations on a Ruse

Vera plopped down on the sofa. It was big and overstuffed and fifteen years old. One of the cushions had a three inch tear in its seam and the whole damn thing was dirty and shabby and needed to be tossed out. One day she'd get around to it. Dusk had darkened beyond dusk to an evening shade of humdrum gray. A shadowy shadow stalked the untidy room. From the corner desk a lamp cast enough light to illuminate Rafe's face and eyes, which were intent on his fingers as they carefully set the pen in place on the handmade display board, the display board his own hands had painstakingly made.

"Three in one trip," she said. "That must be a record."

"One's from a U.S. senator," he said. "I'll stick a gold star on the label and set it next to the one from the federal judge in Chicago. I bet he thinks a smarmy prosecutor stole it."

She took a swig from her beer bottle. "Is there even a chance," she asked, "that you'll take the offer?"

"If a snake promises not to bite you," he replied, "would you believe it?"

"I don't believe a snake can talk," she said, "not even the one in the Bible, and certainly a snake can't promise any promises it's going to keep."

Rafe shrugged and said, "then you shouldn't believe a snake."

"It's not a genuine offer," she said in a way that sounded final.

"The offer is genuine," he said, "the way an invitation to a knife fight is genuine. There's a chance that when you arrive they'll let you pull out your weapon, then they'll stab you in the back."

She shivered at the thought of a knife slicing a gash between her shoulders. Only the worst kind of snaky snake would stab a person from behind. It's exactly that kind of snake she enjoyed punching in the nose, before they could stab the knife into her.

"If you take that seat on the board," she goaded, "you can do a lot of good."

"I can do a lot of good," Rafe countered, "if I stay *off* the board."

She came closer and looked into his eyes as if she'd never done it before. But she had peered into him a hundred times and each time she saw a man who freely admitted his foibles—like his penchant for stealing expensive gold pens which belonged to other people. So what, no one is perfect. She expected whatever man she loved to love her back, too. Otherwise it'd be a foolish waste of her time.

"Let's take a walk," she said. "It's a nice evening out there. I need a smoke."

She grabbed his hand and pulled him out of his chair and led him out of the room and through the front door and onto the porch. There they felt the breeze as it wafted its way from the west, past the leafy elms and the garden geraniums that had grown weed choked and withered from lack of care. They walked down the steps and followed the sidewalk along the potholed side street. A dusky cloud hid the sun as she lit a joint and took a drag.

"What do you think we'll be doing a year from now?"

"Probably the same thing we're doing now," he answered, taking the joint. "You know, heroically fighting corporate greed and urging the People to rise up." He took a drag and then handed the joint back to her. "Or maybe we'll sell out to the too big to fail banksters," he said, letting out the smoke. "We'll become phenomenally wealthy and we'll be totally well invested, and we won't care about anyone but ourselves and we'll wing our way in our Gulfstream to Geneva, to count our pile of shiny, new Krugerands."

She saw the wry glint in his eye, the glimmering that abided there, especially when he was struggling with a problem. That was another thing she loved about him, his sheer, unadulterated humanity. "If we're going to fly in our private jet," she said, "then we better start watching our nickels and dimes. I understand jet fuel went up a dollar a gallon." She knew Rafe valued money the way a landscape painter values his colorful paint: tangible and definitive and absolutely necessary to create something much greater than itself.

"Money," he once said to her, "can make a lot of good things happen, but money never solved one damn problem. In fact, money causes more problems than it ever solves."

"But money can buy some really cool things," she said. "I could go for a new pair of brogans and a half dozen pair of nylons and a case of Dom Perignon and how about a pound of Columbian weed? And maybe a couple grams of coke would be nice, you know, to give us a little bump before we get down to some real nasty, animal sex. And then we'll talk about our future. We can do better than working for a low life public interest gang."

Two months ago an unsolicited contribution arrived in the mail at the Public Cause Group. When the staffer, a young man with messy blond hair and the zeal of a true believer opened the envelop he found a cashier's check. It was in the amount of two hundred and fifty thousand dollars. He also found a sealed note which he quickly took to Rafe.

"The giver demands to remain anonymous," he said reading the message. "That's fine with me. However this individual wants us to use his money for only one thing, to carry out a boycott against a fast food chain. This particular company is feeding the consumer a lot of saturated fat and GMO laced food and artery clogging calories. I'm guessing it's also our contributor's biggest competitor." Then, without a second thought, Rafe ripped the check in half, saying, "the Public Cause Group isn't anyone's hired gun."

"But it's so much money," the shocked staffer said.

"It's so much damn trouble," Rafe replied. "We already have plenty of that on our plate."

When they reached the end of the block, they finished the joint and crossed the pavement. They found their way into a small park. There, they followed a path that took them away from the street lights and to a small pond. They heard the high pitched call from a frantic bat that was swooping and diving in the air above.

"Sometimes they fly into a woman's hair," Vera said. "I hope he doesn't come after me. He'll want to suck my blood."

"Your blood is red and all American," Rafe said. "But you might not want to apply for a job at Wal-Store. You'd never pass a drug test."

She elbowed him in the ribs; he brought her to him. They were people with flaws and weaknesses—imperfect physiques and less than pure heritage and bodies that were vulnerable to all a body's bodily aches and pains—and they accepted each other that way. What other choice is there?

"It's the usual feeling I have," she said. "Whatever you decide will be the right choice."

"Right now," he said, "the right choice is we have a cold beer. There's a new pub around the corner I've been meaning to check out."

Rapid Roy knows all about the Economy

"My friends, it's a fact: the Democrat party is systemically destroying our nation's economy. We all know it, don't we? I ask you, where are the high paying jobs they promised? Are those jobs in Paducah or Pima or Pollard? No! Those jobs are over there in Beijing and Bangladesh and we all know why. It's because this country's corporate tax rate is the highest in the world. And that tax rate was voted in by the Democrats. Anyone with a brain knows that if you put an onerous tax on our fine corporations they'll be forced to go elsewhere to conduct their business. And they'll take their jobs with them. My friends, don't blame our excellent multi-nationals. It's all the fault of the big government Democrats! And here's another true fact: the budget deficit, every dime of it, is the Democrat's fault. They can't stop spending your money on every so-called social safety net program that raises its ugly head. And the national debt, every last penny of it, is the Democrat's doing. My friends, it's a fact. The Democrat party is systemically destroying our way of life and lowering our standard of living. We must do better, people. We have to get rid of the Democrats entirely, for good, forever. Then we'll live the way of life we're entitled to live. So, now that I've made that fact perfectly clear and hit the nail precisely on its big flat head, I'll take a call from a guy in Vermont. This oughta be fun."

"Good afternoon, Rapid Roy. I'm not one of your Me Too-ers, but I listen to your show from time to time. It seems you're not telling your listeners the real facts, the factual kind of facts. For instance, yesterday you said the Democrats intentionally crashed the economy in 2008 by increasing taxes on the job creators. But that simply didn't happen. The economy crashed because Bush started two unfunded and unnecessary wars. He also signed the Medicare bill that gave hundreds of billions to his colleagues in Big Pharma. Then he stopped regulating the banks and he cut taxes for the mega-billionaires and he encouraged the predatory lenders and their sub-prime loans. That's what really crashed the economy. I think your listeners need to know about…"

"No! I can't take that nonsense. As you regular listeners know I keep this program the very essence of civility. There's no question about it. I'm the incarnation of the highest principles of humility and decorum. I keep everything equal and above board. Yet did you hear what that venomous Vermonter was saying? He called me a liar! The leftists are calling me intolerant and uncivil! Why, I'm the fairest minded and most generous man in the universe. I'm open to all opinions and I give every one of them equal time. I do this because I respect your intelligence and your willingness to hear the other side's ideas, even if they're totally asinine and harmful to our country. I'm the one man you can turn to when the going gets tough and I'll never let you down. It's a fact I know more than anyone else, and I'm never wrong. And that my friends, is the most important fact of all."

Chapter XXI
Signs of Trouble Ahead

When she returned to Leadership Place the first thing Dabny did was go to the library. As she entered the room Jamesford was sitting at his desk, deep in thought as he read from a file folder. A pensive frown etched his pensively frown prone face.

"Father, can I disturb you?"

"A daughter has that right."

An odd expression flitted from his eyes, as if he'd been caught reading her secret diary. Maybe he was only tired. "Besides, I need to take a break."

"A father has that right."

She walked to the desk and beheld the man. Here was Jamesford Talbett, the indefatigable man she revered like no other, now battling to keep his empire from further decline. Perhaps he'd taken for granted the entrenched position Atlas commanded, as if no other entity could ever overtake the colossus. But new and unexpected enemies are sure to arise, like rising enemies in the night. Still, he controlled the company and his decisions were not to be disputed. Some of those indisputable decisions were based on information from sources he kept secret and those secret sources were usually correct. That kind of resource takes years to develop. She reminded herself to create her own network of informants. Surely, in the years to come she'd need all the information she could collect on her sneaky competitors, as well as her questionable allies.

"So you've been with Hondo Roache."

Jamesford worriedly spoke with a worried tone, very much unlike him. "I hope your little *jaunt* was purely recreational."

"We hiked in the mountains."

She wasn't surprised her father had found out; yes, his sources usually were correct. "We watched the sunsets and talked about the universe. It's a universal subject."

Jamesford frowned, not convinced. "I'm not sure this is good for you," he said. "That man Roache is a damn slick player. Sure, he's done a lot of good for some of our friends. But he can talk a person into doing things she might regret one day. I've heard he cheats at the games he plays."

"We tried not to talk about business."

She wasn't happy for resorting to a half-truth. Still, she resented this interrogation. "The desert is so earthy. I felt its texture and let a handful of sand run through my fingers, like the sandy sand in an hourglass."

"Sometimes we need to get away," Jamesford said. "But we also need to keep our secrets with each other."

She knew what he meant and she didn't like it. Yes, her father could suspect her, but damn it, he didn't have the right to accuse her. "I've never betrayed our secrets. You know that, don't you?"

"I know what I know and I know I don't know enough," he sighed. "We need to be honest with each other."

"We have Atlas, father," she said. "We both have Atlas; it's a part of us."

At the word her father roused. "Atlas will prevail," he said, "because we will prevail. After I retire, and that won't happen any time soon, you'll take over and when you do, you will prevail. You'll carry the weight because that's how I raised you, with strong shoulders and powerful neck muscles, and a good straight spine. We never had any of that swayback stuff in my family tree. We got great genes, the kind from Roman emperors, you know, the famous ones historians write about in history books, the emperors who lived for a hundred years. They ruled the world and had their way, the way they wanted to rule the world. But you must be patient and learn what you need to learn like knowing when to fudge the numbers and when to cook the books and the best way to blame someone else for your misconduct. Then, after I step down you can take Atlas to the next level, to a faraway place far in the distance, so far that I can't see."

What was out there, Dabny mused, in the distant future where her father labored to peer? Perhaps he glimpsed the rolling hills, all lush and green and perfect and the rising towers of a bright new world where only the giants abide. There, in a place of their own making strode the makers and producers, all those who would live where the individual reigns supreme and no government toady can enter. It was merely a vision now but one day, through her boundless determination she would make it a reality.

"Remember how we've talked about hiring a team of younger Hosts?"

Her voice quivered as she spoke of her gleaming vision. "We'll bring in street smart people, the kind who know their way around the streets. They'll be slick and glib and use the latest slang and they'll say what we tell them to say and they'll say it with a rough and tough attitude. I can hear them now; they'll sound cool and plugged in to the hottest trends. We'll use hip hop music in the sound bed and the Hosts will interview the hottest young movie stars, the right thinking ones who star in films about handsome Navy Seals. They'll increase our audience in the eighteen to thirty-four demographic, and that'll bring in new advertisers and new revenues to our bottom line. And we'll put on bigger promotions and big dollar contests and we'll over exaggerate the ratings the way you did in the beginning. Do you recall those days? They were so terribly difficult and you started with so little, only seven stations in major metro areas. But you never quit and you trashed your competitors' transmitters and you blackmailed their disc jockeys and you grew Atlas into an awesome giant. Now we're going to grow even stronger. I'm going to do what you want, father. We'll make Atlas the most powerful force in broadcasting and nothing will ever hurt us or make us change. We'll make Talk Radio the greatest format that was ever formatted or ever will be formatted, anywhere on the dial, everywhere in the world."

"I never liked that damned rap stuff."

Jamesford was muttering as if to himself. "It sounds like nonsense, a bunch of foolish talking, that's all it is. I swear, if it weren't for Atlas the whole damn radio business would've collapsed twenty-five years ago. But I did what I did and in the end I saved radio from all that foolish talking. I'm very proud of that, too. No other man could have done so much."

Dabny touched his arm. "Atlas will rule forever," she said. "We're the biggest and the best."

"Our stock is down to $195 god damn it," Jamesford said. "What's the matter with those dolts on Wall Street? I'd like to knock their heads together to get rid of the sawdust between their ears. I tell you, they don't know the value of a hard earned dollar or what a tough talking Host can do for the bottom line."

"Let's focus on the future," she said. Yes, the stock price was a growing problem, but she couldn't do anything about it right now. "There's nothing wrong we can't fix and there's plenty of market share we still can take."

"We'll set the bastards straight," Jamesford growled. "They'll be sorry they ever pulled the tail on Atlas."

Then he frowned and said, "the day will come when you'll take what you want to take. But be careful; don't reach so far you can't grasp the thing you want. Don't worry if you hurt people because they don't matter. Do what you must do, but know what you're doing before you do it. Don't let anyone stand in your way, but know where you're going and then walk right on top of them, like they're nothing more than bumps in the road because that's exactly what they are. And don't ever forget, taking and getting is always better than wanting and not having."

"Yes, father," she said. "You know what's best for me, and for Atlas. Of course, I'll do as you ask."

Sighing, he rose from his chair. As he moved to the door he nodded at the file folder he'd left on the desk. "Information is only information," he uncertainly said to her. "It's facts and figures, dates and places and times. And names, of course. Whatever importance it has is for you to decide."

After Jamesford left the room, she picked up the file. She read the heading: Hondo Roache, CEO of HR Consulting. Then she read the report's first paragraph. She saw the name Rebecca Sue Roache and she read the words 'marriage' and 'abuse' and 'messy, rage filled divorce'.

In the next paragraph she read the names Jennifer and Georgie and the words 'hotels' and 'trysts' and 'deviant sexual positions'. Then she sat down in her father's big chair. She pulled out the first exhibit: a slick black and white photograph (taken from a distance, but still the subjects were perfectly framed and in high resolution) showing a secluded cove at what appeared to be a sea-side resort. Hondo was standing on the beach wearing only his swim trunks and in his arms was a tall, lean blonde wearing only the bottom of her bikini. The two were engaged in a fiercely passionate kiss. The time stamp indicted the photo had been taken two weeks ago. Another photo showed Hondo sitting in a booth in a darkened restaurant with a bottle of Dom Perignon in front of him, accompanied by two champagne glasses. Whispering in his ear and looking all snugly and winsome was a brunette with winsomely long brown hair. She was wearing a low cut peasant blouse that displayed the round volume of her voluminous breasts. Still another photo showed him standing on the balcony of what had to be a high rise hotel and in his arms was another blonde, this one taller and leaner than the other and she had a rounder ass and sharper features and what appeared to be a pearl necklace around her swanlike neck. The time stamp on this photo indicated it had been taken the day before Dabny traveled with him to his majestic mountain nest, the nesting where she gave him her greatest gift...the great gift of her newly felt feelings. Then she read the entire file, cover to cover and all the pages in between and all the inky black letters and the not so pleasant words and, oh god, all those horrible, serpentine sentences. And when she finished reading she wasn't happy, not at all.

Gary Bock has a Grand Plan for the Future

"Friends, I've envisioned a glorious vision," he said to his glory seeking listeners who were trying to envision the same glorious vision. "It's an awe inspiring vision of how we'll take back our impure country and make it pure again. Yes, this will be a pristine new place, dedicated to you, the unique Individual. There won't be any freeloaders there, or malcontents or any godless socialists. With your help, I'm going to build a self-sustaining community! It will be clean and dirt free and the sun will always shine on it, so it will always be shiny and clean. We'll own our businesses and we'll have a marketplace and schools that teach our kids the real facts from the Bible and the Declaration of Independence. And really, isn't that all our youngsters need to know? And they'll have their own special playground with fun games like Freedom's Blessed Play House and a Liberty Bell Swing set. We'll produce our own food and we'll have our own pumps to bring water into our homes, which we ourselves will build. There won't be any bureaucrats to tell us how we should behave or live our lives. We'll follow the laws God gave us. Not only that, we'll have a special media park where we'll show movies about the sainted heroes from the battle of Jericho and all of Mel Gibson's fine films and we'll have a studio where we'll make movies about how we suffered hardships to make this new life possible. We'll call our city 'Libertyville USA.' It will have all the best parts of Small Town America, without the poor people on the other side of the tracks, or the garbage dumps and abortion clinics. All I need is your generous contributions, a hundred dollars is a good start or five hundred or even ten thousand! Soon, Libertyville USA will be a reality. Friends, I have the vision and we have the plan and you have the money. I promise you this: my will shall be done. We can make it happen because we're free Americans! We have the muscle and blood and money to make my glorious vision a reality. So please, send your contribution today and before you know it we'll have our very own shining city on a hill, a hilly and clean city where only we'll be allowed to live."

Chapter XXII
A New Continent Discovered, Survived

The Field Goal Tavern was crowded tonight. Leaning against the bar or standing in pairs or sitting at tables in threes and fours were groups of men and women wearing short and long sleeved T-shirts colored blue and white and orange that carried a team logo or a mascot's image or the number and last name of a famous ballplayer. The patrons were mid-twenties and thirties and middle aged. Some had blond hair (tinted and natural), others were brunette (long and short and shaggy haired) and some were redheaded (curly and wavy). Some of the patrons were gray or balding and most had unremarkable faces that were neither attractive nor homely. They were chatting and laughing as they drank beer from long necked bottles or sipped hard liquor from high ball glasses.

Neon beer signs lit the place and the furniture was made of plastic and aluminum. The floor was concrete painted with parallel white stripes over a field of ball field green. The walls held a half dozen super wide TV screens showing the evening's big game between a team of athletic men who were wearing uniforms with white tops and black pants and another team of athletic men who were wearing uniforms with black tops and white pants. The play by play announcer's volume—Rafe thought he recognized the ageless voice of the famous Raymond 'Fast Ray' Limerick—overpowered normal conversation. Mostly the tavern was a place where the all patrons were regulars and they all knew each other by their first name and they all liked the same things and everyone supported the same team.

"We've found Spectator heaven," Vera said to Rafe. "This is definitely not our usual crowd."

"We might make some new friends," he replied. "It never hurts to try."

Vera shrugged. "I'll have my usual," she said. "You know darling, Carling, the tasty lager they brew in Canada."

"With or without a glass?"

"Tonight," she answered, "just the bottle will do."

Vera liked drinking beer from the bottle more than from a glass. A bottle had a certain feel about it, a good hard heft that felt right in her hand and since they were now in a tavern this seemed like a good time to hold a bottle of beer in her hand. She took a table in a corner and watched Rafe as he walked to the bar. When he got the bartender's attention, he ordered Vera's Carling and a Rolling Rock for himself. As he waited for the beers he looked at the pictures on the wall: here was a photograph of the legendary galloping ghost Red Grange straight arming a would-be tackler and there was Joe Montana throwing a long touchdown pass. There was a photo of mighty John Riggins smashing through the line at left guard and one of cool headed Adam Vinatieri kicking a game winning fifty yard field goal, and there were team photos too, of the Giants and Jets and the Redskins and Patriots, and of the Lions and Bengals and the Jaguars and Panthers, as well as photos of teams whose names Rafe didn't know. A good neighborhood pub, he thought, is a welcome discovery. He was glad Vera and he had checked out this place. And he couldn't help but overhear the conversation of the two men to his right.

"It's a god damn, sad shame."

The younger man had an Ace bandage wrapped around his left wrist and thumb. He was blond with ordinary brown eyes and he had a wispy, thin mustache that made him look bland and ineffectual. His face was more oval than round and what passed as a chin was more round than square. His frame appeared solid and he was wearing a lime green t-shirt with a pro sports team logo—it looked like a cross between a mountain goat and a leprechaun. He was drinking domestic beer from a can and was chewing on a leathery strip of poop brown beef jerky.

"The left wing bastards don't give a good god damn," he said. "They don't care if the whole country goes down the tubes. In fact, I think that's exactly what they want."

"That's the way Rapid Roy tells it."

The older man was in his late forties with dandruffy grayish hair and a nose that'd been broken long ago and hadn't mended quite right. "The leftists want to take away our guns, and I don't mean our scatterguns and six shooters. They want to take our sniper rifles and assault weapons," he added, "and our high capacity magazines. Then they'll come after our daughters. Well, I swear to god my whole family will be dead and cold before the Feds get their filthy hands on my eight Croakers."

The other man nodded solemnly. "That's not all," he said as he bit off a length of jerky. "The leftists are planning to take away our red meat. I mean our triple bacon cheeseburgers with an extra slice of cheese and two added patties, with the creamy secret sauce and double the mayo. And then they'll take our foot long kielbasas, and our Spam! And they want to call it 'National Meatless Monday.' Damn, those bastards want to ruin our lives."

"It's just like Rapid Roy says."

The older man took a swallow from a beer bottle. "Sooner or later we're going to have to fight the leftist fuckers. And believe me, it's going to get plenty bloody. Me and my Croakers will see to that."

Hearing that, Rafe turned away from the two men. The bartender was now at the far end of the bar, talking to a pretty blonde and pretty blondes get served first. Rafe reminded himself he'd come here to discover what the place was like, but he didn't have to like it, and he was fast getting not to like the place. But he kept waiting for the bartender to deliver the beers.

Suddenly, a massive groan rippled through the Field Goal Tavern, followed by dejected moans and more groaning groans. On the TV screens, a ballplayer had dropped the ball. His teammates shook their heads with sweaty disappointment. One pointed a threatening finger at a ballplayer from the opposing team of sweating ballplayers.

"It's the same thing with the damn femmy-goons," the jerky man said through his beef jerky. "Rapid Roy said they're going to demand money to screw their own husbands, like the two dollar sluts that hang out at that sleazy Hold 'em Down There Motel. The femmy-goons are going to make us men clean the bathroom, and make us buy the groceries and go to PTA meetings. Rapid Roy said it and I believe him."

"If you ask me," the middle aged man said, "the femmy-goons will come after our sons next, you know, to break them in on the sex thing. That might not be so bad except there's the crud on 'em. Rapid Roy's got it right; the femmy-goons are nothing but stinking trash in short skirts, the kind of trash you throw out on the street."

The patrons cheered at something, probably a bone crushing hit. Then they cheered again, probably at the replay of the bone crushing hit.

"Rapid Roy says we better do something before it's too late," jerky man said.

Rafe looked over to Vera, who was looking in his direction. She couldn't hear the conversation and her face didn't express her usual affection for him. Instead she exhibited an odd look, one of curiosity and then of sudden recognition. Rafe told himself to ask her why as soon as he got the beers. He then motioned to the bartender who was still talking to the pretty blonde.

"The damn queers want to get married," said the jerky man. "They want us to treat them like normal people, like you and me. Rapid Roy says the queers think they have the same rights we do and they even want to adopt orphans. At least they're the mixed breed ones, the kind us good folk won't let into our homes."

"It's nauseating to think about them," the middle aged man said. "I can't help but imagine the kind of sick, unnatural things the queers do to each other in bed. The images get stuck in my mind, like dirty pictures in a porno mag. They're filthy and disgusting. Sometimes, it's all I can think about, over and over and over again. The queers need to be put down like rabid dogs. That's what Rapid Roy says."

Screams and cheers erupted in the tavern. A team had scored. One of the screens showed a ballplayer as he gyrated in a victory celebration; his ball playing teammates triumphantly bumped their chests together.

Finally, Rafe got the bartender's attention, but he only signaled he'd deliver the beers in a minute. Rafe clinched his fist, but kept leaning against the bar.

"The left wingers are trashing this country," jerky man said. "We can't go anywhere without hearing some naggy socialist complain how an oil company is hurting the country, or how a good company that makes a tasty product, say a stick of this fine jerky, is making something that's bad for you. Rapid Roy says the Democrats want us pay for the health care for all the lazy bums who don't want to work, and for those druggy teen age mothers. Hell, no one asked 'em to get knocked up. Damn it, some of 'em even got twins and they live in swanky condos our taxes pay for."

Rafe told himself to stay calm. The bartender would bring the beers right away. He better.

"And it's not only the socialists in the government," the middle aged man said. "It's the whole god damn lot of the greasy worms in D. C....the dickless Democrats is what Rapid Roy calls 'em. He says they're planning to take over all the radio stations in the country. He says the leftists want to make us like those people in that dirty place, North Korea, you know, where they're nothing but a bunch of dirty, ignorant slaves. Rapid Roy says the Liberals are gonna use the radio to tell us nothing but lies and to brainwash all of us."

"You need a brain for that."

The words came out before Rafe could stop himself. "So neither of you has to worry."

The older man's face flushed red, his eyes locked onto Rafe's. "I hope that's supposed to be a joke, buddy."

"I don't believe it was a joke," jerky man said.

"Jokes are supposed to be funny," Rafe said. "There's nothing funny here that I can detect."

Jerky man thrust his face into Rafe's. "I think we got us a weenie sucking left winger here," he said. "What do you think Rapid Roy would do with him?"

"He'd take care of this prick," the older man said. "Rapid Roy wouldn't take this kind of bullshit."

Rafe looked at each man. "What we have here," he said, "is an utter lack of enlightenment. You do know we're living in the twenty-first century, right?"

"I think you're a big asshole," jerky man said. "And big assholes get themselves wiped up, good and clean."

"Hey, I recognize you," the older man said. "You're that dickhead leftist nut job, aren't you? Sure you are, the People's Advocate. Ha! What a piss poor excuse for a man you are."

Rafe didn't say anything. Behind him the patrons groaned in unison; a ballplayer didn't score and he should have scored because the opportunity was there and a professional ballplayer is paid to score when he has the chance to score. In the middle of the stands three face painted sports fans excitedly waved to the camera; another held up a hand printed sign that read

I ♥ My Team!

"So he's famous," jerky man said glaring at Rafe. "He's a famous big asshole."

"That's right," the older man said. "Rapid Roy would say he's a great, big asshole."

Rafe nodded in ready agreement. "Rapid Roy should know about assholes," he said, "because his head is up there most of the time."

He didn't see the fist, but he felt it crack against his cheek. And he felt the concrete floor as his head slammed it. Then he was looking up at the enraged faces while he felt the jolt of their boots pounding his torso. The ceiling was spinning crazily; the lights were blinking off and on. There was a flash of light and pain, and then more pain as more kicks impacted his body. Then he saw the explosion of glistening glass and the beer splashing all over as the bottle exploded against the jerky man's jerking forehead. Then the older man yelped and doubled over as the pigskin brown brogan field goal kicked his two hanging balls, to the right of center, where it hurts the most. Really, really hurts.

Chapter XXIII
Revenue's Fountainhead Revealed

The carpeted hallway, windowless and brightly lit from overhead lighting first passed the Business Office and the Program Director's office, and then it went by the Engineering Workshop and after that it passed the Recording studio and then the Production studio. Inside, a pretty young reporter was sitting at the interview desk. She was reading a binder of notes, preparing to tape an interview with the famous guest who'd arrive in thirty minutes. Then the interview would be uplinked with a satellite four hundred miles overhead, and then downlinked to nine hundred and seventy two radio stations across the country. The interview would then be broadcast on Sunday morning as part of Atlas's commitment to News and Public Affairs. The hallway then passed a drinking fountain and the women's and men's restrooms and the On-Air studio where inside a complex array of electronic equipment was downloading, from the same satellite above, the worrisome voice of Rapid Roy Limerick.

"I need to tell you about my great worry," he was saying to his worried listeners. "The country has gotten so bad we can't let our kids watch TV after five o'clock. I mean it. The boob tube's turned into a funk hole of rank, filthy sex. It's so bad I'm afraid to change the channel when my little nephew is in the room alone with me. I can only imagine what kind of putrid, vile sex we might come upon. My friends, Hollywood is run by the sex crazed left wing. It's them, those dirty leftists who are producing all that filthy sex meant to corrupt our children. This sex stuff has got to stop! We must make Hollywood clean up its dirty act! Call your congressman. Tell him to pass the Purify Hollywood bill and make those lefty's produce only good, clean, family friendly programs."

From this studio Rapid Roy's voice entered a fiber optic feed that, after following a winding course through the building's interior and up through a series of cables and wires, ultimately radiated from a seventeen hundred foot broadcast tower. From there it spread invisibly via the People's airwaves, finally reaching car radios and desk sets and boom boxes and dozens of other kinds of receivers in a fifty-five mile radius. Across that geography hundreds of thousands of men and women and impressionable children were listening. To them the famous Host was a man to be heard and admired and most important of all, believed in and trusted implicitly. Rapid Roy said the things that needed to be spoken and if he spoke them, then the words he spoke were words that needed to be listened to and more importantly, believed.

"You know me and you know what I stand for," he'd tell them. "Only cowards run from the truth, and that is something I will never do. Hell, I can't even run a block if I wanted to! Believe me; you can trust me on that."

The hallway next passed the Research Department and the Sales Department where a crack team of high energy account executives was busy negotiating ad sales over the phone and with instant messaging and then booking millions and millions and tens of millions more in advertising revenue, Atlas's lifeblood and its reason for existence. Rapid Roy delivered the ratings and the ratings drove the ad sales. And the ad salespeople brought in the money that kept the whole profitable process profitably feeding upon itself: a self-sustaining fountain of revenue.

The hallway passed the Conference Room with its long marble table and a dozen leather chairs, and finally it terminated at the General Manager's office. There, when Dabny arrived the door was open and Brody Pullman was pushing up from behind his desk. A concerned look of surprised concern flashed across his smoothly smooth and shaven, blandly bland and quite unremarkable middle-aged face.

"Miss Talbett, I wasn't expecting your visit."

"This isn't a surprise inspection," she said. "I'm satisfied with the ratings and the revenue, but we do need to talk."

Of course, W4's General Manager was happy to hear whatever she had to say. Dabny Talbett and her father owned this radio station and, since she rarely visited her sudden appearance called for immediate attention. Brody had held his position for the last six years, after she'd promoted him from Assistant Manager. Before that he'd been the Sales Manager and before that an Account Executive selling advertising time to local retailers and full service ad agencies. In all those years Brody dutifully followed the instructions from his next superior in the chain of command and now his superior was almost the most superior of them all.

"I'm here to clear up the snag in the renewal process," she said to him. "It's important we have all the pertinent records."

"I'm following your father's instructions," Brody said. "We're collating the logs for the last five years. I'll send them to the Communications Council in two days, like he instructed me."

"I've come to review those logs," she said, now irritated and sounding so. "I will see them now, Brody."

He knew better than to say anything more. He'd heard the stories about other Atlas General Managers: one had suggested the company donate air time to a community clean-up group. That General Manager abruptly lost his job. Another manager wanted to make his station's studio the location for a public auction to benefit the local food bank. That General Manager also suddenly lost his job. No, Brody told himself, this was not the time to question anything Dabny Talbett asked him to do.

He walked to his desk and called the Business Office. "Sarah," he said, "Miss Talbett is here. Please bring the logs to the conference room right now."

In her five years as the President of the Atlas Radio Company, and for all her life as a Talbett, Dabny had spent very little time in an actual radio station. She never spoke into a microphone nor trafficked the tapes and times to broadcast a station's commercials nor did she sell advertising to the unyielding time buying grunts at advertising agencies. Her's was the loftier perspective, from high above in the corporate suite. There, in the insulated confines of Atlas's home office she learned the radio business from her crafty father. She came to know about gross and net revenues and operating costs, about assets and liabilities, about the cost of employee benefits and how to grind down a competitor on the distressed radio station they were desperate to sell. Today, she'd come to examine W4's logs, the legal documents that attested to how much or how little air time had been allocated to those tiresome PSAs. She worried Brody Pullman had indeed followed her instructions, the way he was paid to, and had aired only one per day.

"Here they are, Miss Talbett."

The young lady from the Business Office brought the stack of reports to the conference room and set them on the table. "These cover the last five years," she said. "That's the period the government wants to look at."

After that, Dabny sat alone at the table and picked up the top document. She noted the time given to programming and to commercials and to promotional spots and lastly, to PSAs. The evidence was clear and sworn to by General Manager Brody Pullman and the chief engineer and then attested to by an independent notary public. The logs confirmed her fears: Brody had indeed followed her instructions. Then she recalled her testimony before the Senate committee, how under oath she swore W4 complied with the standard for its license.

"I can deal with this the way I deal with every nuisance," she whispered to herself. "After all, it's not like I murdered someone. And even if I did, I can claim I stood my ground."

Next, she instructed a now agitated Brody Pullman not to send the documents to the council, until she told him to. "We might not need to even send them," she said. "We're working on a plan that will give Atlas all the power we need."

Then she retraced her steps down the hallway, pausing to again peer into the sales room and glimpse the generating of her giant revenues. She continued down the hallway and was passing the door to the Production studio when the interview guest walked up to her.

"Jason!"

Gild was wearing his usual tailored suit with a brilliant white shirt and red and yellow tie. As always, his hero like jaw was heroically set, as if he were set out on a heroic mission. His shiny eyes gleamed with an intelligence she tried to fathom. Yet she'd never been able to fully plumb the deep depths of the man's deeply unplumbable intellect.

"I'm pleased to see you're hard at work," he said to her. "You're such a hardworking professional."

She didn't know Gild was the interview guest and was thrilled to see him. "I only wish I had the time to stay and listen."

"My beliefs are incredibly well spoken," he said. "I've been speaking the same words for three decades so I know exactly how to say them. Say, how's your father? I bet he's doing great at everything he does, which he's great at doing."

"I'm afraid he thinks I'm not ready to run the company," she sighed. "But I know how to make Atlas better than ever. In fact, your words have inspired me to do what I have to, which is what I'm doing here, right now."

A warm smile came to Gild's warmly smiling face. He was known to hold deep empathy for his friends and colleagues. If they succeeded he generously took credit for their success; if they were in trouble he'd urge someone to go to their aid. "Tell Jamesford I think of him often. In fact," he added with his canny tone, "in a day or so I'll have some incredulous news to tell him."

Hearing that, she drew closer. "I want to know now," she whispered. "You've kept me waiting long enough."

"Let's step outside," Gild said. "The walls have ears. Some of them have eyes, too."

They left the building and walked across the street. They found a quiet place in a public park, on a bench away from the publically passing passersby on the public sidewalk. "It's so exciting," Gild said excitedly. "It's exactly what I hoped and planned and worked so hard for. We're coming together! We're a group of people like you and me, the country's true producers. We're proud CEOs and CFOs and smart hedge fund managers and cagy Wall Street bankers and professional sports team owners. We're in the entertainment industry and in medical equipment and consumer electronics. Oh, I really like my new smarty pants phone, it's got such pretty pictures! Yes, it's a fact, the true leaders are coming together to stand up for what we stand for."

"Please, Jason, I want to know the details."

"We're going to unite," he said. "It's like we're taking two different things to make it one thing. We're going to create a new way to conduct our business. No longer will we allow the bad government to tax us. No, we won't abide the regulations that hold us down. We will not produce what needs producing, no, not anything that keeps the country going, not until we're free from the government's illegal taxation. That's right my dear, we're going on strike!"

She saw how his gleaming eyes glowed with gleeful pride. His tone of voice was stonily hard like a stony chunk of rock hard stone; his words were meaningfully spoken because he meant every word he spoke. More than ever she idolized this idol of a man; he'd rightfully earned her idolatry.

"We'll call ourselves the Conclave of Eagles," he gushed. "We'll draw up our declaration of independence and then we'll release it to the world's media. After that, we'll refuse to offer our services, or our keen brains and talents and our awesome intellects. No, not to anyone nor with any business will we conduct our commerce until the government relents to us. I tell you, this is a turning point for us all."

Yes! Here were the historic words, spoken by the one man who could historically speak them, the history making words she longed to hear. They had to be true because Jason Gild was a man who rose above the masses. His words and the truth were one and the same. And as always, he utterly meant every utterance he ever uttered.

"I've been watching your struggle against the hairy goons in government," he said to her. "It infuriated me. It's been a needless war you've had to needlessly wage."

"It's been at a great cost," she said. "I'm afraid I'm using more of our financial reserves than can be maintained." She spoke the way a true hero speaks; her face was alight as if lit with a light from within. "But I hate to give up; I can't do it. I won't do it!"

Gild beamed with his face abeam with excitement. "I urge you not to give in to the government bullies," he said. "Now is the time for you, for all of us to take what we're entitled to take." He paused to peer into her eyes, as if peering into the place from which she peered out at him. There, in a place filled with her fierce determination to rise to the greatest of the greatest of all risible heights, roiled the convincing convictions of the rising Dabny Talbett.

"I'm convinced of my inevitable success," she declared. "But I might need a little support, financially that is."

"I will see to it," he said. "The Conclave will come to your assistance. After all, if Eagles can't conclave in a time of need, then what need have the Eagles to conclave at all?"

The words and the man were beyond doubting, not even for one doubt laden second. Jason Gild had accomplished what no other man could accomplish: he'd brought together the true producers! And now the world could not deny the Eagles their estimable power, no, not their inestimable value, their great hallmark of their greatest of all greatness.

"I won't ask for money from the Eagles," she told him, "unless the need is beyond my other resources."

"I'll contact you again," he said, arising from the bench. "The Eagles will come together and we'll be as one great brain. In the meantime, please express my well wishes to your reliable father. I think of him as my older brother, although we're the same age and we're not related."

As Gild took his leave she remained on the bench. In the unavoidable void the man left behind she felt both alone and exhilarated, as if she'd inhaled a new kind of exultation. The coming days promised more promising possibilities. She'd rise above the petty demands of the Communications Council and their rules about those insipid PSAs. She'd take control of the airwaves and with Jamesford's steadfast support she'd blaze a blazing passage into the future, riding like a fearsome Valkyrie atop the immortal shoulders of Atlas.

Her cell phone buzzed; she quickly answered. "Miss Dabny Talbett? This is paramedic Mike Server, with EMS. It's about your father."

Chapter XXIV
With Death, a Life is Affirmed

She had to pull herself together.

A piercing pain lodged in her chest, like a searingly sharp serrated blade that refused to be extracted. If anything, she needed to know her world would continue; she needed to be assured that yes, her time of destiny had arrived.

"You're going to move on."

Hondo took her hand and spoke condolingly to her. "You have all the genes he gave you. It's in your DNA to take up where he left off."

She heard the words and knew they were true. This moment in her life was bound to come; her father couldn't live forever. Still, he seemed so fit, so very much alive. He'd never once complained of a headache. Dabny wished she'd stayed home this morning, to be there for him, like a faithful daughter. She prayed that with his final breath Jamesford hadn't called out for her in vain, asking for an aspirin.

Hondo and she were now sitting at the table in the casual dining room, the space where she and her father had spoken so many times in confidence. She felt his absence, yes she certainly felt it, but she also felt his presence as if he were watching her. She wondered if this feeling would remain with her. She also wondered if such a feeling might get a little oppressive.

"He wanted you to lift Atlas up to a higher place," Hondo said. "Everything you've planned and worked for, what *we both* have worked so hard for is now at hand. I don't need to keep my work in Congress a secret now. In the next few days I'll have the commitments from Gleason and Brumble and the Senate will vote on our bill."

"I wanted so much for him to see it happen," she said. "I wanted him to know I made Atlas more powerful than ever."

Walking to the window that overlooked the garden, she recalled their conversation. He'd counseled her to move cautiously; to be sure she was going in the right direction. That was just like him: ultimately wise and far seeing. Brilliant. Fearless. Uncompromising. When they spoke that time she had no doubt about her plans or her methods and especially she had no doubts about her abilities, or the final outcome. In her father she saw a once powerful man now sadly hesitant, hobbled by hobbling irresolution. He'd become habit bound. He'd held on too tightly to the time worn past. Yet she worshipped him. Still, she'd defied him and deceived him. But she couldn't allow herself to feel guilty. She never experienced that feeling. Besides, such thoughts were self-destructive. She would do what she had to do. And she needed Hondo's help and, she couldn't forget, he was now her partner, in a minor way.

"I'll support you all the way," he said. "We'll shake the world together." He came to her and took her hand. "After our weekend at the lodge," he said, "I know more than ever that we are meant to be together."

"I want to believe that," she said. "But I wonder about the woman in Richmond. Her name is Jennifer, isn't it? And what about Georgie Fraley? I believe she lives in Cleveland. From the pictures I could tell you were enjoying yourself."

The revelation didn't stun him. When a man keeps many secrets he has to be prepared for the day his secrets are found out. In fact, he expected this conversation, but perhaps not in this particular circumstance. "I won't deny it," he replied as soothingly as he could. But he knew he sounded evasively evasive. "I have a man's wants and needs. You must understand those women aren't important to me."

"And your marriage?"

She was looking at him full in the eyes as if she could see his innermost thoughts, perhaps his innermost duplicity. "Is a marriage not important enough to mention to me?"

"I was younger than I am now and not convinced she was the right woman for me."

He shrugged as if his omission was a shruggable oversight. "It happened and then it was over, like a marriage is supposed to be. Thank God there weren't any children. They would've made a mess of it."

She stepped back to assess the whole of him. Yes, in the past few days she'd learned much about this gifted man named Hondo Roache. She'd come to know how he'd shrewdly used his family and political connections to obtain his sought for rewards. At a young age, Hondo learned how to charm and cajole and when the need arose, how to deceive and intimidate. He could look you in the eye and say words that sounded true but were as false as the falsest falsehood. Suddenly she worried he might turn against her. Perhaps, with Jamesford gone, Hondo was plotting to take more than the ten percent he now possessed. Still, he'd found a way into her once impenetrable being and for the moment she'd allow him to stay. Right now she had no choice. But one day there'd come a reckoning.

"After last weekend," she said, "I believed I could trust you with my plans for the future, for both of us. I want to keep believing that, but I have to wonder about your loyalty."

"I've never felt about a woman the way I feel about you," he said. "You're truly a superior woman, one whose affection I dearly cherish."

Okay, his words sounded truthful enough, yes they did, and heartfelt and well meant. But Hondo Roache was a skilled manipulator. Hadn't Jamesford warned her about him? That's why he'd kept a file on the lobbyist. Men like Hondo hold a part of themselves away from the world's curious eyes. She wondered if there were still more women, in other cities and other countries. Would he simply leave one day to be with one of them? Worse, he could hurt her in other ways. If he so desired, Hondo could advise the senators to vote against privatization. That would damage the stock price and leave Atlas vulnerable to a takeover. But no, she'd made the right decision. In Hondo Roache she joined forces with a man equal to her in resolve and intelligence and in the determination to ultimately triumph. If now, when destiny at last had arrived she couldn't rely on him, then everything she believed in might not be true. And that was one thing Dabny Talbett couldn't let herself fall prey to: doubt her doubtless ability to judge a man's real character.

Rapid Roy offers a Heartfelt Paean to the Dearly Departed

"I know who killed him."

He breathed mournfully into the microphone. "I know it like I know my own famous name. Jamesford Talbett was killed by the assassins in Washington. It was the senator from Illinois and the representative from Wisconsin and all the leftists who want to take from the best and dole it out to the moochers. I blame them…the lying Liberals for making it so damn hard to run a business these days. I know for a fact the government has been trying to kill him. The other day they sent a thug to his house to threaten him if he didn't do what they demanded. And we all know who that thug is, the so-called People's Advocate. Really? That guy is nothing but a leftist henchman. He's the creep the government uses so it can keep its hands clean of the dirty crimes it commits. But Jamesford Talbett wouldn't back down. Like the hero he was he kicked the goon out of his house. He told the creep to tell his government overseers that Jamesford Talbett was not to be screwed with. And that's the shame of it. Jamesford Talbett fought to the death against the parasites that came after him, all of them grabbing to take his business, the business he'd made with his own two hands and one big brain. It's a sad, sad day my friends. A noble man has left us and I for one will try to make up for his absence. I know I can do it too, because I've got more than enough brains for any two men. And I've never failed at anything. In fact, I can do whatever I want and no one is going to stop me."

Chapter XXV
Dabny takes the Reins; thus begins her rightful Reign

"I didn't want to do this…at least not this way."

She was gazing at the six others now seated around the board room table. "But with my father's passing I must now assume leadership of Atlas. I know you'll give me all your support in this unfortunate time of unexpected transition."

In unison, the directors nodded in agreement. They were five middle-aged men, all white and balding and overweight, along with a svelte forty-three year old woman with highlighted brown hair, Dr. Helena Pecker. She'd been a board member for ten years, ever since Jamesford had recommended her. She was smart and savvy about business and she had hands on contact with the big boys on Wall Street. Not only that, she'd seen a part of Jamesford that no one else did. Helena was a leading urologist in New York City with offices a block from the stock exchange. She was married to a Park Avenue gynecologist named Payton Paxton Pecker and they'd failed to produce any offspring. It was well known, but never spoken of in Dabny's presence that Dr. Helena Pecker and Jamesford had carried on an affair for eleven years. And Dabny never asked Jamesford about it because she respected the widower's privacy. Besides, she didn't care if her father was bedding a married woman.

"The doctor is pretty and intelligent," Dabny once said, "and she's already had her hands on him."

Dabny knew that since her mother's death Jamesford had flings with other women, all of whom were married. She guessed he chose them because he didn't have to worry about them asking for a wedding ring and of course, if they became too clingy he had the leverage of exposing them to their husbands. Her father was entitled to do what he wanted. Nothing took precedence over Atlas, that is, nothing except his devoted daughter.

Her assent had been foreordained for many years. The cause of her ascension, the founder's death was also not unusual. Still, the suddenness of how life had fled the great man stunned the group. Jamesford Talbett appeared superhuman, immune to death's deadly influence. He'd created an empire and his own shining destiny. Nature herself seemed too feeble to bring him down. To die of an aneurism with a Readers Digest in hand while sitting on the commode was less than a noble way to leave the world behind, especially for one so august as Jamesford Talbett. He might have better shrugged off his mortal coil while working at his desk, using his massive (albeit vulnerable) brain to the very end, devising his next earth shaking campaign.

"We're a nervous wreck about the stock."

Director Culbertson Craven said that. He'd been on the board for thirteen years. "It's down to $100. The analysts say it's because of Jamesford's death. I don't think it's fair," he added. "His dying shouldn't cost us money. But then none of us actually do any real work for Atlas. So don't worry. We'll stand by you, Ms. Talbett, and we hope you'll keep us on the board."

He and the other directors looked nervously toward Dabny as she stood at the head of the table. Before continuing, she moved her eyes over those six distressed faces. They were so alike in their stylish yet understated business suits, all of which were dark gray, and their manicured nails and erect postures. They were, she thought, as well bred and educated and connected as any board of directors in the country.

"As CEO," she replied, "I'm aware of the stock's price fluctuation. I plan to reverse the downward trend. I'll also assess the board's strengths and weaknesses. I'm sure you understand. In the days ahead I'll have to rely on your support."

"We've never failed to sustain whatever Jamesford asked of us," said Director Wesley   Rather Weasely. "There's no reason to think we won't support you."

It was true, of course. She had no reason to think these people would vote against anything she proposed. This board of directors, like most boards which directed most corporations functioned as an eager facilitator. Hand selected from a group of networked cronies from families with the oldest money, the board would ratify and later justify whatever the CEO wanted to do. And, since these members were members of other boards of other corporations, with the same other members on the board, everything worked out to the advantage of everyone else. No, she needn't worry about their loyalty. And if Rafe Nailer did agree to join them, well, his voice and words would be politely heard but never agreed with or acted upon.

"The first order of business," she said, "is the situation regarding W4 and the Communications Council."

"I hope we're not in any trouble," said Director Beasley Bentover. "I don't like trouble. The doctors say trouble is bad for my nervous system."

This member, Dabny remembered, had sat on the board for five years, the shortest time in the group. He'd taken the seat after his predecessor, an ultra wealthy scion of a chemical dynasty named Wally 'the Wellborn' Wallace was killed in an automobile accident. He'd driven his fire engine red Ferrari into a thousand foot ravine, outside a little town in Lichtenstein during an Amsterdam to Genoa road rally. To commemorate his plunge into eternal equity, the Atlas board of directors draped his chair with black crepe for the entire month of May.

"I can tell you without a doubt that we will retain W4's license," Dabny said. "The ratings for the station continue to be strong and the revenues are meeting the monthly targets. So, we have every reason to expect a healthy bottom line going into the next quarter."

"There's a rumor going around that a great deal of Atlas money is in play in the market." Director Harold 'Shirker' Comfort was uneasily looking at Dabny. "It's said the Crystal ComCo Hosts are being approached by a secret intermediary and being offered large sums to come back to our side."

The rumor was bound to arise. When she'd entrusted Rapid Roy with the assignment, she knew it was a big risk. The man, like anyone with the need to glorify his importance would find it hard, no impossible to keep a secret. But then, he was also the one man who could persuade the Hosts to return to Atlas. She'd weighed the risk against the potential gain and taken the necessary action, which any smart business leader would do.

"Rumors like that," she replied, "are in the nature of our industry."

"Is it true?"

Dr. Helena Pecker's worried face wore a look of deepening worry. "Is Atlas spending money to bribe the people who betrayed us? If the shareholders hear about it they'll be up in arms. "

Dabny riled. She shouldn't have to listen to the fretting of a mere director, especially one who'd slept with the previous

CEO. "My father," she said, "was engaged in a strategy that will make Atlas impervious to our opponents. I won't say if he was, or was not pursuing the CryCom Hosts. But I will tell you that he and I developed a plan, one that I am in the process of carrying out to total completion."

The directors looked at her with curious eyes, but incuriously not with any doubt. If Dabny Talbett said she was following her father's plan, then they'd plan to follow her, doubtless of the direction they followed. Following the leader…even to the edge of the abyss…is preferable to striking out on one's own path. After all, the path one may strike out on might lead to an even scarier abyss around the next corner.

"How can we help you?" asked Director Poltroon Rugg. He'd been on the board for fifteen years. In all that time he'd never said anything that mattered to anyone.

"In the next few days you may hear more rumors," Dabny answered. "Some of those rumors may be about our efforts to privatize the airwaves. I will tell you my father intended to win this battle. We are about to gain the needed votes in the senate. So I will continue to pursue this initiative. And I'll pay whatever it costs, because that is what my father asked me to do."

Michelle Fang identifies the Real Problem with Women

The outraged Host was making an outrageous point to her outragable listeners. "It's the naggy women who call themselves 'feminist'," she snapped into the mike, "who are dragging us down to the gutter, down with all the other naggy sluts and the money grubbing, filthy prostitutes. Sometimes I'm so ashamed of my gender I wish I could change it. Now, hear me out. There are women in our country, like the representative from California

194

who I don't have to name and the one from New York, too, who are little more than prostitutes for the leftists. And what about that woman from Michigan who claimed a policeman raped her? I'll tell you what: that woman is lying like the lying trash she is. If anyone deserves to be thrown in jail it's her, not him. She was trying to get out of the traffic ticket, wasn't she? She forced oral sex on him. She's another example of how the whores of the liberal left are trying to destroy our morals. Well, my friends, we've been too tolerant for too long. We have to say 'no' whenever a filthy homeless slut asks for help. They don't deserve our help. The only thing they deserve is to be thrown into the hooker prison and left to rot with all the other sluts and meth addicts and the filthy, filthy whores."

Chapter XXVI
Keeping an Eye Out, Rising Up

"I'll get an ice pack for your eye," Vera said. "Lie down on the sofa. You need to get horizontal."

"I was horizontal on the bar floor."

Rafe was swallowing a handful of painkillers. "From there the world looked like a cowboy movie, like a scene out of Shane. But I wasn't the one throwing his fists around like Alan Ladd. Damn it, you had all the fun."

Vera leaned over and, avoiding his injuries tenderly kissed her fiancé. "I only acted in the heat of the moment," she said. "Besides, the old guy was a stinking, beer swilling, belligerent bully and the other one was a creepy, ad copy writing jerky jerk."

"It's a good thing you can run fast in those brogans," Rafe said. "For a minute there I thought they were going to catch us."

Vera was fluffing a pillow to slide under his head. "We lost them in the third turn into the alley," she said. "I bet they're still looking for us in the dumpsters."

"It's times like this," Rafe said, "that make me glad I've got a good lady."

"It's times like this," Vera replied, "that make me glad I am one."

Six months earlier at a Bookworld Book Store in the UpScale Mall in Plano, Texas, (a few miles up the freeway from Dallas) Rafe was autographing the first page of his third book on civil activism, titled The People Will Rise Up. It was a Tuesday evening, the last event of a three week promotional tour and he was weary from the never ending series of airports—the delayed departures and bumpy flights and the late arrivals—and the bouncy, jostling taxis and the hotels that all the looked and felt and smelled the same and the early morning interviews and the tasteless, unsatisfying lunches and the late night drinks in hotel lounges that also all looked and smelled the same. Tonight the turnout was very good—a lot cf eager twentysomethings and middle age activists and retired people who fondly remembered the '60's. As he sat at a table in the center of the store—next to a shelf full of books he'd written—Rafe was happy to take the extra time to sign every copy a customer lay before him. After all they'd paid good money for it and even if they'd shoplifted it he was still happy to put his signature on it. Sitting next to him was a fidgety Vera Standfore fidgeting with her fingers, acting as supporter and body guard as she had at every signing in every city during the exhausting tour.

"I think you're doing a fine thing, young man."

A little old lady with short cropped gray hair was looking at him with reverent eyes. "I only wish I was spryer so I could fight alongside of you."

"I'll think of you," he said, signing her book, "the next time we stand on a picket line."

The next customer in line was a clean cut man in his late twenties. He said, "I joined Public Cause last week after I saw you on Democracy Now. If it weren't for you I don't think we'd have a chance against the corporate bullies. But I believe in you and like your book says, the People will rise up. "

"I'm only a messenger," Rafe replied. "The message is that people like you are going to rise up because you can't do anything else."

"That's right," Vera said. "We don't a have a choice. The People have to rise up *now*."

The last two people in line purposefully approached. The woman was fortyish. She was wearing a bright white blouse with a lacy collar that reached her chin, a navy blue jacket with a gold cross lapel pin and a navy blue skirt that fell to a half-inch above her knee. Her shoes were black and heavy. Her hair was the color of a pile of straw and it was piled on top of her head just like one. Her face had blue, blue eyes separated by a nose which was thin and long and her mouth pinched up in the middle, right below that funny little groove. The man was fifty-ish. He was wearing a painfully white shirt with a blue tie that had little crosses which matched the gold cross pin on the lapel of his dark blue suit. The shoes on his feet were black and heavy and his large head was balding badly, from the back toward his brow and the comb over didn't quite cover his shiny dome, no it didn't, not at all.

"I haven't read any of your books," the woman said to Rafe.

"So nice of you to say so," Vera cheerily replied.

The man cleared his throat. "I haven't read any of them either," he said. "But I understand they're very inspirational. One of the members mentioned he saw you were coming to town so we had to meet you."

"I appreciate your effort," Rafe said, smiling modestly.

The couple looked at each other. The woman said, "we came in late and missed the reading."

"We were stuck in traffic," the man explained.

"I understand it's bad around here," Vera said. "A lot of people must want to get out of the Big D very fast."

The man looked at the woman and then he turned to Rafe. "We'd like to make a purchase," he said. "We want to buy three hundred copies of your new book."

Rafe beamed grandly. "I'm delighted," he said, "that you think so highly of my work."

"This will make it a Best Seller," Vera exclaimed. "Our first one!"

The woman nodded as if that were an important milestone to her, as well. "The store won't have that many copies in stock," she said. "Can we buy them directly from you?"

"We'll be happy to take your order," Vera said eagerly. "Give us a credit card number and an address to send the shipment to."

The man pulled a business card from his breast pocket and handed it to her. "We'll leave a sign on the front door," he said. "It'll give the delivery guy directions on where to leave the boxes. Sometimes we're not there, you know. Often, we're out toiling in the field, tending to our flock."

"This location," Vera said as she read the card, "is the Glory Avenue Church of the Lamb's Sacred Blood."

"Jimmy is the pastor and lead shepherd."

The woman nodded with great admiration at the balding man. "My name is Sister Mary Ruth. I play the organ and sing in the choir. Our membership is over three hundred strong and true, and each one of us will do the right thing when the time comes. It's a personal commitment we've made to God Himself."

Vera looked over to Rafe who was looking back with a mystified expression. He turned to the man and said, "it's good to know your church is so active with civil disobedience. Will your members use my book as a guide for the actions you've got planned? If I'm available I'd like to join your demonstration. Or are you planning to occupy a too big to fail bank?"

Pastor Jimmy looked at Sister Mary Ruth, with an expression as mystified as Rafe's. Then Sister Mary Ruth said, "oh no, we plan to use your book in our fellowship meetings, which are a kind of book reading club. We'll use it to learn about the coming ascension."

Rafe tensed, Vera did too. "Are you going up somewhere," she asked. "Is it a place that's really high?"

"We'll read your book as we prepare for the Rapture," Pastor Jimmy said. "As you know, it's expected to commence within the next six months. Perhaps it will begin even sooner. That's what my favorite radio Host Gary Bock says, and I believe him. I think of Mister Bock," the pastor added with a sly giggle, "as a 'Heavenly Host', you see."

Vera murmured, "Uh, oh."

"I can hardly wait," Sister Mary Ruth enthused. "My little sister Lilith Eve is already up there. I haven't seen her since we were teenagers. We lost her in a DUI crash, you know. It was so terribly sad because the day before it happened I told her to always buckle her seat belt. I guess she was so drunk she forgot. It's too bad she ran into that school bus and all. I'm so looking forward," she said, "to learning what you say about who all we'll meet up there."

Rafe looked at Vera who looked back at him with a really mystified expression. "It appears," Rafe said cautiously, "there's been a misunderstanding."

"I think it's a big one," Vera said.

Pastor Jimmy said, "we'll use your book as a kind of instructional for our flock to follow. I believe they will embrace your words with great enthusiasm."

"Exactly when," Sister Mary Ruth asked, "do you believe the people will rise up, Mister Miller?"

"Nailer," Rafe corrected.

Vera said, "but sometimes I call him sweetie. Other times I call him just plain silly."

Pastor Jimmy looked at Sister Mary Ruth and then back at Rafe. "The people will rise up very soon," he asked. "Won't they? I mean, they'll be ascending up to God's own Heaven."

"Actually, the People will be staying right here on good old Mother Earth," Vera said. "They'll be kicking some corporate ass and making a big fuss about it."

"Oh dear," Sister Mary Ruth said.

Pastor Jimmy frowned. "Are you some kind of atheist troublemaker?"

"Don't worry," Vera said, "he's the blessed kind of atheist troublemaker."

"I try anyway," Rafe said. "Lord knows."

Sister Mary Ruth flushed crimson. "You must come to our church before it's too late," she urged. "We'll give you all the support and love you need to get you back in good graces with the Lord. You know, He's very forgiving when you come to Him in great humility."

"We'll show you the way," Pastor Jimmy said. "It'll be hard work and it'll take a lot of prayer and contributions to our church, but you'll find your way back to Him, I promise, both of you."

"That's quite alright," Vera said. "He knows where we are if He wants Rafe to sign His copy."

Rafe sighed. "Those were the good old days," he said as he held the ice pack to his wounded eye. "I only wish we had a photo of that little consecration. It'd look great on a press release."

"I still have Pastor Jimmy's business card," Vera said. "I can give him a call and ask if he'll write a blurb for your next book."

Rafe pulled her to him. "I wonder," he said, "if Sister Mary Ruth ever has to put an ice pack on Jimmy's raptured face."

"I hope so," Vera said. "Because that would mean somebody like you wasn't quite so polite." Then she started to unbutton Rafe's shirt. "Let's see," she whispered, "what kind of rapture we can rise up to."

Chapter XXVII
The Price of Inheritance

"It's damn tough about the big guy."

Rapid Roy was consoling Dabny. "Your old man was the kind of man a guy like me looks up to. I mean he was three inches taller than me. You know, if it weren't for him I might not be where I am, that is, I'd still be a Host of course, the best in the whole world too, but I might not be talking for Atlas. I could be talking for the damn bull dyke if ol' Jamesford hadn't ponied up the big bucks to keep me on your payroll."

Not replying, Dabny looked away from Rapid Roy's rotund face. She had to concentrate on Atlas. New responsibilities weighed upon her. Besides that, she had to be careful of what she said, here in the Greener Pastures reception area. In the funeral home's next room her father was now alone. The great man was at peace in his silver and gold casket, magnificent in repose like a departed autocrat who'd bequeathed a dynasty to his only heir. Dabny had stood beside the casket and peered down at his noble face. She felt alone, cast adrift and a little frightened. How could he die like that, without giving her any warning? He'd been the most important person to her; more than that, he'd created her entire universe. She hadn't expected this day to come so soon yet she had no choice but to keep moving forward. Her plan was close to completion and then her domain would be greater than her father's. After that, she'd turn the radio industry into her own personal fiefdom.

Currently, in her black dress and matching black pumps she was talking with Rapid Roy and three others—Dr. Helena Pecker, Brody Pullman and Leona Parks, the executive assistant—the last mourners remaining after the showing of the deceased's remaining remains.

"Considering the circumstance, he looks pretty damn good," Rapid Roy had said. "It's like he's not really stone cold dead but only taking a little snooze. Hell, if I didn't know better I'd expect him to sit up and take a look around and then climb right out of that shiny ol' box."

Dabny ignored him and turned to Leona, saying, "you need to transfer my papers and files into my father's...I mean into the CEO's office. I'll want you to stay on, of course. My father trusted you implicitly."

"I've been with him for eighteen years."

Leona could hardly speak; tears filled her eyes. "He was such a strong man, a man who worked very hard. I thought of him like an uncle. Now that you're taking his place," she said to Dabny, "you'll be like my...cousin."

"I'll have a new set of procedures for you to follow," Dabny replied. "That way you'll know exactly what I expect from you. And I'll want a new desk, mahogany I think, in the Art Deco style, one that's at least eight feet wide, and order a new couch. I want one that's chrome and black leather, with a matching chair. I want the walls painted too, cream with light blue trim and the floor needs to be refinished, as well. And I want an area rug, hand woven and Persian, of course, with a soaring eagle as the motif."

After that Dabny moved across the room to stand close to Dr. Helena Pecker and whispered, "I expect you to support me, Doctor. My efforts in congress are coming to a head and very soon the spectrum will be in my hands. This is the time we must pull together."

"You're playing with a risky hand."

Dr. Pecker's eyes were red and her face was puffy. She seemed lost, as if she didn't belong with these people, but she had to be there, if for no other reason than to feel involved, or to quiet her guilty conscience. "As a director I consent to your actions, but I don't believe Jamesford would have persisted with the fight. He told me the cost is straining the company's finances."

"My father didn't confide everything in you," Dabny said. "Our bond surpassed all others. So, in the future please keep your opinions a secret, better than the way you kept the secret about your affair."

Without waiting for a response, she crossed the room and walked toward Brody Pullman. W4's General Manager was standing in the doorway and was about to leave. When he saw Dabny approach he quickly walked back to her.

"If anyone asks to see the logs," she told him, "even if they're from the council, tell them to come to me. You will not release those logs until I instruct you."

Brody nodded, saying, "of course, I'll follow your instructions."

"You're on notice," she added. "Don't do anything until I tell you."

"Yes," he said. "I'll do anything you ask."

She dismissed him with a nod and watched as he left the room. From across the reception area came Rapid Roy's voice, saying "so long, you guys, see you at the service." Then he came up to her and whispered in her ear. "I've got to tell you something," he said. "It'll make your day."

"We'll talk outside," she said.

They made their way out of the building and stood in the shadows like two shadowy conspirators. "It's been a damn weird kind of week," Rapid Roy said. "First your daddy up and dies and that's a real sad thing. Damn, who knew he had a bad thing inside his brain? I bet he could've lasted another year if he'd tried to. Maybe he didn't care anymore."

She wanted to slap him but she didn't.

"I had a little chat with good ol' Anne Caldron," Rapid Roy continued. "Damn, if she isn't one wigged out, totally empty headed air head."

"What is it, Roy?"

She hated standing so close to this man. She didn't like listening to him talk about the harpy Host, who she also couldn't stand. "Is Anne coming back to Atlas?"

"I'm making progress," Rapid Roy said. "But I gotta tell you, that woman's not right upstairs. I mean, when we were talking...I met her at a sleazy bar down on the south side, one of those places you go to meet people you don't introduce to your mama...and I tell you, she was skanky drunk or high, OxyContin maybe, I know what that stuff can do to you. Her hair, you know it's colored a weird pink shade right down to her scalp. It was ratted up to one side and she was wearing this flimsy top, it was frazzled and I could see one of her nipples and her breath damn near knocked me over..."

Dabny yanked his arm. "Is Anne Caldron coming back or not?"

"Hell," Rapid Roy answered, "she might be going to jail if the cops pull her over."

"Did you give her the offer," Dabny said, "the twenty percent bump?"

Rapid Roy grinned. "Ol' Anne said twenty per cent wasn't the only bump she was getting. I think she meant she'd take the offer, but I'm not sure she'll even remember talking to me."

"Talk to Brilly," Dabny said. "Get him to commit. I want him and Anne out of CryCom and back on Atlas, next week."

"You'll have to sign some big checks," Rapid Roy said. "I hope that won't be a problem, what with you spending the company's money on our bonuses—I sure do like getting those fat checks—and then there's the fifty per cent lift you promised me, and whatever you're paying that shifty lobbyist and all the other bills I don't know about."

She again resisted the urge to slap him. Yes, money was an issue, but she could handle it. And with Jason Gild's offer of financial support from the Conclave of Eagles, she didn't have to worry about the cash that was hemorrhaging out of Atlas.

"We're good for it," she said. "I have all the cash I need."

"If that's the case," Rapid Roy said, "I'll want a sixty per cent lift in my comp package, along with a seven per cent cut of the company."

She refused to let anger overcome her. "Atlas isn't a chunk of meat to be doled out in scraps," she snapped. "You can have the raise, the sixty per cent but not a piece of my company."

Rapid Roy leaned into her face, like a schoolyard bully harassing a wounded opponent. "I earned a piece of the action," he said. "I consider it an insult that you don't want me at your table."

Damn him, this arrogant thug. Her noble father built Atlas. He had the vision and the guts and he took the risks and most importantly, he'd bequeathed his great creation to his only offspring. How could she consider giving a part of Atlas to this brute, especially with Jamesford lying in the next room? But this was not the time to argue.

"Please Roy," she said, choking back her anger as if it were grief. "With my father's passing I've been so terribly full of distracting thoughts. I'm sorry," she whispered like she meant it. "I'll look at the books, after the memorial service. Perhaps I can find a way to bring you in with us."

If that wasn't good enough he didn't say so. "It's not like I'm robbing you," he said. "I made a fortune for you and besides, the company is big enough to carry me. Think of ol' Rapid Roy like I'm a sweet little baby boy, out for a ride on the fatherly shoulders of Atlas."

Chapter XXVIII
Dabny Eulogizes, Others Ponder

Every pew contained a mourning, mournful row of mourners. Most were dressed in black and middle-aged and older. In the rear a standing crowd filled the available space. Everyone looked straight ahead, toward the pulpit and at Dabny as she walked up the steps and into and out of a soft ray of purple light that slanted through the stains in the stained glass windows. She came to the lectern and somberly gazed out at the somber gathering.

"Jamesford Talbett was my cherished father."

Of course, everyone knew that. She just wanted them to appreciate her grievous loss. "He knew that to succeed you must believe in yourself. No one, he'd say to me, can do what's only in you to do. My father dared to test himself against the most daunting obstacles. He simply ignored the parasites and the silly do-gooders. The moochers and welfare cheats surely had an enemy in Jamesford Talbett. He struggled for years to make something of lasting value, and now Atlas towers above all the others. If he were here today he'd ask that we not mourn his passing as much as we celebrate the behemoth he created."

Looking up at her from the first row were Hondo Roache and Leona Parks, Brody Pullman and Jason Gild and all six members of Atlas's board of directors. As she listened to Dabny's eulogy, Dr. Helena Pecker thought back, across the eleven years she'd known Jamesford Talbett. He'd been her patient for a year, coming in for an annual checkup when he asked her out to lunch, saying it was for business purposes only, with no romantic intentions. It was during that lunch he brought up the subject of the board of directors. "Since you know all about my plumbing fixture," he told her, "you ought to know about my other business." Ever since then she couldn't decide if he'd been trying to be funny.

During the following years he'd take her to his magnificent property by the ocean. There, he taught her how to shoot skeet, although she didn't enjoy it and wasn't very good. She couldn't understand the pleasure one might take by blowing colored discs into little bits which then lay scattered like corpses across the grassy grounds. Besides that, she didn't enjoy shooting a gun. What's so great about pulling a trigger and hearing the blast and feeling the jolt against your shoulder? It's an action anyone with minimum intelligence can perform; it doesn't demand any actual ability and it yields nothing of any real value.

Jamesford took her to his private beach and they walked through the woodlands on the Talbett's sprawling estate. They'd fly in the Atlas Gulfstream to sunny Miami and Aruba and to the pleasant Virgin Islands and one time they flew to Paris. There, Helena remembered, Jamesford told her he loved her over a dinner of steak tartare and lobster bisque and a bottle of '61 Chateau Haut-Brion. But afterward, after a session of not so torrid lovemaking he'd whispered, perhaps to himself that he'd never loved any woman and he never would. And that made Helena more sad than angry, but not so sad or angry to stop bedding him. His wealth and strength of character, she told herself, made up for his lack of human warmth.

During the affair's decade she never confided in Jamesford any secrets about her husband and Jamesford never spoke about his relationship with his daughter. It wasn't until three weeks ago he'd told the doctor about his concerns about headstrong Dabny. "She loves Leadership Place and our jet and our money," he said. "She also loves her closets full of trendy clothes and her lifestyle and who wouldn't? But I fear I made life too easy for her. I only had seven radio stations when I started Atlas, but she's got nine hundred and seventy three. My daughter has never failed at anything," he sighed. "But scoring a goal on the lacrosse field isn't the same as running a billion dollar corporation."

Helena remembered Jamesford's worries about Dabny as she eulogized her late father. It wasn't so strange, the doctor thought that his daughter used words like 'stubbornly stubborn' and 'rightfully entitled to succeed' when describing the dearly departed.

"My father would say if a person doesn't follow the crowd, doesn't take the easy way or give in to temptation, then that person will go into the world and make something big, something very big happen. He taught me everyone has the inalienable right to work hard for what they want."

Those words were familiar, thought Leona Parks. In the eighteen years she'd worked as his executive assistant, Jamesford often said she, like any legal American citizen had the absolute right to work as hard as she wanted. To this day she didn't know if he'd been trying to be funny. The Jamesford Talbett she worked for was seldom intentionally funny. Oh yes, sometimes he'd try to make a joke, usually about the sniveling bureaucrats in Washington or about his deceitful competitors, especially the cunning lesbian who ran that other radio company. Jamesford rarely used humor, saying he had little use for it. He sometimes swore and occasionally he'd mutter a dirty word. But mostly he simply told her what jobs to do and left her to figure out how to do them. Leona now wondered what her job would be like now that she was working for Mister Talbett's spoiled young daughter. In the past Leona had seen Dabny take off an afternoon to go clothes shopping or treat herself to the luxury of her favorite spa. Sometimes she'd leave work early to drink wine at a bistro where she had her own private table and was treated like royalty. Leona didn't understand how the young woman had earned that distinction. It was odd, she thought, well not really so odd that Dabny never spent an afternoon with her friends. From what Leona knew, Dabny didn't have many friends, if she had any at all. Dabny treated Leona the way she treated all Atlas employees: with cool detachment, little better than an indentured servant.

"Father taught me to focus like a laser on the problem at hand and to stay on task," Dabny said to the gathering. "He'd say a good company is operated by people who want to make a good profit. But a *great* company is run by people who excel at everything. They don't settle for what's merely good enough and if they have to, they make their own rules along the way."

When he heard that, Brody Pullman wondered if Dabny Talbett would make her own rules now that she was running Atlas. He already knew she wouldn't follow the existing rules if they didn't suit her, like the way she ignored the rules about PSAs. He told himself that perhaps he should've tried to persuade her to adhere to the industry standard, but he'd worked hard to get the job as General Manager and he wasn't going to rock the boat. However, the Communications Council was demanding to see W4's logs. As soon as it was revealed he aired only one PSA per day his reputation as a competent broadcaster, and probably his career would get switched off like a used up radio. But damn it, like any corporate manager he'd followed his superior's directions, to the letter. It was she who'd lied to the senate committee, too. No, he wasn't so foolish to believe she would protect him now. The Talbetts hadn't made Atlas a giant by sacrificing themselves for the sake of their employees. To Jamesford and Dabny Talbett, employees were interchangeable and when the situation demanded, employees were expendable. God damn it, he wasn't going to take the fall for her! As soon as this service ended he'd rush back to W4 and send the logs to the council. Then he'd call his lawyer.

"My father held himself to the highest standards," Dabny said to the gathering. "He taught me society's laws are made to keep the population in its place and most of the time those laws work fine. After all, if the People are allowed to do as they please then who will do the work nobody wants to do? But Jamesford Talbett held himself to a higher standard. A true leader, he told me, will make his own laws. Those laws will be strict and demanding and most people would not be able to live by them. But a true producer will abide by the laws of his own making because he expects more from himself than he does from the masses, those who don't possess the same entitlements he's entitled to."

Listening to Dabny's moving tribute, Jason Gild recalled a particular day and place. It was nine years ago, a Thursday afternoon in a private meeting room on the second floor of the Silverman and Gold National Bank. Sitting at the table were James E. Mammon, the bank's CEO, Jamesford Talbett and Gild. The issue at hand was Mammon's current dilemma: he'd leveraged the bank's assets far beyond its balance sheet and one of his markers had been called in. Mammon had contacted Gild, because they'd been friends since their days at Essex Preparatory School for the Financially Well Inherited. Jamesford Talbett was asked to attend because he could easily float an undisclosed loan to Mammon. Gild recalled the conversation, which transpired in a businesslike way. "Of course," Jamesford had said. "I'm happy to make the loan to you. I won't ask for interest, either, only return of the principal and a peek at the accounts of a couple of my competitors."

To Gild it was smart to help the banker in his time of need. It was smarter to take advantage of Mammon's dire dilemma. In that way Jamesford gained confidential information about the competition's financial difficulties. Six weeks later Mammon paid Jamesford back in full. And Jamesford scooped up eight distressed radio stations at an unheard of low, low price. The man who made Atlas great, Gild understood was a man who followed his own rules when the opportunity arose. Truly, Jamesford Talbett was an inspiration to all who aspire to soar like aspiring eagles into the aspirational skies of commerce.

"He was a man with the clear eyed vision and bravery," Dabny said to the gathered mourners, "to stride across the world and never run from a fight. And he never gave in or surrendered to the government. My father made history; he lived every day like the noble man he was."

If Jamesford Talbett had been so damn noble, Hondo Roache was thinking, why did he keep confidential files on other people? Before Dabny had told him she'd found out about Jennifer in Richmond and Georgie in Cleveland, and about his rancorous marriage, Hondo suspected Jamesford had been spying on him. Hondo guessed it began a year ago. That's when Jamesford had come to the offices of HR Consulting to discuss his project to privatize the radio spectrum. However, Jamesford refused to pay Hondo's price, calling it 'an insult to me as a shrewd businessman.' Then Hondo replied, too sharply he realized, that, "a shrewd businessman is never insulted. He learns from his mistakes and he knows the value of another man's expertise."

Perhaps Jamesford took offense at being spoken to that way. Or perhaps he merely wanted to know more about a lobbyist who refused to lower his price for a famous business titan. Either way, Jamesford added Hondo to his list of people to know all he could about. Hondo wondered how much Dabny had known about her father's confidential files. All along she planned to use him to get the spectrum, and then she'd jettison him like a once needed but now depleted asset. Dabny had given him—grudgingly he recalled—ten percent of Atlas. But the stock had plummeted to $65. That signaled big trouble ahead. Not only that, she was writing checks the company couldn't back up. Hondo had seen her use people to get what she wanted, the way Jamesford used people with little regard for their well-being or their careers. The Talbetts didn't follow the rules or traditions or the protocols of the business world. They took what they wanted and left only wrecked lives in their wake. If Jamesford or Dabny wanted something then no one was safe. Suddenly, Hondo felt a cold foreboding. He'd never been a patsy and he wasn't going to play that role now! He had to find a way out of this trap.

"Lastly," Dabny said to the gathering, "I will tell you this: during his final days my father looked upon his life and he wasn't yet satisfied, as all great men are never satisfied. He intended to push on, to go to a place where only the immortals are allowed to go. My father, Jamesford Sanford Beauford Talbett was on his way to a place that few people are entitled to enter. I want to think he's there now, looking down on us. Yes, my father would do that because he was that kind of man…the kind of man who looks down upon those less fortunate than he."

Dabny took a moment to allow the mourners to digest her meaty words. Then she returned to her seat. A round faced Presbyterian minister offered the benediction. "Dearly beloved," he chanted, "we now say farewell to a great, great man. And while we do so, we should remember that men such as Jamesford Talbett do the good Lord's work. And their good works will live after them for generations to come. It's the way God intends for all of us; yes it is, to live the way that benefits all of mankind and to walk in the path He leads us. So, let us celebrate his life and reflect on how much better the world is because of Jamesford and all his long life's labors. Reflect on this and you will understand how the Invisible Hand moves us all in the right direction. So, reflect deeply upon my deep and reflective words and say, Amen."

Hondo took Dabny's hand and when they reached the outside they made their way past a gaggle of reporters and gawkers and the hecklers who carried signs that read 'He didn't take it with him' and 'Now Radio is Free Again'. Ignoring them, Dabny and Hondo reached their limousine at the curbside. As they entered the vehicle Jason Gild joined them and the car pulled away from the crowd.

"Your words moved me movingly," Gild said in reverence. "I'll surely remember them for as long as I live, and then some."

"She's a strong woman," Hondo said. "There's never been a more loyal daughter."

She squeezed both men's hands. This was a trying day, but it was also a day that would burn forever in her memory. "I have the strength that comes from my father," she said. "And I have the strength you both have given me. You are such big, strong men."

"This will make you feel better," Gild said. "Everyone is talking about you at the Conclave of Eagles. They've seen how you've shown the world what a true leader can do in a difficult time. They've watched your father and you battle the goons in the evil government. Your efforts are most remarkable."

"Have the Eagles drawn up their proclamation?"

Her eyes were dry now; her face was set like a warrior readying for battle. "Can I rely on them if I run into trouble, the way you and I discussed?"

Her question brought a gilded frown onto Gild's frowning face. "The Eagles are the rarest of humanity's rarest humans. They've succeeded because they've successfully soared above the common flock. They're the smartest people in the country and they will not submit to any threats. So," he sighed, "they are even now debating, as you can understand, exactly how they can join together and become an invincible force, yet remain the uniquely unique individuals that they are."

Hondo murmured, "that doesn't sound right."

"Eagles must soar," Dabny said. "But they must come to earth to take their prey."

"I urge you to continue the struggle," Jason Gild said. "Our watchful eyes are watching you and soon we'll see all that's there to see. I promise you, the Eagles will do what we must do, and we must do what we will do, because we must do what we must do, and we will do it, too. Mark my words, my dear. Our time to take all that's rightfully ours to take is now closer than ever at hand."

Chapter XXIX
A Pleasant Interlude

The presidential suite at the Hotel Crown Diplomat usually didn't host presidents or vice-presidents, prime ministers or premieres. In fact, on most nights its occupants were ultra wealthy pleasure seekers who stayed under names other than their real ones. The hotel's General Manager, Biff N. Numbnutter III allowed such evasion, in fact he encouraged it.

"If our guests want a sensual and well-appointed playpen, one with all the gadgets and lovely toys," he'd say, "then the Diplomat will be delighted to accommodate them."

Biff enjoyed having VIPs stay at his world class establishment and, with the images he collected from the suite's five hidden cameras, he kept the visual evidence of the guests' actual identities and their sometimes peculiar pastimes. It never hurts to possess that information in case someone is curious, and is willing to pay a king-sized price to get it into their hands.

Tonight, lounging in the luxury suite's luxurious furnishings, surrounding a table top that held several liquor decanters and shiny crystal tumblers were Rapid Roy Limerick, wearing a flowery Hawaiian shirt and Brilly O'Neal who wore a green turtleneck sweater that made his large head appear even larger. Joining them were three bottle-tanned middle aged men in stylish Armani suits: Steven "Trigger Man" Stalker, the President of the National Gunfire Organization, Austin Spiller, head of the

Petroleum Producers Syndicate and Ransom P. Stealer, CEO of the Too Big To Fail Chamber.

"Our little gabfests won't be the same without poor ol' dead Jamesford," Rapid Roy said, as he puffed on his Cuban cigar. "His sources came up with some hot gossip, especially about the scum bag in the White House."

"It's a damn tragedy."

Steven Stalker was fretting in a fretful manner. "Jamesford was going to kick in a million to our smear campaign against that bastard...what's his name...you know, the sniveling prick who's suing the Croaker company just because his wife and kid happened to catch a few stray slugs in a silly shopping mall shootout."

Austin Spiller leaked a secret. "Jamesford was going to call in a couple congressional IOUs for me, to get enough votes to open Yellowstone for our mega-fracking drill rigs. I hope his not so hot blooded daughter will stay with the program."

"She's too busy trying to buy those two jack-ass senators," Ransom Stealer said. He bent over the tabletop and inhaled a line of white powder through a rolled up $1000 bill. A pile of more powder awaited inhalation. "Little Miss Talbett is running up a pretty big tab, too. If she's not careful she'll crash her daddy's company right off the bandwidth."

"I'll tell my fifteen million listeners the government is out to destroy her," Rapid Roy said. "It's amazing what I can get those fifteen million dolts to believe."

Brilly O'Neal untied the rubber tube around his bicep and set a now empty syringe on the table. "Your listeners will believe anything," he said. "My listeners are much smarter. They only believe what *I tell them* to believe."

"I need you both to tell your listeners this," Steven Stalker instructed them. "If that sniveling prick wins his suit against Croaker, then the government will take away the guns from all the proud patriots in this country. Tell your listeners to call their congressmen, in both houses. I want those spineless peons so scared they'll never let a bill get out of committee. Then my clients at Croaker will write me a check for a cool five million. That's enough to redecorate the master stateroom on my yacht which, by the way I've christened The Salty Spree Killer."

Austin Spiller was busy chopping six fresh rows of powder. "After you've done that," he told the two Hosts, "I want you to tell your listeners the greedy Chinese are stealing all our oil, so we've got to drill five thousand new holes right away." Spiller paused to inhale two rows, then said, "if those holes need to be drilled in the middle of downtown Crackerville or smack dab on the beach of the Red Neck Riviera then that's where we'll drill them. Tell your listeners it's very patriotic to have a pipeline run through their front yard, right past the pick-up truck on cinder blocks and the stone cold dead blood hound lying in the crabgrass. Hell, they can even paint a nice big red, white and blue flag on the pipe and make it look all nice and star spangled."

"And tell your listeners this."

Ransom Stealer paused as he took another snort of powder. "If the government tries to regulate the banks then the whole damn, shit bag economy, I mean all the cigarette factories and stock car race tracks and liquor stores are going to close up. I want you to get your riffraff listeners scared and worried and keep the riffraff scared and worried."

Rapid Roy was swallowing a handful of OxyContin capsules with a gulp from a decanter of tequila. "I have to be careful how scared I get my listeners," he said. "They can't hold more than one scary thought in their brains at a time."

"My listeners are better than that," Brilly mocked. "Their brains can hold two scary thoughts while they walk and chew gum, except most of them chew tobacco."

"Tell them to run, not walk," Steven Stalker said. "Tell them to run to their neighborhood gun store and buy another Croaker, and maybe an assault rifle or two, and a carton of high capacity magazines and a thousand rounds of hollow points for good measure."

Austin Spiller chuckled. "Whatever you say, don't tell your listeners about the new oil slick off the coast of South Carolina. The experts tell me the damn thing is thirty five miles across, but it's still too far to see from the beach, so the good ol' boys can still hunt their crawdaddies in blissful ignorance for another couple of weeks until that slick washes ashore."

"Start working on a new script," Ransom Stealer said to the Hosts. "Tell your listeners they'll lose their jobs, and then they're going to get thrown out on the street and they'll have to live under a bridge and eat road kill armadillos if the banks don't get another bailout."

"Tell them the whole god damn country is falling apart," Steven Stalker said. "Make them so scared they'll shoot their own mothers in the face if they think it'll save their sorry asses."

An hour later, after the pile of powder had been ingested, Stalker, Spiller and Stealer took their executive leave, with ten minutes between each departure. After all, they didn't want to be seen together, especially by anyone in the press. A report of their secret meeting would send Wall Street into befuddled, bewildered and terrified chaos.

"We should demand another million apiece."

Rapid Roy spoke with a voice rounded by OxyContin and made gruff from his prodigious intake of straight tequila. "Those three snakes got more than they'll ever spend. In fact, I think we should demand another *two* million each."

"You and me are the king of kings of radio."

Brilly spoke with his usual flat tone, now somewhat slurred. His lips drooped at the corners and his eyes were glassy like a pair of rain spotted eye glasses. "I can get a raise easy enough from Abby Watsamore, but why should I? I'll only have to pay more taxes. The cash from those three snakes is unreportable and tax free and it gets direct deposited in my sweet little account in the Caymans."

Rapid Roy giggled. "I bet your bull dyke boss keeps a secret account too, one where she can run off to with another hairy ol' bull dyke. Then they can live in harmony with all the other bull dykes, and do the nasty stuff that bull dykes do to other bull dykes."

"At least my boss isn't a damn cold blooded robot."

Brilly was trying to drink dark rum out of a crystal decanter and the liquor was running down his chin like a rivulet of warm brown spittle. "My boss's got more balls than any five men, ten if they're Democrats."

"What would your big ol' bull dyke boss do," Rapid Roy asked, "if she walked in on us right now?"

The question ruffled Brilly. "Abby would want to know why we didn't leave any blow for her," he said. "Then she'd probably kick our butts to prove she can do it. That's something the robot couldn't do."

"Dabny Talbett can't stand the sight of you." Rapid Roy said. "But she wants you back on Atlas."

Brilly shrugged and took another gulp from the decanter. Another drop of dark rum trickled down his chin and stained his turtleneck with a greenish brown spot that curiously resembled a large headed man in a green turtleneck sweater.

"The robot will pay you the big bucks," Rapid Roy said. "Twenty per cent on top of whatever the bull dyke puts up."

"I've heard the latest rumors," Brilly said. "Gossip says the robot is spending her daddy's money like a rich spoiled brat on a nose candy bender. If she really wants me back at Atlas," he went on, "she's going to have to make me very happy."

"I'll be glad to take her a counter offer," Rapid Roy said. "I bet ol' Dabny will be thrilled to hear what you want from her."

Brilly said, "you've got an opportunity too, Roy boy. My beneficent employer will be happy to have you come over and play with us good guys at CryCom. She can be very generous, too."

"She's a damn bull dyke carpet muncher," Rapid Roy said. "I don't work for manly girls; they'll cut off your balls and hang them on a plaque on their office wall."

"She doesn't care about your oversized nuts," Brilly said. "Abby will give you twice what the robot is paying you."

Rapid Roy tossed three more OxyContin caps into his mouth and washed them down with a gulp of tequila. "It's hard to say how much it would take for me to work for the big ol' bull dyke. Now let's call in the hookers. I'm ready for some serious playtime."

Gary Bock's passionate Plea for Action

"God sees what you do."

The heavenly Host was speaking as if his listeners' heaven ready souls were hanging on his every word, which indeed they were. "God sees your every deed and He hears your every thought. He knows every sin you ever committed and the sins you thought about committing but didn't. And if He knows what you're thinking, He knows what your congressman is thinking, and the president and all the other members of the government. Now then, since we know that's true, it's also true we must cement the final bond between our churches and the government. It's the only way our beloved country can pull itself together. Then, once again we'll be one God fearing nation under our one, fearsomely fearsome God. Friends, imagine how spiritual our lives will be when our evangelical ministers write the nation's laws. We'll be living in a new Eden! It'll be a place where everyone loves God and obediently obeys His will. Yes, we'll be proud of this country, again. It'll be clean and pure, without crime or lewdness and socialism will be forbidden, under penalty of death. Just think how our schools will teach the real truth about God's creation of the universe, which he accomplished in a mere six days, sixty-five hundred years ago, this month. And there'll be more wonderful things for us to take joy in. Contraception and abortion will be outlawed and polygamy will be mandatory and we won't have to pay taxes. Only God will rule us! Think about this shining vision and pray hard so it will arrive as soon as possible, because as far as God is concerned, soon as possible isn't soon enough!"

Chapter XXX
Kilroy mulls, Rafe motivates, Ted talks

"That's a badass shiner."

An impressed Leonard Kilroy was gazing impressedly at Rafe's injured face. "It makes you look like a movie tough guy, like you stepped out of the ring against Rocky."

"If I stepped anywhere," Rafe replied, "it was in front of the jerky jerk's fist. I hope his knuckles are killing him today. That's the best revenge."

His elbows were resting on the lunch counter, and Kilroy's were too as they waited for their coffee and sandwiches. Around them the diner was filling up with the lunchtime crowd who had to eat fast and get back to work. The cramped space was noisy but not so noisy to drown out the radio the cooks were listening to in the kitchen. From there came the country fried voice of the nation's favorite folksy talker, none other than talkative Ted Brundy himself.

"It's the sure fire truth," he said. "The Feds will take everything they can from us hard working folks and give'n it to the Mexicans and Indians, not the kind that live on reservations but the billions of 'em on the other side of the world. The leftists want to make a government that runs everything. Now, I may not be the prettiest pea picker in ol' Farmer John's pea patch, but I know our rightful freedom is at stake. The Liberals are planning to take all they can from us. If we let 'em, they'll steal your paycheck before you even see it!"

"Frankly, I'm nervous."

Kilroy ignored the background chatter. "I haven't heard from Senator Brumble, but I have heard about Dabny Talbett. She's not letting her daddy's death slow her down, or for that matter keep Hondo Roache from closing the deal."

Kilroy looked up as the counterman delivered their coffee, which turned out to be hot tea. Kilroy corrected the man and turned back to Rafe. "The council is meeting tomorrow," he said. "The chairperson will try to make us vote without considering the logs from W4. The two Democrats won't go for that and the two Republicans will try to stand their ground. The council has never been this divided. The session may turn into a slug fest."

"If that's the case," Rafe said, "don't give them a warning; sucker punch them first. That's the best way to win a fight, or a vote."

"Crystal ComCo is pushing the council to revoke W4's license," Kilroy said. "They want that prime dial position, too. I don't think the council chairperson will look favorably at that, but he may not have the votes to stop it. Frankly, I don't know what to think about the chairperson. He seems both peevish and puppet like, and not in a good way."

Rafe nodded seriously. "This chance won't come again," he said. "You've got to push him and if he doesn't move, you've got to push him harder. Make it happen while you can."

In the kitchen talkative Ted was still talking. "The big government boys are working on a scheme that will make us all their cowardly slaves…not the colored kind who used to work in the cotton fields, when the right folks were running things. No, the government wants us to do the kind of work no real citizen should have to do. Now, I may not be the brightest boy in the Remedial Ed class in the schoolroom no one talks about, but I know our kind of people should never do menial work. We've got to stand up on our hind legs and fight back, with every tooth and claw we've got. That's right! It's the only way folks like us will stay the way we are. And that's the way we're entitled to stay."

Kilroy looked down at the mug of coffee the counterman delivered. It was in fact, coffee this time, which Kilroy intentionally over sweetened. Then, after a first sip he said, "my guess is the chairperson will attempt to postpone or cancel the meeting. He'll try to buy time in order to find a way to grant W4's renewal without us voting on it."

"You have to prevent that," Rafe said. "Make the chairperson take the vote."

"In the Communications Council," Kilroy replied, "the chairperson has a lot of power. Last week he adjourned the meeting and told us to go shopping. It seems his penny stocks in Penny's had lost three points. They were worth pennies on the dollar."

Rafe gazed at the plate the counterman set down in front of him. The tuna salad he'd ordered looked suspiciously like egg salad and the potato chips he expected had come out as French fries. He shrugged and picked one and bit into it.

"People get distracted," he said to Kilroy. "Your job is to make it clear the vote has to be taken. Then make the chairperson take it."

"He said a council's vote isn't as good as the marketplace."

Kilroy studied the BLT that was supposed to be a ham on rye and the cole slaw that was supposed to be potato salad. He sighed and picked up the sandwich and took a bite. Then he said, "the chairperson also said the Republican Party is better than the Democrat Party because Republicans will pay more for the pretty ladies who jump out of the birthday cake. He also said his daddy promised him the biggest party of all for his next birthday. His daddy also promised him a painted palomino, or it may be a picture perfect pony."

Rapid Roy tells it like it is, for Sure

"Now then," he grunted into the microphone. His head pounded from the previous night's indulging and his mouth was sandpaper dry like paper encrusted with sandy, dry sand. "As I was saying before the break, we know for a fact the Social Security Administration recently purchased two hundred thousand rounds of high powered ammunition. What purpose could they possibly have for all that killing power? I don't need to answer that for you, do I? It's a well-known fact a human can take only so much abuse before he has to hit back. It appears to me, good friends, we've reached that limit. The plain truth is we're going to fight back and it when we do, it won't be pretty. And pretty is, you know, as pretty does. Now we'll hear from one of my pretty fine listeners in beautiful Athens, the faraway land of the peachy keen Georgia Peaches."

"Rapid Roy, you're telling it like it is! Take it from one of your biggest Me Too-ers, I know what we have to do and I mean to do it. The gov'ment can't keep stealin' from us and calling it 'revenue'. We know the truth, don't we? And we know it 'cause you're the only man who's telling it to us, the way we want to hear it. The South will rise again and you're the man to lead us. God Bless you, Rapid Roy. The eyes of Dixie are on you!"

"That man knows his facts! So I'll leave you with this thought: keep your muskets loaded and ready for action because the Feds are marching on us; they're out to steal our rightful rights and they have to be stopped, right now. I know you can take 'em down, just like I know I'm the only man who can make the Democrats give up their lousy games and leave us good Americans alone. Yes, I'm the one man you have to believe in because I'm in the right and I'm on the right side of every argument. Don't ever forget that. And friends, don't forget I know more than you do. And that's a great, big true fact of life."

Chapter XXXI
Striking Out, Nothing Spared

Once they were inside the building, Hondo pointed down lane number five. At the far end stood an upright formation of ten red collared objects, unprotected and primed for demolition. "The secret is to aim behind the head pin," he said to Dabny. "If the ball hits there, all of them will go down together."

"It doesn't look so difficult," she replied. "I bet I'd be the best bowler in no time."

"Since you've never actually played the game," Hondo said, "you shouldn't make that assumption."

She looked around. Pins were crashing and people were yelling and laughing and drinking beer from strange brown bottles and eating potato chips out of the bag and biting into foul looking hot dogs that were oozing mustard and blood red ketchup. This was a foreign world; a raucous and crude environment filled with the commonest of people with bad haircuts and cheap jewelry and pock marked skin, people wearing garishly designed shirts that weren't properly tucked in and grotesquely colored shoes. The sound system was blasting an awful kind of noise—she'd never call it music—and the continuous crashing of the pins was quit jolting. She'd never visited this kind of place and she never wanted to and no doubt, she wouldn't want to ever again.

"I don't understand it," she said. "Why did Brumble choose this place to meet us?"

"The senator grew up with the game," Hondo said. "He feels comfortable here and besides that, no inquisitive reporter is going to see us together." He swept his hand across the scene. "If it weren't for these good people," he said, "the Hosts wouldn't have an audience."

"I now have a better appreciation," she said, "for the science of qualitative demographics."

Throughout the building more pins were crashing and people were yelling, some in delight and others in frustration. Dabny and Hondo made their way to a lane near the far end and watched as the bowler made his approach. His movement was fluid as the ball left his hand and rolled in a perfect line, with a precise arc into the pocket behind the head pin. All ten pins flew in a crashing, flying jumble and disappeared into the dark space at the end of the lane.

"Not bad," Hondo said, "for a guy his age."

Dabny saw the bowler was Senator Kenneth Brumble. He looked up at them and didn't express any recognition. He walked to the return machine and scooped up his ball when it appeared. Then he repeated the approach and release, the ball rolled down the lane and nine pins exploded from their positions.

"That's the tenth frame."

Hondo was looking up at the score which was projected onto the screen above the bowlers. "Brumble rolled a one eighty seven."

Pins crashed. A bowler yelled, "that's a double!"

"One eighty seven," Dabny said. "I thought the usual score is 300."

Hondo hoped Senator Brumble was happy with his score. Experience taught him a happy man is more open to hearing, and thoughtfully considering an offer that promised a great reward.

A happy man might even agree to do as you ask, as long as he remained happy. A happy Senator Brumble might even commit tonight and that would make Dabny very happy. However, Hondo wasn't so happy. The more he thought about his deal with her and the way the stock price kept dropping and how she was squandering the company's money, the more Hondo unhappily fretted. Ten percent of an empire is big; ten percent of a failing empire isn't such a good deal.

"Remember what I told you," Dabny said. "I want you to close the deal tonight."

Pins crashed and people yelled, some drunkenly, others excitedly. Senator Brumble sat down. He looked at them, back and forth. "Condolences, Miss Talbett," he said. "Your father was a one of a kind man."

"He thought very highly of you, Senator," she said. "He'd often say you'd make a terrific member of our board of directors."

Behind them pins crashed and children screamed.

"I've got another year in office," Senator Brumble replied. "Then I'll be available."

Hondo knew Dabny wasn't really offering a position on the board and the senator wasn't really interested in taking it. Hondo knew she would make any promise to get the spectrum and those were promises she didn't intend to keep. And Hondo knew one more thing: this wasn't a good idea. Somewhere in the lobbyist handbook it must be written to never meet a politician in a noisy bowling alley. And he knew to never, never do a deal with a politician in a bowling alley with the client by your side. Dabny may be his new business partner, at least in a way she was, but she was still his client. Usually, a client knows what they want but they don't know how to approach the politician in a productive manner. Putting the client and the politician together was courting disaster. However, Hondo had conceded to her demand to meet with Senator Brumble in person. And Hondo was committed to obtaining the senator's commitment and most important of all, Hondo Roache was personally committed to deliver this politician's commitment.

"We can make your retirement very pleasant," he said to Senator Brumble. "If there's something special you'd like to take away with you, when you leave your government service."

"I'm sure you'll be relieved to get out of that wretched cesspool," Dabny said. "It must be an awfully dreary, unpleasant place. I can't imagine working with such backward, stupid people."

Hondo heard her say it, yes she did say it, and the words couldn't be shoved back into her mouth. "What Miss Talbett means," he said to the senator, "she's sure you'll be happy to find a new career elsewhere, perhaps as an upper level manager in the private sector, even a CEO of a multinational. You might consider becoming a lobbyist. The remuneration is quite satisfying."

"I think," Senator Brumble said, "I know what Miss Talbett meant."

Pins crashed and bowlers yelled. The smell of cheesy nachos and greasy burgers and stale beer wafted past them like a toxic cloud from a clamorous train wreck.

"I want you to understand this," Dabny said to Senator Brumble. "I can do many things for you, and you only have to do one thing for me. That can't be so hard to understand, can it?"

Hondo heard that, too. He wanted to kick her but it was too late. "What Miss Talbett means," he said, "is she'll be happy to return a favor in a way that's agreeable to you. And let's not forget that Atlas has many resources to draw from. When the spectrum is secure with Atlas we'll offer the country the highest quality programming on every dial position, and more Hosts, with more entertainment for the listener. It will be a win-win for everyone."

"It certainly sounds that way," Senator Brumble said. "I prefer to achieve a win-win outcome in all the projects I work on."

Pins crashed behind them. A man walked by carrying three bottles of beer. "It's splitsville, bros," he yelled to the bowlers three lanes away. "We got one hell of a drunk on the way!"

More pins crashed and the men yelled back with unintelligible and probably indecent words.

"Do you like the new BMWs?"

Dabny was looking eagerly at Senator Brumble. "The new models have a wider wheel base than last year's," she said. "They've got updated GPS, and redesigned cup holders. There's waiting list, of course, but I can get around it."

Hondo glared at her, and then turned back to Senator Brumble. "You know sir," he said, "this is a chance for us to trade thoughts on what each of us can do for the other. It's up to you to tell us exactly what is appropriate for the issue at hand."

"If I give you my vote," Senator Brumble said, "then the bill will pass and your Atlas will own the airwaves. That's a very big favor."

"Atlas will thank you," Dabny said. "And I will thank you, as well. In fact, I can do many things in many ways. Remember, I can make you very happy, in a manner you can't imagine right now."

Pins crashed and the men three lanes down were chugging their beers and belching. A fourth man was spitting his tobacco chaw into a paper cup.

Hondo cleared his throat and said, "the House is ready to pass the bill."

"The *Republicans* in the House," Senator Brumble corrected, "are ready to pass the bill. But they have the majority by only one vote."

"It's all we need," Dabny said. "And your vote is all we need in the Senate."

Pins crashed. An ill dressed little boy ran past yelling, "I have to go poopy!"

"It's a matter of the present state of the industry," Hondo said to Senator Brumble. "The future must take over from the past. A new era is here and the old rules are holding back a modern business model. I would think you'd want to move with the times. And you'll be acknowledged as the farsighted leader who made it all possible."

"You'll be a national hero," Dabny enthused. "I'll commission a statue, or a portrait that will hang in our corporate lobby."

Hondo glared fiercely at her but she didn't see, but Senator Brumble did. "We're talking about a massive hand out the government would make to a corporation," he said. "It would mean giving you the final power to control what can be said on the airwaves, and what news stories to report, or cover up. There won't be anyone to protect the People's right to know."

"You can trust us," Dabny said. "The market will decide what's in the listener's best interest. If an item is entertaining and people like it, then it will be broadcast. But if it's information that will upset people, then it won't go into the airwaves. That's the way the marketplace works and the market makes the right decision, every time."

Behind her pins crashed. A woman screamed, "that's a turkey!"

"I'll let you know my decision," Senator Brumble said, "when I've decided to make it."

Anne Caldron knows Who's the Problem, and Why

"As usual, it's the Liberals' fault," she sputtered angrily to her sputteringly angry listeners. "They get this country into trouble, and I'll tell you why. It's because Liberal men have small penises. The Liberals are too afraid to fight so they let our enemies take whatever they want from us. Liberals are afraid of the dark and they're afraid to go out at night. They want to be coddled and fussed over by the government. That's right, and they cry when they don't get what they want, like little, spoiled babies. Whaa, whaa, whaa. It's time we elect strong Republican men to lead our country. We'll make a new country where all the men are virile and they stand erect and they have lots of muscles and hair on their chests and they'll tell us how to live like good Americans again. Yes, I'm telling you the truth. Republican men are the only hope we have for the future of our nation!"

Chapter XXXII
A Reflection on Lost Thoughts

Dabny was unhappy. She missed her father and his wise council. She missed his insightful comments about business matters and his level, guiding hand. More than anything, she missed having him close by when she needed to talk. Now, she fiercely clutched the walnut steering wheel of her brand new yellow Lamborghini. She cut in and out of the sleepwalking traffic lumbering along the Thru-Town Expressway. Her parting with Hondo hadn't gone well, like the meeting with Senator Brumble hadn't gone well. How dare that old man, a mere politician—one whose days in office were numbered—keep her, no not only her but Atlas too, and the entire radio industry, keep all of them on hold while he 'thought more about it'? Damn him! And damn the whole rotted out system of moochers and parasites, the stubborn bureaucrats and the incompetent clerks and the functionaries who slouch and mewl like indecisive children while the true producers must show them patience. This was the very quagmire she'd pointed out to her father. And yes, he believed Atlas should never be restrained. In Jamesford Talbett's day Atlas took the needed resources and assets, took the talent and the revenue, took whatever had to be taken. No man held Atlas in check.

But she had to wait.

This wasn't worth the ten percent she'd given to Hondo Roache. The deal was supposed to be done by now. She wouldn't second guess her prior deal making. No, she'd done what she had to do. But results were to be forthcoming and certainly, they weren't forthcoming at all. Hondo Roache had failed her and was still failing her and now it appeared he'd fail her in the future. This was not going to stand! She'd devise a new plan, one that didn't include Hondo and she'd make it work without him.

She swung the Lamborghini past a lumbering, unwashed city bus. It was crammed with sullen service workers, maids and servile waitresses and janitors in dirty clothes, and poor immigrants from places she'd never visit and they were going to a place she refused to think about. But she couldn't refuse to think about the current price of Atlas stock, which was now down to $55. In the last two weeks it had lost 78% of its value which meant she'd lost 78% of her inheritance. She was still rich, but she wasn't the mega-wealthy heiress she'd been a few short weeks ago, or the mega-wealthy heiress she'd planned to be from now on. Suddenly, her throat tightened around her windpipe as if constricted by a hungry boa constrictor. She gasped for breath. For a moment she panicked and feared losing control of the car. But no! She refused to let emotions overtake her. She was Dabny Talbett! Her intelligence was greater than all the adrenalin that was flooding her brain and athletic body. Yes damn it, she would prevail. She'd do whatever was necessary to pull Atlas stock back up to its former price, when her father was running the company. She would ultimately triumph. Atlas would continue to dominate the airwaves!

Her next appointment was in fifteen minutes and though she didn't mind being late, she worried the other party wouldn't wait for her. She gunned the Lamborghini, passing all those identical looking, crappy American made cars as well as slower moving imported autos. They all should be going faster because that's what they're made to do.

Rapid Roy has an Idea

"As always, the facts are on our side."

His head throbbed from his last night's bender and his tongue felt like he'd licked a rusty cheese grater. "The Democrats hate what America stands for. It's also a fact they hate our great presidents like Hoover and Nixon. They hate the First Amendment which clearly says our religion and government should be one and the same. And they hate the Second Amendment that gives us the right to carry our Croakers wherever we want. Look it up! It's a fact the Democrats are conspiring with Nazis and the Commies. They plan to disarm us so we can't fight them when they come for our children to make them work on their truck farms and in their baking soda factories. Just yesterday I read a hard hitting article in a news journal named the Onion. The story reported how the Democrats are so jealous they're going to prevent us from singing our national anthem at our patriotic NASCAR races. It's a disgrace and it's a fact Democrats hate the leaf blowers used by the Mexicans who mow our lawns. It's a fact they hate our beloved Hummers. Democrats hate our rightfully earned wealth and our tax attorneys and the camouflage pants our sons wear to their grade schools. So now that we have those facts clear in our minds it's time we do something about it. Now, I'm not going to tell you to take your spray cans of red paint and go to the Democrats' homes and cars and businesses and mark them with a great big 'D' so the world knows where they live and work. No, it might be wrong of me to tell you to do that. But if good Americans did that, then everyone would know who to look out for. And when we know where the Democrats live we'll be better off. Of course, I'm better off than you are, and I should be because I'm entitled to be. I'm the biggest star and the biggest Host in the entire country and I'm better than anyone. In fact, I don't even know how good I am! And not knowing that makes me the biggest star of all."

Chapter XXXIII
A Meeting of Minds, and Fists

A Porsche Carrera is sleek and nimble and it accelerates like lighting. It handles curves like a race car and it's designed to achieve maximum performance. It's made of the highest quality materials with the finest engineering and the highest level of workmanship. And like any internal combustion driven machine, it needs gasoline to keep its motor going.

A Toyota 4-Runner looks exactly like what it was made to do: carry passengers and cargo through the harshest elements. It's sturdy and reliable, made from the highest quality materials and with its 4 wheel drive it can take on the roughest terrain. And like a sleek Porsche Carrera, a Toyota 4-Runner needs gasoline to keep its motor going. Both cars will sometimes have drivers who might forget to buy that fuel. They'll keep driving for as long as they can until the warning light nags them to finally stop at the next gas station. That's what happened at the corner of East Congress Avenue and the T. Roosevelt Bypass.

Hey ho, let's go. Shoot 'em in the back now. What they want, I don't know. They're all revved up and ready to go.

The Ramones' pounding resonance was silenced as Rafe turned off the 4-Runner's motor. Climbing out of the SUV he tossed his empty Rolling Rock can into the trash bin. The price of regular, he noted, had gone up seventy-five cents since his last fill up. He made a mental note to study the price fluctuations for the past three years and the latest quarterly reports from the five biggest oil companies. But right now he needed to fill his empty tank.

As he was sliding the nozzle into the fill hole he looked up as a black Porsche Carrera pulled into the station. The sports car stopped across the pump island and the driver emerged from the stylish interior. The well-dressed man looked annoyed, as if this task wasn't planned for and certainly not one he enjoyed. He also looked familiar. Rafe tried not to stare but he had to figure out if he knew the guy. He could be someone from the local media, perhaps a beat reporter or one those pathetic sycophants of the White House press corp. He might even work in the Capitol. But no, he was too smooth looking for a government employee. Then Rafe recognized him. Well, well. If this wasn't a fateful coming together of two dedicated foes then it was at least a coincidental passing. At first he didn't care to take advantage of it. If he broached a conversation with the noted Hondo Roache it might not proceed in a manner that was either productive or useful. In fact, Rafe might lose his temper. Then, after a moment of reflection he decided a chance meeting was exactly what Roache didn't expect and wouldn't enjoy. If nothing else it'd be fun to see the look on the irritated lobbyist's face.

Rafe finished with the nozzle and replaced the gas cap. Then, as he was taking the receipt out the printer he heard the pick-up truck with the radio turned up to the maximum volume, blasting from the open driver's window.

"This is it."

Rapid Roy was revealing the truth to his truth seeking listeners. "This is the time when the Liberals have to admit they're wrong. That's right, they're wrong when they say Americans will accept legalized pot for so called medical use. Ha! We know what they really mean. If Americans wanted to get hooked on hard drugs like marijuana then it'd already be available in Bon-Bon and WalRite drug stores. It'd be like buying a bottle of aspirin. But pot's not for sale in those stores and that's why it's illegal, and it will continue to be illegal because that's what good Americans want."

The recently polished black C-50's brakes squealed as it rounded the gas pumps. Then came the jarring, jagged sounds of metal rasping and tearing against metal: American brutishness sideswiping German high technology. Then came other sounds.

"God damn it!"

Hondo yelled at the driver who was stumbling out the pick-up. "You hit my car and Jesus Christ, you're stinking drunk."

"And you're an uptight, pussy-faced rich fucker," the pickup driver slurred. "Why don't you park your god damned Kraut toy out of the way so a working man can get around it?"

The man was broad shouldered and plaid-shirted with rolled up sleeves and his forearms were thick like an oak tree, with a blue tattoo on his right arm of a smoking Croaker on the muscle below the elbow. He was also six-pack slow to duck when Hondo landed the first punch, a glancing blow to the chin, but the truck driver's fists carried a lot more force and he put Hondo down with two fast blows, both to the lobbyist's face. The drunk then stood over the fallen man and began to viciously kick, with his steel-toed work boots the expensive suit and the hurting lobbyist inside it. An arrogant grin crossed the drunk's unshaven face, which was pudgy and round and needed a shave. But his grin disappeared when he realized another man had run up to him.

"You knocked this man down fast," Rafe said. "He didn't have much of a punch, but I do."

Rafe's fist smashed the drunk's nose which spurted blood in a bright red stream. The man took the next one in his beer belly and then he struck back, smacking Rafe on his left cheek. But the drunk failed to dodge Rafe's next punch, a blow to the left side of his face which sent him sprawling to the ground, and almost out cold.

"That's going to a big ol' shiner," Rafe said. "I recommend an ice pack for the eye and a good woman to nurse you."

Then he attended to Hondo who was coming to. His face was bruised, his lip was cut and blood was running from his nose. With eyes that weren't quite focusing, he looked up and stared into Rafe's damaged face. "So the bastard got you too," he groaned and then he looked over to the fallen drunk. "I've heard about you, Nailer," he said. "Gossip says you're a tough guy who's always looking for a fight."

"Sometimes I punch people for the hell of it," Rafe replied. "You were already on the ground so the drunk was the next closest guy."

He helped Hondo get to his feet. Each man looked at the other with suspicion, and a grudging kind of respect. Hondo produced a handkerchief from his coat and, while holding it to his nose, he unsteadily walked to his car. With a sad shake of his head, he assessed the damage to his prized Carrera. Then he walked back to Rafe who was on one knee, talking to the still downed drunk. The man seemed dazed, as if he couldn't figure out what he was doing there. Hondo stood over them and pulled out his cell and called 9-1-1.

"We can't let this son of a bitch get away," he said. "He caused enough trouble tonight."

"This is a first for me," Rafe said. "I've never been on the same side with a lobbyist."

Hondo took a position next to the drunk and Rafe crouched down. They weren't going to let the man get to his feet. "I never expected to meet you," Hondo said. "But I never avoided you, either."

"We were bound to cross paths," Rafe replied. "But perhaps not like this."

Hondo wiped a rivulet of blood away from his upper lip. "I've heard you've been busy."

"I've heard that about you, too."

"You're talking to some people," Hondo said, "who I happen to know."

Rafe shrugged. "We're playing in the same ball park," he said. "But we're on different teams."

"At this point in the game," Hondo said, "we need to check the score. It may be closer than we think."

It may have been the perfect time for one of them to mention the name Atlas or Dabny Talbett, but neither did. Hondo managed to stop the nose bleed and Rafe allowed the drunk to get up on an elbow. In the distance a siren was wailing, heading in their direction.

"The boys in blue are on their way," Hondo said.

"They'll want to tase the drunk," Rafe said. "After that he'll be happy to go to jail."

Jail. The thought of it spooked Hondo. Jail meant a degrading loss of freedom and having to follow the orders of thugs and bullies in uniform. Nothing could be worse than to lose control of one's power to act for oneself. Yet, wasn't he now chained to Atlas and to Dabny Talbett? She was directing their shared destiny, their co-joined fate. Hondo couldn't know what that fate might be or where Dabny might lead him. If at first he wanted to own a piece of Atlas, he now knew the company was never going to prosper after the death of Jamesford Talbett. Dabny might lead the way into a revenue rich future; she also might drive Atlas into the ground and worse still, she'd drag him down with her.

No, he told himself, Dabny Talbett would prevail. Atlas would rise up and take command of the radio industry. The stock would regain its lost value and the entire spectrum would be under Dabny's command. And Hondo would gain the profit; his ten per cent would yield him millions. But if W4 lost its license and if Brumble didn't commit then Hondo's ten per cent would become a liability, worse, it'd become a chain that would confine him to years of wasted time and effort. That would be, he realized, another kind of jail.

"It's not a pretty sight."

Rafe was gazing at Hondo's bleeding lip. "You need to take care of that."

They looked over at the police cruiser as it pulled into the station's lot. The siren ceased blasting but the flashers kept flashing while two cops jumped out and jogged toward them.

"We're done with this stinking drunk," Hondo said to Rafe. "I guess our job here is done, too."

"That's funny," Rafe said, "I was thinking about all the work I still have to do."

Chapter XXXIV
A Mindless Meeting, Gone Mindlessly Awry

This wasn't her kind of place.

Walking through the crowds in the crowded midway Dabny avoided contact with the rabble who surrounded her. There were throngs of them, like the unwashed hordes in teeming Mumbai or Shanghai or even downtown Boston. To her right stooped an old man without any front teeth and a scar across his cheek. He was operating the controls of a rickety roller coaster. To her left she saw a young girl and boy squeezing each other's buttocks as they happily made their way toward the Ferris wheel, which appeared ready to collapse. Dabny saw a woman with short cropped orange hair squatting on the littered ground, eating a melting ice cream cone and she witnessed a man in a torn shirt rubbing his genitals as he leered at the children riding the merry-go-round. She saw a young girl spew cotton candy pink vomit and she heard a carnival barker dare a young man in a dirty t-shirt to sink three basketballs through a hoop that was clearly rigged to defeat the attempt. She kept walking through the crowd until she arrived at a building whose interior was made up of mirrors and reflective glass. Inside, the occupants' distorted figures looked like the warped images in a psychopath's worst psychopathic nightmare. Standing next to the building lurked the man she'd come to meet. He was wearing a dark green trench coat, a dark gray fedora and oversized dark glasses and a scowl on his jowly face.

"I've been waiting for five god damned minutes and thank God," Rapid Roy sulked, "none of the riffraff recognized me. You know they'd start nagging me for an autograph, which I'd never give to them. Hell, most of this crowd can't read. I was going to give you another minute before I got the hell out of here."

"Don't you dare give me an ultimatum," Dabny said. "I can make you regret it."

Rapid Roy shrugged. "You might like to know," he said, "Brilly O'Neal said he'll never come back to the asylum where the crazy broad named Dabny Talbett is bossing all the other whack jobs. He further said he wouldn't come back to a place that can't pay him what's he's worth and he wouldn't come back anyway to work for a black haired robot."

"I can pay any price," Dabny replied, "even for an overblown ego like Brilly O'Neal."

"So," Rapid Roy said grandly, "it looks like the big two timers are keeping their two timing butts at CryCom. That makes me think your plan isn't working out so good. What's more, that nosey troublemaker Rafe Nailer is making a stink with the Communications Council. He's getting to be a big pain in your ass, isn't he?"

Dabny flushed. "Nailer isn't going to make a difference," she snapped. "I've got him right where I want him."

"If that means you're going to pay him to shut up," Rapid Roy said, "then I want the same treatment. An eighty per cent lift in my comp and a fifteen percent stake in Atlas will make me happy. Of course you can give me more if you want. I'm worth every shiny penny."

"You are an ungrateful, pompous buffoon," Dabny retorted. "If it weren't for my father and me you'd be nothing more than a small town cattle caller."

Rapid Roy smirked. "This cow will be coming home, alright," he said. "But he might not be moseying to Atlas. Ol' Elmer might stroll his way over to CryCom to chat with his cud chewing girlfriends in their pretty little corral on the bright side of the dial."

"You can't frighten me," Dabny said. "Abby Watsamore can't come up with the kind of money you want. Besides, you have a problem with her orientation."

"Orientations are funny things," Rapid Roy said. "They can look weird until you get close to them. Then, when you've got a new perspective they can all of a sudden look perfectly normal. And sometimes they look downright inviting if you look at them from the right angle and the person is handing you a check with eight figures on it."

A scream came from Dabny's right. A little girl with pig tails scampered past and a little boy was close behind brandishing a rubber snake that appeared frighteningly authentic. Maybe it was. Dabny glanced over at the funhouse. The distorted shapes in the mirrors looked more like ghoulish freaks of nature than human beings. How can that possibly be enjoyable?

"I look at it this way."

Rapid Roy's smirking face was full of smirks and bluster. "A dyke is a dyke and she'll never stop being a dyke. But a god damn bull dyke with a whole lot more money than you think she has is the kind of dyke I can sidle up to, real nice and cozy."

"You'd never do it," Dabny snapped. "Your listeners would call you a hypocrite."

Another scream emitted from the funhouse. Down the midway a siren howled and the merry-go-round's groans sounded like the soundtrack from a Freddy Krueger movie. "My blessed listeners," Rapid Roy said, "are convinced I have their interest at heart. If I move my ass over to CryCom my listeners will come with me. Besides, they don't know, and they don't care who runs the roost. That kind of thing is way over their vacant skulls. All they care about is getting entertained by people like me. And I'm the greatest entertainer there is."

"I'll smear you so bad," Dabny said with a cracking voice, "you'll be nothing but a bunch of static on the far end of the dial."

"There is nothing," Rapid Roy said with a great big grin, "that can damage me in the ears of the multitudes who worship me."

A fly buzzed by Dabny's ear and landed on her forehead. She brushed it away and worried what its tiny feet may have left on her skin. Flies go everywhere and everywhere seethed the offal of humanity's unclean pleasures and ugly perversions.

"There's the matter of your little playpen at the Hotel Crown Diplomat," she said. "I'm not really surprised to learn I'm only one of your employers. You're also working for the boys in Big Oil, aren't you and for the Big Banksters and for the Big Weapons guys. And then there's the issue with what is it called, OxyContin? I understand it's a controlled substance. But you're out of control with it, aren't you?"

"It's god damn amazing."

Rapid Roy's beaming face beamed with unchecked pleasure. "That stuff can make you feel all warm and fuzzy and it gets you in the mood for some very enjoyable fucking. You ought to try it, Miss Robot. And if you don't have a partner of either gender well then, you can go home and happily fuck your-self to death."

She'd never slapped a man as hard as she slapped Rapid Roy. Then she slapped him again, even harder. After that she turned from his beat red face. She walked back down the mid-way, through the rabble and the shabby riffraff, the trash and squalor and the crying babies and the all the vile, noxious children with dirty faces and the disfigured old man with no front teeth.

Chapter XXXV
An Unexpected and Meaningful Meeting

When Hondo pulled his damaged Carrera into the WalRite parking lot he took a slot away from other cars to protect against door dings. His Porsche still had one good side and he was going to make sure that side remained pristine. After turning off the motor he took a moment to mull the events of this muddled evening, and he wasn't happy, not at all. Senator Kenneth Brumble had shown neither a favorable or negative disposition about his upcoming vote. That disturbed Hondo. Usually he could read a politician's thoughts from his facial expression or the tone of his voice, but Senator Brumble was expert at cloaking his intentions.

"That place is worse than hell itself."

Dabny was fuming after they left the bowling alley. "It's noisy and there's so many dirty people who smell bad and they have rotten teeth and Brumble is a lousy prick. He doesn't deserve any gift I give him."

"He may be a lousy prick," Hondo replied, "but he knows he has the vote you need. That makes him a lousy prick you have to play nice with."

Dabny didn't take that well. She also didn't take well Hondo's advice that they should give the senator more time to make his decision. "Pushing him too hard," he'd said, "will only piss him off, and what we don't need is a pissed off lousy prick who has the vote that will get you the spectrum."

Dabny didn't take that well, either. "I can't understand it," she fumed. "Why you don't make something happen. I thought you're the best in the business."

Hondo didn't take that well. Dabny may have been frustrated but she didn't have to insult him. He was working the senator the way an experienced lobbyist works any politician. They were making progress, whether she could see it or not. Before they parted Hondo had said to her, "these things sometimes are more complicated than they appear."

"Then you're not doing it right," she snapped. "I want you to work harder, and smarter. That's why I gave you ten percent of Atlas. I expect you to earn it."

That's when Hondo got into his Carrera and blistered his way out of the bowling alley's parking lot. Three miles later, going seventy in a forty zone he finally relented to the fuel indicator's nagging warning light. He saw a gas station ahead and turned in and then came that unpleasant business with the drunken pick-up driver. The punch he'd thrown seemed to hit a chin made of concrete and his hand still hurt from the impact. His lip was cut and bleeding and his face throbbed with a pain he didn't know was possible. The only thing that made the event interesting was meeting Rafe Nailer. He didn't seem like such a bad guy, maybe a little brash but still, not such a bad guy at all. And damn, he could throw one hell of a mean right hook.

After entering the drug store Hondo let his eyes adjust to the bright fluorescents. He scanned the signs hanging over the aisles. He saw the sections for Face and Body Lotions, and Cosmetics and Creams and Hair Care products and fingernail polish and fingernail polish remover and there, near the far side wall was the First Aid section. When he arrived there he saw three rows of brightly colored boxes of cotton swabs and bandages for burns and minor cuts and bruises from everyday activities. Perplexed, he stared at the assorted products, deciding which would best treat his injuries. As he considered his options a tall, lean woman with short blond hair and vivid azure eyes walked up the aisle and stopped beside him.

"Damn," she murmured, looking at his face, "you've been in one hell of a fight. Are you okay, sir?"

"It's not worth mentioning," he said.

"You need to clean that cut lip with hydrogen peroxide," she said looking closer at his wound. "Use an antiseptic cream, too. Here this one's the best and," she showed him the box of bandages she'd come in to buy, "put one of these on it." She gazed at his bruised cheek. "You're getting a black eye, too," she said. "You need to put an ice pack on it and get horizontal. I know it'll help you feel better because my fiancé had to do the same thing. Honestly, he lets people bother him too much."

"Some guys are like that," Hondo said.

The woman shrugged. "Some guys can take a punch better than others," she said. "And other guys don't know when to duck when they should."

"I'll be sure to remember that," Hondo said, "the next time the opportunity presents itself."

Vera graced Hondo with her lovely smile and said, "I hope you feel better soon." Then, carrying a box of bandages she walked away, back down the aisle to the checkout counter.

Watching the movement of her hips, Hondo thought the young woman was quite sexy in an authentic, down to earth way and certainly she was charming and, yes, very different from Dabny Talbett. It's funny; he was proud of his knowledge of women. Yet maybe he'd been too fast to see an inner beauty that might not actually be there. Worse, he'd been blind to the subterfuges that lurked behind her icy eyes. A worrisome notion came over him: he'd failed to gain a commitment from Senator Brumble and so far he hadn't closed Senator Gleason and now he was beginning to doubt his ability to judge a woman's character. She'd cannily used his desire to own a piece of Atlas against him. Perhaps the best thing to do was go home and pour a double scotch on the rocks and put the ice pack on his face, like the pretty lady with the azure eyes suggested.

He took the box of bandages, the antiseptic cream, the hydrogen peroxide and the ice pack to the counter, paid for them and walked out of the store. Returning to his car he saw a beat up pick-up truck had parked close to it, but not so close to ding his Porsche when the truck's door opened which it did, emitting a gray haired man wearing dirty overalls accompanied by the sound from the radio, that of Michelle Fang's impassioned voice.

"Some women," she was gasping, "are no better than trampy, dirty slaves to their filthy cravings and dirty carnal desires and they'll stop at nothing to get all the deviant pleasure they crave. You can't trust anything they say because sex is their drug and they'll lie and cheat to get all the raunchy, filthy sex they can't live without."

"She's got a nasty hole in her," the man in overalls said. "Right there. See?" He was pointing to the bashed in front quarter panel, at the gash the C-50 had gouged into the Porsche's sheet metal. "A nice car like this," he sighed, "shouldn't get holes like that. It makes 'em look cheap and tarty."

Hondo opened the Carrera's door and tossed in his shopping bag. "It's not a pretty sight," he said to the man. "I hope the dealer's body shop can fix it."

The man shook his head. "You need to get this car to a great body shop, like the one I work at. We can make that panel as smooth as a baby's behind and the color, why it'll be exact with the original. You won't tell the difference."

"I'll use the dealer's shop," Hondo said. "But I appreciate your advice."

The man shrugged a shrug that was shruggingly sad and knowing. "Sometimes when you fix something," he said, "it's even better than new. But mostly no matter how hard you try it'll never be as good as you think it will be. You shouldn't expect too much from people who say they'll do something they won't do, because they don't want to do it."

Rapid Roy gives Credit where Credit comes with Interest

"You have to know your enemies," he said to open his show, "because you have to be prepared for when they attack you. And your enemies will attack you any way they can. For example, even as I speak the Democrats are taking bribes from radicals to pass laws intended to bring down our respected financial leaders. The Senator from Oregon is rumored to have accepted a petition from a leftist group, one that wants congress to establish a so-called Consumer's Protection Bureau. Now really, what kind of socialistic scheme is that? I'll tell you. This so-called regulatory bureau will come after the people who take the risk and lend money to bums who'll foolishly spend it on goods and services they're not entitled to. And the Democrats think those loans don't have to be repaid! They'll even refuse to allow a modest forty-five percent interest rate on credit card balances. The Democrats are out to get our fine bankers and our generous pay day lenders. The Democrats are trying to destroy our Capitalism which is the country's perfect way of life, the very system that made this great country great. We have to stop it now! Write to your congressman; no, call him today. Tell him to kill the Consumer Protection bill because it's a bad bill. It's socialistic and unfair to our patriotic bankers. Remember, your enemies are out to destroy you, so you have to destroy them first."

Chapter XXXVI
Mind over Meeting, Pensive and Peckish

The Federal Communications Council usually met in a room large enough for its five members plus representatives of the national press corps and for interested private citizens, and for broadcast industry personnel and their accompanying lobbyists. But this morning the council meeting was being held behind closed doors by order of the pensive Republican chairperson, Peter P. Proper.

"We have a pressing proposition to powwow over," he told the other council members. "This demands our most secret secrecy. It's possible this issue will cause the kind of peer dissension the public shouldn't see in a federal agency. That wouldn't be very nice to read about in the Journal. I know for a fact my daddy wouldn't approve."

Thirty eight year old Peter Prescott Proper was the scion of the very proper Propers of Providence, a patrician and plutocratic dynasty which owned a portfolio plumb full of private investment banks and Wall Street brokerage houses and insurance underwriting companies. Through the preceding five generations the Proper's wealth came from owing the parchment like paper that proved they owned the income from the selling of products made by many other people, people who were in fact not as proper as the provident Providence Propers. Peter's father, Pierpont Pere Proper worked for the previous Republican president as chairperson of his election committee and secured for his precious offspring the prized position of Chairperson of the Federal Communications Council. Though Peter had a proper degree in Business Administration from Princeton (he'd graduated at the bottom of his class) he'd never earned an actual paycheck and certainly he'd never properly punched a time clock.

"This will give me the opportunity," he said when learning of the presidential appointment, "to get my hands a little dirty. I'm going to like having something to do with my time."

Today Chairperson Peter Proper was going to hold the first meeting when he might have to make a painfully painful decision. Before he made that decision he'd rely on for support and guidance from the other Republican member, fifty-nine year old J. Dillard Dorker. Growing up in a wealthy, Midwestern linage which owned newspaper companies in a dozen states, J. Dillard fiercely believed that big media companies are better than small media companies and the biggest media companies are the best. He studied at the University of Chicago where he learned about the wonders of the unfettered free marketplace—the infallacy of pure Reaganomics—and all about the upside benefits of supply side economics.

"The economy of this can-do Capitalist country," J. Dillard once said in an interview in The Weekly Standard, "must never be tampered with by the so-called professional economists in big government. The only efficient way to distribute this nation's wealth is to let it trickle down slowly so a tiny portion eventually reaches those less deserving and if the truth be told, to those who don't do anything of value and besides that, they're not entitled to have any wealth and they don't pal around with important people like I do."

J. Dillard Dorker passionately believed the smart people who ran the broadcast industry should never be regulated by anything other than the marketplace. "It's great men like Jamesford Talbett," J. Dillard once wrote for an Op-Ed piece in the Journal, "who bring the fabulous Talk Radio Hosts to our free airwaves, and they make this country's radio industry the envy of the world." J. Dillard Dorker's term on the council was coming to an end and this might be the last meeting he'd have the power to make a statement that would become a precedent that might stand forever, and forever influence the license renewal process.

"This is a meeting," Peter P. Proper said when he opened the session, "that we'll look back upon and remember. I think it's nice that we can remember meetings like this meeting. I hope so, anyway. Memories can be good if you can remember them."

"But the press won't remember this meeting," Angela Even said. "Because the press won't be here to see it."

Angela Even, a lifelong Democrat, was forty-three and held degrees in Communication Technology and Public Policy. She'd worked at radio and television stations in small and medium size cities, then in the Top Ten metro areas and finally in New York City. She learned the technical side of broadcast engineering and the craft of newscast production and the vagaries of advertising time sales and commercial standards and general management and all the laws and regulations that govern the broadcast industry. "She is," a reporter for the Economist wrote when she was appointed by a Democratic president, "the most qualified and capable person to ever serve on the council."

"I demand we take a vote."

William Fair was the other Democrat on the council. "I want the press in this room, as witnesses if nothing else."

"I'm the presiding chairperson of this council," Peter P. Proper peckishly replied. "That means I can overrule you, Fair, and I will do it right now. So there."

Peter Proper had overruled Fair before. And before, Fair had contested the overruling and wrote a memo of dissent which went into the council's secret file, and then it went nowhere else. Still, Fair always pressed for more transparency and more public access and always Peter P. Proper pooh-poohed Fair's proposals. But today, this meeting was going to be very different.

"I want to be clear," Leonard Kilroy said. "We're going to either renew the license for the radio station called W4, or we'll reject the renewal and revoke the license."

"If you and Angela hadn't made such a fuss over those silly station logs," Peter P. Proper replied, "we could have made the process easy, like we're paid to do. We could've held the usual meeting and approved the license without any trouble. But no, you had to make it a big deal. I hope you're satisfied with yourself."

Peter P. Proper commenced sweating bullets, the kind made out of perspiration. He looked around the table at the four other members. J. Dillard Dorker looked back at Proper and nodded conspiratorially. Angela Even gazed at Chairperson Proper with more than a little distrust, bordering on contempt. William Fair kept his face blank like a wiped clean slate and Leonard Kilroy was trying not to show his giddy expectations.

"The logs show W4 did not adhere to its promises," he said. "It's clear Atlas didn't follow the rules of broadcasting. In fact, W4 never followed any accepted practices. Need I remind you that we're the people the country trusts to protect the People's airwaves? It's this council's responsibility to enforce the rules."

"Any so-called 'rules'," J. Dillard Dorker said, "aren't necessarily the final standard. In the past this council has relied on the marketplace when renewing licenses. And I will remind you Kilroy, since you're still new at this little game, we normally allow the market to make our final decision."

Angela Even raised her voice. "I'm damn sick and tired of hearing about your screwed up market, Dorker. We're supposed to follow the law here."

"The so-called 'law'," he calmly replied, "isn't as important as the marketplace."

"J. Dillard is right," Peter P. Proper put in. "Laws can change when they feel like it but the final decision is made by the marketplace. I learned that from my daddy. He said the market makes the best decisions of all!"

What happens, Kilroy asked himself, when the market can't decide? Perhaps the market had a bad night and isn't in the mood to make a decision. Or maybe the market doesn't have enough information, or the market wants to take a moment to think things over or maybe the market doesn't think at all, or maybe the market doesn't care about anything today because no one cares about its real feelings and all everybody ever does is take what they want and leave the poor market alone and friendless, like a bullied stepchild who can't find enough to eat and a safe place to hide from his evil half siblings. Damn it, the market just might want to go outside and play and forget about making decisions.

"The former General Manager of W4 is a man named Brody Pullman," Kilroy said. "After he received immunization, he admitted W4 aired only one PSA per day. Further, Mister Pullman confirms he was ordered to do so by the station's owner, Ms. Dabny Talbett. It's perfectly evident," Kilroy summed up, "the license for W4 must be revoked."

"The Talbett family," Peter P. Proper rebutted, "are perfectly nice and impeccable people. I mean Jamesford was impeccable before he passed away. And that's a sad thing. I sure don't want to die like he did, you know, with a bad thing inside my brain. But his daughter is nice and impeccable, too. I'd hate to make her sad, what with losing her daddy and all."

Everyone peered at Peter P. Proper. J. Dillard Dorker shook his head in pure disgust. Angela Even glared at the chairperson and said, "Proper, you're not so much a paid for political toady as a pathetic, pain in the ass nincompoop."

"I second that," William Fair said.

"You're too worried about those PSA thingies," Peter P. Proper posited. "Now, let me get this straight: they're the commercials that don't sell anything, right? I guess they're for the poor people, the ones who live in cardboard boxes and don't have as much money as I do."

William Fair said, "Proper, you're not only a pathetic toady, you're blithering, asinine, over-privileged toady, and I call for a vote."

"I second the motion," Leonard Kilroy said.

The room fell silent. Peter P. Proper sighed pensively and peeked at J. Dillard Dorker who peered back and sighed pensively as well. The other three members looked at Peter Proper too, and everyone was on edge, as if perched atop a pointy precipice. It was a moment in time like no other for the Communications Council and Peter P. Proper didn't like being there. In fact, he didn't like being the presiding chairperson and having to ponder this piercing predicament. Maybe he could feign a sudden illness and call for a hurried postponement. But no, the others wouldn't believe him; they never did. Yes, he'd suffer their derision and vocal punishment. What if he used his chairperson's gavel and pounded the meeting to a premature close? That way he'd buy some needed time to figure a way out of this prickly pickle. No, the damn Democrats would squeal to the press about how he, Peter P. Proper had failed in his job and in his prestigious position and a proper Proper from Providence never failed to do his prescribed duty. He'd be pilloried in the papers. Pierpont Pere, Peter P.'s pater, would be profoundly disappointed, and that was the one thing a peerless son like Peter P. Proper could never let transpire.

"I need to remind the council of another matter," Kilroy said, "In her sworn testimony before congress, Ms. Dabny Talbett testified W4, as well as all the Atlas stations, follows the agreed upon standard and airs the customary number of PSAs. I purpose this council explores the legal precedents pertaining to Ms. Talbett's obviously perjured testimony. I also purpose, Chairperson Proper, we take the action the Law requires. After all, the preponderance of proof is there to see and ponder."

Gary Bock knows the Reason why People are so Strange

"Is it right to ask," he rightfully asked into the microphone, "why God created the homos and the butchy dyke lesbians and the freaks of nature who don't know what they are? I must tell you it's a question that has perplexed and puzzled me. It's odd, don't you think, that here we have a few repugnant people who are so terribly crippled in their sick pursuit of animal pleasure. It's hard to understand what God is thinking. But after much prayer and communion with the Holy Spirit I've received the One True Truth. You see, if we didn't have knowledge of that kind of twisted malformation of the human soul, then we never would appreciate His magnificent gift to us. And that gift is the sexual love which He intends to be only between a man and his submissive wife in the unbreakable bonds of holy matrimony, which He demands be between a man and a subservient woman. Can't you see the truth of it? God is showing us the sins of the unforgiven and the unforgivable. This is His great lesson for us to learn. We'll be free from the freaks and the butchy dyke lesbians and this will again be the greatest country on the face of the earth, which He made for us good God fearing Christians…and for us good God fearing Christians only."

Chapter XXXVII
Meeting, Sweet, Sweet Meeting

Her hair was lush and golden and silky gorgeous. Expertly trimmed and impeccably styled it tumbled dramatically over her shoulders. Her cheeks, with those model perfect high cheek bones were lightly blushed, her lips were lined and colored a luscious shade of red and her eyes were cobalt blue and bright. She was slim like a fashion model and she was wearing a crimson Armani dress which was draped stylishly around her narrow waist. Moving with the grace of a dancer, she walked past the whispering diners in the Café De' Le Aura and arrived, all smiling and dazzling and beautiful, at her counterpart's private table.

"Oh my God."

Dabny was gazing wonderingly at her guest. "You always make such an exquisite entrance."

"And you, my lovely love," Abby Watsamore gushed, "give me such lovely compliments. But I sometimes wonder my dearest, if they really come from your innermost heart of hearts."

Each woman assessed the other's hair and attire and graciously kissed the other's cheek. Then, as she sat down next to Dabny, the head of Crystal ComCo said, "I've so wanted to do lunch with you for such a long time, my darling dear, however time is such a challenge. But of course, you know that, don't you, my dearest pet?"

In reply, Dabny sighed. "We have very difficult jobs and our time is so limited and of course, we're too much alike, you and I."

"I hadn't heard the news," Abby purred, "that you've come over to our side."

Dabny knew exactly what her competitor implied. "I still prefer men to women," she said, "even those men who might listen to CryCom."

Neither cared for the other; neither expected a girly kind of tête-à-tête. Dabny knew that when she invited Abby to share her table and her time. Maybe her rival would divulge a useful bit of gossip, or she might exhibit her knowledge or lack thereof, of Dabny's plan to steal back the Hosts who'd deserted Atlas for CryCom. That would be valuable information, worth going through the next excruciating hour of syrupy, bitchy sweetness.

"It's so terribly sad about dear, dear old Jamesford."

Abby sighed with what sounded like real feelings. "He was the kind of man I envision when I take the time to envision men in general. I bet he'd not be happy with the current price of Atlas stock, would he? But I'm sure you're doing something smart about that, aren't you, you crafty little fox. I bet you're buying it up by the wheelbarrows full. "

Dabny sighed, too. "I miss my father terribly," she replied. "But I'll keep Atlas number one, for no other reason than that's what he would want. And our stock will take a giant leap in the coming future. Atlas will be bigger than ever."

"You better be careful, my honey dear," Abby said, oozing sugary deference. "Atlas might get so big you'll fall off and hurt yourself."

Abby Watsamore was seventeen when she decided to make her career in broadcasting. It was also the age when she admitted to herself, but not yet to anyone else that she wasn't interested in boys; she liked other girls. It wasn't so bad, she told herself, to want to be near another girl and touch her and join their dreams together. And, as she grew older and open about her dreams, both personal and professional she found the way to achieve success. The secret lies in doing what she wanted to do and to do that thing better and faster and more productively than any other person, male or female, straight or gay or whatever. She learned how to write news stories and advertising copy and to how to work the production board in the control room. She sold advertising time and even recorded the ads for playback over the air. Most importantly, she learned how to work with others. She made more admirers than enemies and when the opportunities arose she made the most of them. Now, she was the CEO of the nation's number two radio company and she wasn't content with that.

"I hate to pry during your time of grief, my dear sweet sweetie," she said. "But I've heard you've been spending a lot of your departed daddy's dollars. It's rumored you're trying to acquire property that belongs to other people. Frankly, that has distressed me dearly, my dear sweet love."

"We play by the same rules," Dabny replied. "If one is robbed of something she values then she's going to find a way to take it back, one way or another."

Abby's eyes remained on her devious competitor. "Dear, dear Dabny," she said. "I've done what any smart CEO would do, what you would do, in fact. You see, I intend to make CryCom the biggest radio company in the country. And that means, well of course you know what that means, don't you my dear, lovely love?"

Before Dabny could reply, the waiter walked up to their table. Dabny ordered her favorite wine, Château Cheval Blanc and Abby ordered a double vodka martini, straight up and extra dry with two green olives. It was the drink she was famous for drinking, the concoction which rumor said she could consume six of and still make love like a sex-crazed amazon and then after leaving her exhausted lover, manhandle her black and chrome Harley like a devil may care Hell's Angel, all the way up to the waiting gates of heaven. Even when on the drunker side of sober, Abby Watsamore could look a woman straight in the eye (or a straight man if the pickings were slim that night) and see whatever frightened or delighted them, what made them want the things they wanted, what they hated and what they feared and what they yearned for or their darkest desires, the desire to get closer to her.

"Don't be surprised," Dabny said to her, "if one day soon we find ourselves working together."

"I bet you're referring to how Atlas is going to own the spectrum," Abby said. "It could be you're looking in the wrong direction, my sweetest pet."

Dabny shrugged away her rival's insolence. "It's inevitable," she said. "One company is going to be the boss of all the others."

"Perhaps that's true, my lovely sweetie," Abby said. "But that company might not be Atlas."

Dabny never envisioned a world where Atlas didn't rule the airwaves. For the last forty years Atlas had stood astride the industry and all the others could only look up in wonder. Of course, Abby Watsamore would challenge her but CryCom was too small to take on Atlas. Certainly, Abby and CryCom were too weak to bring Atlas down.

"Let's not quibble," Dabny said. "I'll see to it that CryCom gets the best dial positions. That is after Atlas is suitably taken care of. I'll split up the big metro areas and divvy up the medium and smaller towns. I won't disappoint you, I promise."

"But as you well know," Abby said, "CryCom has some of the country's hottest Hosts. I believe they're entitled to the best dial positions in any size city. However, I prefer the biggest ones."

In the cobalt blue of Abby's shining eyes shone a slyness Dabny couldn't decipher. She wondered what this beautiful lesbian was thinking, or scheming or daring to accomplish. Abby Watsamore possessed an intellect equal to Dabny's and equal skills and motivation, as well as the determination not to settle for second place. It was rumored, but never proven that one night last year she'd taken a tax lawyer who'd deceived her on a motorcycle ride to a secret place in the bog lands, five miles south of town. Later that night, when the moon was new and dark, only she returned. With Abby Watsamore, Dabny was dealing with a woman as shrewd and cunning as herself. And Dabny hated anyone who tried to be as shrewd as she.

"If we work together," Dabny said as earnestly as she could, "both of us will have the best dial positions."

"If Atlas is number one," Abby replied, "CryCom can only be number two. I must tell you quite frankly my dearest dove, I prefer to be on top."

"We can work a deal," Dabny said. "I'll give you the best dial positions in five cities if you give me back Brilly O'Neal and Anne Caldron."

Abby frowned. "If you take my lovable, sweet lovely two timers," she said, "I'll be without the stars I need. And that would make me very, very sad, indeed. Oh, woe is me."

"You can find other stars," Dabny said. "After all, sooner or later we'll both need new Hosts. Even a big talker like Rapid Roy will run out of words one day."

"He thinks he'll be around," Abby countered, "for a very long time to come."

Dabny raised an eyebrow. "You've spoken with Rapid Roy?"

"He and I had occasion to chat, not long ago."

Abby smiled her sultry smile, the smile that broke hearts by the hundreds. "We discovered we have wants and needs in common. It seems my dear sweet sweetie," she added with a purposeful pause, "you've hurt the poor man's tender feelings. He asked me if I can make him feel all better again."

Rapid Roy knows all about the Sweetest Taste of All

"Revenge is a good thing."

He was speaking as clearly as he could so his listeners would clearly understand. "Revenge is good when you know you're in the right and the other guy is wrong. Let me say that again so it's crystal clear in your mind: revenge is good. Yes, revenge is good because it makes us feel better. Revenge is Nature's way of leveling the playing field and if Nature wants anything, it's a level playing field. Let me add that when somebody lies to you, or when they take advantage of you or when they steal from you the only thing you can do is get back at them. You have to hurt them as much as they hurt you. No...you have to hurt them worse! You have to make them wish they never hurt you at all. Then, when you hurt them and you've taken back what they took from you, you can feel proud of yourself. You've righted a wrong and you made them sorry for what they did. So remember, if somebody does a bad thing to you then you're entitled to hurt them as badly as you can. And that's the way Nature wants us to live. That's the way I want you to live and let's face it, you want me to live that way too. After all, I'm entitled to get what I want and I want all I can get. And that's what I have and I feel good about it, too. And that's why revenge is Nature's gift to all you good Me Too-ers and most of all, to me."

Chapter XXXVIII
Tis Meet They Do Thusly, and Rightly So

"The chicken pot pie looks good," Leonard Kilroy said. "So does the baked white fish."

"So does the beef stroganoff," Senator Kenneth Brumble said. "The meatloaf looks tasty, too."

Rafe saw the look on Kilroy's face and couldn't read it. Then he looked at Senator Brumble. His expression didn't give any indication, either. Standing in line at the capitol cafeteria they looked like three normal men in business suits taking their usual noontime lunch. Yes, they looked normal and mostly that was true.

"Chicken or beef or fish," Rafe said. "Sometime we have to make tough decisions."

"I try to avoid them," Senator Brumble said. "Making decisions gives me a headache."

Rafe looked at the green and yellow vegetables and the pieces of pink and red fruit swimming in thick syrup and the broiled entrees and something, the pan fried trout he thought, was looking back at him.

"What happened," he asked Kilroy, "in the council meeting this morning?"

"I think the roast beef looks a bit overcooked," Kilroy said. "And the white rice looks kind of soggy, don't you think?"

Senator Brumble decided on the meatloaf and mashed potatoes with cream gravy. "I had a headache," he said, "after I talked with Dabny Talbett. I tell you, that woman has a way of irritating a man. It was like some kind of buzzing insect was trying to get inside my skull to bite me on my brain."

"Speaking of brains," Kilroy said as he set the pot pie on his tray, "or lack thereof, Chairperson Proper's brain must have a pulsing pain from getting calls from his pissed off Republican playmates. I bet they won't invite him to anymore of their pretty little tea parties in the park."

"Tell me now."

Rafe had chosen a grilled cheese sandwich and cole slaw with a dill pickle on the side. "How did the council vote?"

Kilroy and Senator Brumble were walking off to a table and Rafe paid for their lunches. Then he joined them. Senator Brumble tasted his meatloaf and appeared satisfied with his selection. Kilroy sipped his iced tea in a very deliberate manner. "It's a funny thing about headaches," he said. "They come and go like they have a mind of their own."

"What happened this morning," Rafe demanded. "How did the council vote?"

"It's not a state secret," Senator Brumble said to Kilroy. "We'll know soon enough."

Kilroy grinned. "I wonder if Ms. Talbett will get a headache," he said, "after she hears the news about W4. She won't see our decision as particularly positive."

Rafe beamed. "I knew it," he cheered. "History is made every day." He couldn't wait to hear the details. Then he'd call Vera. They'd dash off a Public Cause press release and send it to the members and to the corporate media, though the corporate media would probably ignore it. He remembered when Vera

Xeroxed her butt cheeks to use as the image on the front of a press release titled The Blunt End of Civil Activism. Only one astute reporter, from the McClatchy service called to ask if he could interview the subject.

"What you did today," Rafe said to Kilroy, "was truly historic."

"The weird part came," Kilroy said, "when the chairperson said he'd vote with the Democrats, because a proper Proper from Providence is never on the losing side. Then J. Dillard Dorker called Proper a pathetic, pinheaded punker and threw a water glass at him. Proper dodged the glass and started to pout like a petulant preppy. And then Dorker lunged across the table. He got his hands around poor Proper's windpipe and I thought I was going to see a good old fashioned Republican death match. And then," Kilroy added as he took a breath, "that's when Angela Even punched J. Dorker in the temple and knocked him clean out cold. I tell you, if Fair hadn't pulled Angela off of Proper I would've joined in the fun. As it was the only thing we accomplished was revoke W4's license. We didn't debate if the Senate should indict Dabny Talbett on two counts of perjury. But all in all, we did the properly proper thing."

Rafe would like to have witnessed the behind closed door party of punching party partisans. Perhaps Peter P. Proper had anticipated a perilous fight; that's why he kept prying eyes from peering into the proceeding. Still, the rightful result had been attained and that was what Rafe had hoped for. But there was another item to discuss. "The part about Ms. Talbett's lying to the Senate committee?"

"That's for the chamber to decide," Kilroy said as he looked over to Senator Brumble.

The senator was nodding with a serious expression. "This is a problematic proposition," he said. "She's not the first witness to confuse the truth with the facts before a congressional panel. It's possible she meant what she said but she didn't know what she was saying."

"I think she was lying," Rafe said.

"She was lying," Kilroy said.

Senator Brumble shrugged. "I'll talk to the committee chairperson. It's possible a perjury charge can be made. This might turn out poorly for poor Ms. Talbett."

"She has a lot on her hands right now," Rafe said. "If she gets to own the spectrum her hands will be even fuller."

"But Atlas has great, big hands," Kilroy said with a straight face. "The spectrum can fit nicely in one of his powerful palms."

Both Rafe and Kilroy were staring at Senator Brumble who tried to ignore them. He took a bite of his meatloaf and began to chew it pensively. If he had something to divulge he didn't portray it.

"I hate to ask," Rafe said. "Actually I don't hate to ask. What are you going to do, Senator, about the bill to privatize the airwaves?"

"Yes," Kilroy said, "how are you going to vote, Senator?"

The senator had chewed his meatloaf to the point he couldn't chew it anymore. He had to swallow and when he did he looked from Rafe to Kilroy and back to Rafe.

"My vote, gentlemen," Senator Brumble said, "is not yet properly committed."

Chapter XXXIX
A Luncheon Like No Other

Hondo arrived first and followed the maître de to a private table in the far corner, the best location in the room. He looked across the lavish dining area at the august collection of well-heeled patrons, some with white hair and solemn faces, others were middle aged and were speaking in hushed, important tones, these, the wealthiest and well connected, the very best-bred and most entitled, the elite of the city's finest elite. Hondo took note of the two-hundred year old stained glass lamp shades and the English silver services and the Royal Copenhagen porcelain plates, all of which made Café De' La Aura look like a second rate chop house. Indeed, The Emperor was the town's most exclusive restaurant, noted for its gourmet entrees and faultless service and stately, subdued atmosphere. Its wine list was ranked as the finest in the country and no prices were listed on the menu. This was the kind of place a shrewd lobbyist would bring his most sought after legislator and a wealthy CEO would meet her capable partner. Hondo wondered if that partnership would stand the test of time.

Last night he'd mulled the same thing. The old guy in the drug store's parking lot, he was a plain looking man with axel grease on his face and wearing dirty overalls had said to Hondo, "most things never turn out as good as some people tell you they will."

That got Hondo to thinking. Nothing about Dabny's plan was working out the way they expected. The price of Atlas stock was now $15 and still falling, which made his ten percent not equal to the value of the time he'd exchanged it for. Worse, he'd learned the Communications Council had revoked W4's license. That was an unexpected and terrible blow, one that would hobble Atlas for many years to come. Hondo didn't know if Dabny had heard the news but when she did nasty words would be spoken and worse actions would surely follow. And what about her, his erstwhile partner and possible mate? Their relationship wasn't working out the way he'd hoped and he didn't see how it possibly could. What had he been thinking?

Today he had a black eye and a swollen lip and his ribs were killing him and the only thing to show for all the pain was Senator's Brumble's lack of commitment and Senator Gleason's refusal to take his calls. And the gossip about Dabny's squandering Atlas's assets was coursing through Wall Street and spoken of in the offices of bankers and brokerages where decisions on whether to loan her more money were being made in the negative. No, Hondo thought, this whole project which had started out so promising was not working out, not at all.

"I hope you haven't waited long."

Dabny arrived wearing a white silk blouse and blue jacket that perfectly coordinated with her pressed black pants. Then she exclaimed, "oh my God, look at your face!"

"It doesn't hurt to look at it," he said, "as much as it hurts to wear it."

She looked closer at his injuries. "Who did this to you? What did they want? I bet they were a gang of meth addicts, like the filth I hear about from Michelle Fang. Did you fight back?

Oh, of course you did, didn't you? I bet you hurt them worse than they hurt you."

"Don't worry," he said. "Plenty of people got hurt."

"You should carry a gun, one of those Croakers they write about in the Times," she said. "Bad people are everywhere these days, like the subhuman thugs who attacked you. They should be shot dead, right there in the street like the filthy scum they are."

Before replying, Hondo looked up as the sommelier arrived. "Château Cheval Blanc for her," he said to the man in the clean white shirt and perfectly fitted black vest. "Glen Finnegan on the rocks for me, and make it a double."

"You're drinking hard liquor at lunch."

She was worriedly looking at him. "Is that for the pain?"

"At least for that," Hondo said.

She sulked. "We need to talk, about what happened last evening."

"Before I got beat up, or after?"

"I'm not happy," she said. "I'm not satisfied with the way you've handled our cause. You should have obtained a commitment from Brumble by now. And we still haven't heard if Gleason has pledged his vote to us. Perhaps I expected too much from you. But no, I recall you persuaded me that you're the best there is. If that's true, why haven't I seen the results you promised?"

He'd expected to hear this, still he didn't like it. "The senators can make the process take longer than you expect," he said. "But that doesn't mean we won't get their votes. I bet we'll have Brumble's commitment by the end of the week."

"I don't want to wait that long."

Right then her cell phone buzzed. "Oh, it's Senator Brumble now," she said, looking at the ID. "He's going to give us his answer."

"I'll cross my fingers," Hondo said. "This is it, I know it."

"Senator," Dabny cooed into the phone, "I've been so anxious to hear from you."

Hondo watched and listened as she then said, "last night I meant to tell you that I can make it possible for you and your wife to enjoy some special time in Tahiti after you've escaped from the Senate." Hondo kept watching as her tone changed, from one of unctuous patronizing to that of growing anxiousness.

"No, Senator," she said, "I only meant there are many wonderful ways that I can....what?"

Hondo saw her eyes grow wide. "I didn't mean it that way," she said and listened to what the senator said next. "You weren't listening to what I told you," she said, and then her lips curled upward like an enraged serial murderer and then she hissed, "god damn you, you backward hayseed son of a bitch." And she hurled the cell phone right at Hondo's head. He ducked and it sailed passed his ear and exploded against the wall behind him.

And that's when she screamed, "god damn it all to hell," and hurled her water glass which also exploded against the wall behind Hondo's head. Then she hurled his water glass against the wall. Then she threw the crystal water pitcher which exploded in a hail of wicked, wet, jagged shards. Then she thrust herself up from the table, which she kept pounding with her fists. Then she turned around as if confronting a stalking stalker. She kept turning back and forth, looking to the right and left for the closest human target, any man, woman or child she could pummel with her fiercely clinched fists. Everyone in the restaurant, all the well groomed gentlemen, the bankers and lawyers and the well-funded investment brokers and their oh-so proper wives and the model gorgeous mistresses, the cream of the cream of society's most entitled looked at her with mouths agape and eyes wild with worry and wonder. Then she swung back to Hondo.

"You fucked up," she rasped. "You fucked up, you bungling, incapable flunky."

"We need to talk," he said, calmly. "We need to act like adults."

She leaned across the table and slapped him hard across his face, right on his injured lip. "I want you to feel the pain," she hissed, "like I'm feeling it right now, you massive, inept fuck up."

"Madam!"

The alarmed waiter appeared next to her. "Madam, please. Are you in distress?"

"She's a little upset," Hondo said. "But she'll get a grip, won't you, Dabny?"

"God damn you," she hissed at him. "You screwed it up, you, you worthless plastic doormat."

"Madam?" The waiter pleaded, "Please, allow yourself to calm down. Please, this is The Emperor."

Dabny swung around to attack the cowering man then she managed to regain her sense of place. She looked around the room and saw the astonished peerage peering back at her. "Oh, God," she groaned. "I'm in The Emperor. These are my people."

"She'll be alright now," Hondo said to the waiter. "Forget the wine. Bring her a double Glen Finnegan, like I'm having. And bring them right away."

"Oh my God," she moaned and slumped into her chair.

Hondo didn't say anything but merely gazed at her. He remembered their first meeting at Café De' La Aura, what now seemed like a lifetime ago. What was it he found so attractive, her cheeks, her mouth, her lips? No, it was there, in the depths of those roiling green irises. Yes, in those emerald eyes he'd seen her cunning and sly artfulness, all that shrewd deviousness that beguiled him like an awestruck acolyte in the presence of his perfect idol. Or was it her deliberate manner, or her overpowering determination? Maybe it was her reputation as a woman who never failed at anything. A woman, he'd fondly and erroneously imagined who would lead them to a place where only the deities dare to go.

"We don't have to give up," he said. "We can try again. Brumble may be playing you for a bigger payoff."

"He said he'd rather stick his head in wood chipper," she replied, composed but still stunned, "than give the airwaves to me."

That sounded pretty definite. And with Senator Gleason not returning his calls, Hondo conceded he'd failed dismally in his mission. It was an odd feeling but not exactly horrible, more like the way shock takes over after a massive bodily injury. "We can develop a new plan," he said and knew he didn't sound hopeful. No, he really sounded downright stupid and stupid never suited him.

"Atlas is bled dry," Dabny murmured. "I have to meet the next payroll, in a week. Christ, I have to make a report to the pain in the ass shareholders. And those suck-up hanger-on directors will want to know what's happened to their compensation package. Damn them. They're nothing but a bunch of spineless leeches. Oh, there's a payment coming due on our refi loans, and on our self-funded insurance plan and the contribution to the executives pensions, and I need to send checks to Tiffany's and Bergdorf Goodman, and that damn Italian car dealer."

"You can sell your shares in Atlas," Hondo said. "Surely you have enough to cover the margin."

Dabny grinned smugly. "Fortunately," she said, "there are financial resources I can tap into. You may recall Jason Gild promised to support Atlas with funds from the Conclave of Eagles."

Hondo shook his head. "I haven't heard anything about a conclave of eagles or sparrow hawks or prairie chickens or any other feathered creature."

"It's been kept a secret," she said. "Jason plans to surprise the world with their proclamation of independence. They're going on strike! The Eagles will refuse to do any work until the government agrees not to tax them."

"You can't really believe that," he said. "That's the stuff of deluded minds."

Dabny glared at him. "Damn you, you're such a pathetic loser. You promised me the spectrum, damn you, and I relied on you to deliver it. Well, you didn't deliver it and Atlas is broke. But you'll see what a real producer can do. I'll get the funds from Jason Gild."

"I want out of the deal," Hondo said. "I'm selling my ten percent for whatever I can get."

She glared more angrily at him. "I expected as much... you're running away like a simpering schoolboy who tried to play with the grown-ups. Well, you need to grow up; be a man, damn you, if it's even possible."

"You can have my ten percent back, for nothing. That's what it's going to be worth." He got up from the table. "And oh, one more thing my dear, you might be interested to hear the news about W4."

Rapid Roy reaches out to his Admirers, from his New Home

The big leather chair with its contoured high back and wide, padded seat had been designed and built especially for him. The desk was shiny and new and the microphone and production board were state of the art and new, as well. In fact, the entire on-air studio was brand, spanking new, like he'd demanded.

"Here's a fact you need to know," he said to his loyal listeners. "A man as smart as I am…and I'm one very smart man… knows a good deal when he sees it. And that's why I came over here to CryCom. That's right. You're hearing me on a different station but I'm the same big brained Rapid Roy, the man you trust to tell you what you need to know. I came here because the good folks at CryCom ponied up the big bucks I'm entitled to. So now that I've made the move, it's time I told you the real truth about Atlas. It's a fact Atlas is rotted out inside. It's crumbling! It's going broke and I sure wasn't going down with that sinking ship. Who can blame me? When the CryCom boss asked if she could help me, why of course I'd let her. She's a gorgeous dame, by the way, and she's wicked smart. She knows how important I am and when she offered what's more than you'll ever make…more than you can imagine…I asked myself 'how can I refuse this woman's heartfelt generosity?' That's the kind of honest man I am. And that's what makes me a big star, yes the biggest star of all. So in the days and weeks and months to come you'll hear me on this station. I'll be the same heroic man I've been in the past, because why should I change? I'm the best thing you'll ever hear on the radio, in your entire life. And that's a fact that's as real as a real fact can get."

Chapter XL
Vera Shrugs

"Do you know what I think is funny?"

She was looking over to Rafe. He was sitting at the kitchen table sipping a Canadian rye on the rocks and studying a Journal article. It was a report on the cataclysmic change in the radio business and how that created a paradigm shift in the entire broadcast industry which produced a tidal wave of speculation that drove a tsunami that engulfed all of Wall Street. Stock prices rose then fell then rose and fell and then rose once more and kept rising to a dizzying an all-time record high. A dividend dazzled stock broker was quoted saying, "this is like riding a nervous kangaroo with hiccups down into a gold mine and then shoveling a pile of nuggets into its pouch." Another broker who'd lost everything in the panic jumped out of a twenty-seventh story window in midtown Manhattan. Nobody cared.

"I think it's funny," Vera said, "that the people who think they're better than other people have to go so far out of their way to prove it. But when they do that they sometimes come to a cliff they often fall over."

"It's because," Rafe said, "they think they know where they're going. Problem is, they're wrong as often as they're right."

Vera shrugged as she came to him and stroked his hair. "I only know where we're going," she said, "and that's to bed."

Rapid Roy is the Very Best, just ask Him

When he spoke to his listeners he sounded like he knew exactly what he was saying. The talent came from years of practice. To him it didn't matter whether or not he actually believed his own words, in fact he didn't know what he believed in, if indeed he believed in anything at all. Sometimes he didn't know what he was saying. He merely let out his words in a steady stream of conscious intended to enthrall his eternally enthrallable audience.

"This is a fact," he told the millions who were tuned in to CryCom. "Capitalism is the best system the world has ever invented. Look at what it's brought us: the greatest country in the history of humanity and magnificent supermarkets with shelves full of tasty foodlike snacks and disposable paper products and super-size sodas your kids can drink all day. It's brought us Botox and the best professional athletes in the world and yes, even the best radio Hosts who ever talked into a microphone. Ha! I know you think I'm patting myself on the back, and why shouldn't I? It's a fact I can out talk anyone on the planet. Why, I use only half my wits and I still have more to say than the other guys put together. Now then, I'll also tell you this fact: the radio business is a capitalistic business and that's way I want it. I earn my money…it's a lot of money by the way, and I deserve even more…by providing you with a service you can't find anywhere else. My interns dig into the reams of reports and newspaper articles so you don't have to, then they give the information to me. That way, I do your thinking for you. It's a fact most Americans want to be told the truth the way they hear it from me. I know because I talk to you every day and I even read one or two of the thousands of emails you send to me. It's flattering how you believe whatever I want you to believe. And I can make you believe just about anything, can't I? I am that amazing. I really am. I'm probably…there's no doubt about it…I *am* the greatest person alive today and I can't see how anyone better than me will ever come along. And that's a fact you can take all the way to your highly profitable and totally trustworthy, too big to fail bank."

Chapter XLI
Excellence Undone, now the Truth is Revealed

This was the first time Rafe had entered Atlas. The mammoth building, all glistening glass and shining structural steel stood like a brooding colossus at the corner of First Street and Foremost Avenue. Inside its mighty walls great plans had been devised and executed and from those grand schemes an immense fortune had been forged, as if arising from the flaming coals in Vulcan's fiery furnace. A powerful entity arose and took command of an entire industry. Now, that seemingly bottomless fortune had been squandered and the great entity was mortally wounded, teetering, on the brink of collapse. Or, Rafe thought, a better metaphor might be Atlas was already dead and its shattered spirit was fading into the airwaves, never again to be found on the radio dial.

After he passed through the metal detector and the security guard's pat down he came to the first floor receptionist and said, "I have an appointment with Dabny Talbett." Then he took the elevator up to the seventy fifth floor where he passed another receptionist and followed a carpeted hallway, passing the marble busts of Julius Caser and Claudius Caesar Augustus Nero and Julius Caesar Augustus Caligula and into the ultra-modern office suite of the new CEO.

"I'm here to see Dabny Talbett," he said to Leona Parks. "I believe she's expecting me."

"She told me to show you in as soon as you arrived," the executive assistant said. "I think she's having a bad day, poor thing."

Behind the oaken door he entered an office furnished with chrome and black leather furniture with floor to ceiling windows that looked out to a sprawling landscape of lofty spires and gleaming towers and glimmering, glinting pinnacles. The floor was polished hardwood upon which spread a handsome rug with an artfully woven likeness of an immense eagle soaring over majestic mountains or, Rafe thought, the large bird might instead be a circling scavenger buzzard. The freshly painted walls held an oil painting of Jamesford Talbett wearing his trademark double breasted navy blue blazer with an amber Ascot. He was sitting like a brooding titan behind his oversized mahogany desk and broodily staring at the viewer with his famously cold as steel, steely cold, brooding stare. Beneath Jamesford's portrait was an actual mahogany desk sculpted in the Art Deco style and behind it sat Dabny Talbett. She had on a white satin blouse and a double breasted navy blue blazer and an amber scarf around her throat. She was wearing a look of steel hard determination with a smile that seemed pasted determinedly on her face.

"Rafe my dear friend, I'm so glad you came by," she said. "Oh my, you've been injured. Have you been fighting?"

"It's not worth talking about."

She shrugged as she accepted his evasion and motioned for him to take a seat. "I know someone else who had to defend himself from a mob of left wing drug addicts. He fought them gallantly and he beat them very badly, with his own two fists. But he and I have parted ways. Frankly, I discovered he's something of an incompetent liar and an out and out fraud."

"Some guys are like that," Rafe replied.

"But you're a man of integrity," Dabny said. "I knew that about you from the very beginning. I also know you have a keen sense of duty to the people of this great country. That's why I invited you to join our board of directors. I'm so terribly disappointed you declined my offer."

Rafe didn't like being there. This was the very room where Jamesford Talbett had planned his failed takeover of the People's airwaves. From this room he'd issued directives which ruined the careers of hundreds of people. He broke laws with abandon and he crushed anyone who dared to question his methods. He'd bought off senators and representatives and bribed inspectors and blackmailed disc jockeys and rarely kept his promises. Now he was dead and missed by hardly anyone, perhaps only by his only daughter. In a way, Rafe thought this office was a continuing crime scene.

"The double perjury charge will be filed tomorrow," he said to Dabny. "That'll make your job as CEO even more challenging, and not to mention your reputation will suffer. But then, a felony charge hasn't hurt other CEO's. However, jail might take away from your time in the salon."

"There is no challenge I cannot meet head on," she said. "In fact, I welcome the opportunity to present the facts. I know I will prevail."

"It's good to be confident," Rafe said. "It's better to know when to duck."

She looked sincerely at him. "You may have heard an unfortunate rumor," she said, "that Atlas is in trouble. It's true we are currently experiencing a minor problem with cash flow. And we're undergoing a minor change in our operations and programming."

Rafe knew about that. "I bet you're referring to Rapid Roy Limerick and the other Hosts who went over to CryCom, and to W4 losing its license which is also going to CryCom, and to the senators who'll vote against you taking over the airwaves and, oh yes, to the fact that Atlas stock is down to three bucks a share, and the board of directors have filed a law suit against you and then there are the rumors that you're on the brink of personal bankruptcy."

"I will make Atlas stronger than ever," Dabny snapped. "The situation is merely temporary."

"Time is relative," Rafe said. "A sixty second commercial can seem like an hour, and that hour can seem like a lifetime spent in purgatory."

Dabny flushed. "Atlas still owns nine hundred and seventy two stations with current licenses. I will initiate a new kind of programming which will attract a new audience. Frankly, it's something I've planned ever since the idea came to me. All Atlas stations will carry the unique sound called white noise. It's prefect for mediation or simple relaxation. This will cut down on our promotional and payroll costs, as well. I think it's an absolutely brilliant concept."

"White noise is the hissing sound a station makes," Rafe said, "when it's off the air."

"There will a commercial break at the top and bottom of the hour," Dabny said. "Advertisers will love not having to compete with music or the tiresome voices of the Hosts. I'll be able to charge a premium for our ad time since our air will be clutter free."

For one fascinating moment the idea almost made sense. Yes, there are times when white noise can help one fall asleep and certainly it's preferable to the rasping of an angry, sputtering, mindless Host harangue. But…Rafe looked at Dabny and said, "so you'll have plenty of time to air the proper number of PSAs."

"That's why I invited you," she said. "It would be such a fine gesture if you relented and ceased your campaign against Atlas. We'll be so very quiet now, and after a while Atlas will become like a reliable friend to all our listeners. They won't want to hear anything that will make them feel uneasy, like the pathetic PSAs from the No Kill animal shelters or those terribly disturbing messages from the Habitat for the Homeless. I never liked that dreary stuff and neither do the people who listen to Atlas."

"That's exactly the point," Rafe said.

Dabny shrugged; she didn't understand, nor did she care. "Atlas is still a mighty force to reckon with," she said. "And with our white noise we'll bring in millions of new listeners who will bring in new advertisers who will write big checks to Atlas." She paused to show him her most earnest smile. "So how about it Rafe, will you give me time to rebrand our image and rebuild our audience? I bet you would do it for me, wouldn't you?"

Rafe shrugged as if he were throwing a weighty weight from his strong but weary shoulders. He got up from his seat and moved toward the door. "I've learned a lot from you, Ms. Talbett," he said. "I've learned that the best and the brightest will always rise to the top and I've learned to take what's mine to take and let everyone else fend for themselves and most important of all, I've learned to never help someone who's weak and needy, because they're not entitled to any help."

The previous night Dabny discovered all about the people who are weak and needy, or rather about the people who refuse to lower themselves to help the people who are weak and needy. It started when her limo pulled up in front of the Hotel Crown Diplomat. In the evening's gathering darkness, the centuries old stone structure rose out of the earth like an enormous mausoleum, where the residents stayed for all of perpetuity. If she weren't sure of her location she might think this was some kind of cloudy, filmy, troubling dream. But she never believed the images in her dreams, or in her nightly nightmares. The horrid things that came at her in her sleep, the ghost of her reproving father, even the worst of her night time terrors and the giant, horrible, blood dripping monsters that never stopped stalking her, weren't really real. However, a new and awful reality had overtaken her. But now, in this time of dire distress one particular man could pull her back from the abyss of utter disaster.

"I can't tell you," she said to him on the phone two hours earlier, "how much this meeting means to me."

"I would never want you to feel abandoned," Jason Gild had replied. "You're the strongest woman I know, and I've known some very strong women. But then again, I've known some miserably weak women, too. Actually, I've never understood your gender. In fact, I don't know how to understand anyone, and no one else does either."

She didn't know what to make of his words, but she was certain an inscrutable truth hid inside them. She committed them to memory. Now, as she walked through the hotel's somber lobby, where curiously only a handful of guests were lounging and sipping cognac and chatting quietly, the thought came to her: the moment of redemption had arrived. Yes, when she entered the Grand Festival Ballroom there'd be assembled the fabulous Conclave of Eagles. This would be a night when her rescuers would also become her collaborators. Together they would rebuild Atlas and then the world would know and would stand in awe of the unyielding power of the incredible Conclave of Eagles.

With her heart pounding in expectation she opened the double doors and entered the Grand Ballroom. She held her breath, waiting to see the faces of the most accomplished people on the planet. Yes, she expected to feel an electrifying thrill.

"Where are they?"

She walked further into the cavernous, empty space. She saw the stage and the lectern bathed in spotlight. She approached it. Perhaps a great speaker would soon appear. Yes that was it. The Eagles would quickly assemble to hear a message of defiance and their proclamation of independence. It was true; the mighty Eagles were going on strike!

"Ah, my dear Dabny."

Indeed, the great man now entered from stage right. His grand silver hair was swept back from his noble forehead, which was circled with a gold headband. He was wearing a flowing white robe cinched at the waist with a purple sash. His feet wore Roman sandals.

"Is this the new you?" she asked. "I approve, of course."

Gild laughed knowingly. "There is much you'll learn tonight, my dear child," he said. "I'm delighted you've come to our fateful gathering."

Dabny looked around. "The Eagles are missing."

"Missing? Oh no, the Eagles are even now watching and with their keen ears they hear every word I speak."

She again looked around the empty hall and then climbed the steps. She walked across the stage to Gild who was standing at the lectern, preparing to deliver the greatest oration in humankind's history. She came close enough to see into his glimmering eyes. As before, in those gleaming blue irises gleamed the bottomless depth of his depthless vision. She saw a man who stood above all others. Within his chest

throbbed the heart of a man who would stand like a mighty titan, resistant to the government's coercion, defiant to the end.
And in his hand was the strength to hold her future and the future of Atlas, together like two shimmering diamonds, both of
them unique and hard as diamonds; perfectly diamond shaped
in every way.

"This a difficult time," he said to her. "But you must take
hold of what Jamesford left behind. You must insure it will continue as a monument to his great work. He did what he did because he could do it and he left it to you to keep on doing it. I can
only imagine what he's thinking right now."

"There's nothing I won't do in his memory," she said.
"My father wanted me to make Atlas even stronger. I've been
trying to do that but the forces of tyranny are attacking me."

Gild kindly patted her hand. "I have only the highest regard for you," he said. "Indeed, I have the highest regard for all
of us. We'll continue to wage our valiant war against the bureaucrats and the niggling, rat faced moochers. It's a war that we can
win and we will win it because all wars are winnable, by both
sides. I say it's a war we must win!"

"Yes," she said, "we'll win the war."

"We producers are about to take our gallant stand," Gild
said. "We'll show the country what it must see, that we are the
people who make everything possible. We are the fierce engines
and the determined drivers of the nation's economy. We're the
only job creators who matter. We are the makers of the marketplace and the marketplace knows all there is to know, all that's
knowable in the whole known world. I like to think of us as a
great, glowing crystal ball that's never wrong and its glowing
glow never stops glowing, not even when the light comes back
on, and chases the scary darkness away."

She wondered if Gild might be talking a bit too grandly, as if giving an interview to the Wall Street Journal. But he'd brought together the Conclave of Eagles, hadn't he? If anything, Jason Gild was simply stating that a brilliant new world order was now at hand. And they were going to rule it! She hoped that's what he meant. She also wondered where the Eagles had gathered at this moment.

"I can't wait to join with the others," she said. "When I can meet them, the other Eagles?"

"The whole country will look upon us," Jason Gild said. "The moochers and the parasites will all see us. And they will be afraid of our strong strength…of our powerful power…of our mighty might."

He really didn't have to talk that way. She got the message. She was on his side. "When will the Eagles deliver their proclamation of independence," she asked. "I've been looking forward to hearing it."

"The Conclave of Eagles is the greatest gathering of great minds that has ever gathered," he proclaimed as he swept his hand across the empty room. "We're the most talented and smartest people in all the country, probably in the whole world. Most likely we're the greatest people who ever lived. When we refuse to do our jobs the entire economy will crumble into a dusty pile of dusty dust. The nation will become a wasted wasteland. It will be flat and dirty and unfit for humans, at least for the weak and stupid and those who can't work for a living. But the Eagles are the best and smartest people there are. We shall create a new and brilliant world. It will be a place where only we will live. And we will prosper and live free, above all the laws and tiresome, fussy bureaucrats."

"I'm wondering," Dabny said as she nervously looked out at the vacant ballroom. "Have the Eagles set a date when they'll tell the world what they intend to do?"

Gild flung his hand across the high ceiling, now very dark. "The stars in the heavens shine no brighter than the Eagles," he exclaimed. "And neither are those stars any grander nor do they reach further into the cosmos than the soaring Eagles. We're the only people who make all things possible and we can take those things away and when we do humanity's dregs will come to us and they'll beg us to make their pathetic world all better again. But will we do that? Ha! The Eagles don't acknowledge the existence of altruism. Why, it's nonsense, I say. It's futile beyond all futility."

"But right now," Dabny said, "what exactly will the Eagles do? I mean, what's going to happen next?"

"The Eagles will soar like soaring eagles," Gild exclaimed, louder. "We're the most gifted and talented and smartest people there are. We have the brilliant brains and the able ability to do as we please and that's what we shall do...what we're pleased to do."

Dabny again looked into Gild's gleaming eyes. She wanted to assure herself that it was indeed depthless wisdom she saw glinting in those gleaming blue irises and not something else. "I hoped I wouldn't need to ask," she said. "But I will accept your offer of financial assistance from the Eagles."

"The Eagles are the greatest individuals in this country," he said. "We're the rarest of the rare, the canniest of the canny, the most shimmering and shining minds that have ever thought a shiny thought inside our massive, unbreakable craniums."

"I need the Eagles to support Atlas in a financial way," Dabny said. "Of course, we can structure a schedule for repayment. I'm sure everything will work out to our advantage."

Gild laughed from deep inside. "Ah, we Eagles are so very rare, so very magnificent. We're independent individuals; we're powerful people with plentiful power, the power of the potently powerful. It's impossible to imagine how such grand people like us could surrender to a worthless collective. Why, such a giveaway of our unique identities is utterly preposterous. It's utter madness, I say, madness!"

"Please Jason; I've got cash flow problems."

The words nearly choked her. "Atlas needs the help of the Eagles."

"The Eagles are uniquely unique," Gild cried. "We can't be compelled to labor for something as sordid as a common goal. Why, it's an insult to the very nature of what the Eagles stand for. We are stronger than the strongest strong man. Yes! We're even stronger than that!"

Dabny grabbed his arm and shouted at him. "Jason please, Atlas needs help. The Eagles have to help me."

"The Eagles will soar into the sky high sky," he cried again. "Eagles can't be brought to earth by the needs of the needy, of the weak kneed weaklings and the miserable, second rate failures. There can be no assistance to those who don't create wealth or those who don't produce a product. The very idea is abhorrent to the individual. It's true! We are the makers not the takers. We are truly grand and the losers are frail and despicable. There is nothing but ourselves...me and you...but there can be no us. No, the Eagles will not abide such horrid collectivism!"

Dabny saw the glowing gleam in his gleaming eyes and the way his face contorted, how the flesh stretched taut across his cheek bones. She looked out at the dark ballroom. Now, she wasn't sure how to ask the question. "Jason, is there really a

Conclave of Eagles? I mean, it seems there might be some kind of misperception somewhere."

He stared at her with his gleaming eyes, all gleaming and glinting and glowing. "The Eagles are the very greatest of the great," he proclaimed. "We're the smartest of the smart and the best of the best people in the entire world. We are the producers who produce and the doers who do all the doing. Yes! We're better than anyone! We'll take what we're entitled to take and we'll go where we want to go and nothing can stop us because we're unstoppable. We are the great achievers who achieve the unachievable. We'll never be made to do what we don't want to do and we'll make everyone see how noble and smart and wonderful we are. The parasitic masses try to bring us down to their mediocrity. They're jealous of us and our incredible minds and our magnificent mindfulness. They want us to be like them in their useless, small minded way with their weak little brains and all that ugly hair on their forearms. Oh, how can they possibly know the regal thoughts of Eagles? It's impossible! Only Eagles have the intelligence to conceive the inconceivable. Only Eagles see the world the way that we have seen it, from high, high above. Only we Eagles have the great flapping wings to take us far, far away, beyond the puny, mooching crowd of losers and pedestrians and the slobbering, feeble minded freeloaders. Yes, the Eagles are rising up. Yes! Yes! Nothing can stop us because we are unstoppable. Nothing can hurt us because we are unhurtable. Yes, yes it's true, oh great Minerva! The Eagles will never be brought to earth!"

"You're crazy if you think Atlas can't withstand your attacks," Dabny screamed at Rafe. "You just wait and see; Atlas has the strength of a giant, and that giant will rule the world.

Nothing has changed," she shouted. "I've only become stronger and smarter!"

"There's no need to call me," Rafe replied. "I'll be sure to stay in touch."

Then with Dabny's roiling green eyes burning a hole between his shoulders, Rafe left the CEO's office and walked back through the outer office, nodding goodbye to Leona Parks. He made his way through the glass and chrome door and down the Roman emperor lined hallway to the elevator that took him back to the first floor and from there he emerged from Atlas. And waiting at curbside was Vera Standfore at the wheel of her candy apple red Dodge Charger, smoking a joint and laughing at what she was hearing on the radio. When she saw Rafe she turned off the radio and unlocked the passenger door.

"You're smiling," she said to him. "I bet that means you've got a new pen for your collection."

"It's pure titanium," he said. "Dabny Talbett is entitled to the very best."

Vera giggled. "You wouldn't believe," she said, "what Rapid Roy has been saying today."

She turned the radio back on.

"I'm telling you the true facts," the big talker was talking to his listening listeners. "There are those, many of them who would destroy me if they could. They resent my courage and my intelligence and my stamina in the face of unrelenting personal attacks. But I will persist and I will continue to persist to bring you the Truth as I know the Truth to be. And I tell you right now the vile, evil rumors about me are not true. Why, I'm totally incapable of lying. So believe me when I say the vicious smears about my so called drug abuse are intended to make you question my integrity. It's impossible! Do you actually think

I'd self-medicate with prescription pharmaceuticals? Yes, it's a crazy idea. In fact, I've never heard of OxyContin. And there's more lies too, about me being on the take from big business. Nonsense! If I was secretly taking millions from the suntanned boys in Armani suits then how I could tell you the facts the way I've been telling them to you? You know the real truth. Those lies are coming from the lying, leftists Liberals who would drag me down to their sordid level. Remember my friends, life is hard and that's how Nature wants it! That way, only the best of us are entitled to get what we want. You can't trust anyone who tells you anything different because they're all liars and treacherous left wingers and they'll never be as good as you and me. But you're not as good as me. No one is! And another thing....

The End

Acknowledgements

A tip of the hat goes to my ol' writing buddy Clif Nixon; the man can tell a damn good story.

And many thanks to Amy Kennedy-Graham who always supported me.

My appreciation goes to Angi Palm and Jessica Nelson for their efforts in editing some fearsomely ugly early drafts.

Thanks too, to Peter Biello and the members of the Burlington Writers Workshop.

And thank you Marcia Blanco for the image that graces this narrative's cover.

Thanks to Jim Gamble for his PR efforts.

And as always, my appreciation and affection goes to the redoubtable R.K. Dandy.

Lawdy, that lad sure knows his way around a book.